THE WEATHER IN MIDDENSHOT

EDGAR MITTELHOLZER (1909-1965) is often considered to be the first novelist from the West Indies to earn an international reputation for his fiction, as well as the first professional novelist to emerge from the English-speaking Caribbean. Beginning with his first book, *Creole Chips*, which he self-published in 1937, Mittelholzer would go on to publish more than twenty volumes of fiction, as well as two volumes of nonfiction, including the autobiography *A Swarthy Boy* (1963). His best-known works include *A Morning at the Office* (1950), which one critic cited as having begun "the great decade of the West Indian novel," the *Kaywana* trilogy (1952-58), and the ghost story *My Bones and My Flute* (1955). His macabre classic *Eltonsbrody* (1960) is also available from Valancourt.

I0633108

EDGAR MITTELHOLZER

The Weather in Middenshot

VALANCOURT BOOKS

The Weather in Middenshot by Edgar Mittelholzer
Originally published in Great Britain by Secker & Warburg in 1952
First U.S. edition published by John Day in 1953
This edition first published 2025

Published by Valancourt Books, Richmond, Virginia
http://www.valancourtbooks.com

The Valancourt Books name and logo are federally registered
trademarks of Valancourt Books, LLC

ISBN 978-1-960241-51-1 (trade paperback)
Also available as an electronic book.

Cover by Roderick Brydon / KLRCovers.com
Set in Dante MT

It may be well to note that Middenshot, with its human contents, is a village entirely fictitious. Should anyone imagine that he or she has been depicted in this book such a person would, indeed, be imaginative.

E. M.

THE WIND

I

The wind whined and whooped down the chimney like some lewd demon leapt out of the apple tree in the back garden and determined to hurl a hoarse coughing horror through the cottage.

Grace shivered not because it was cold in the room but because she could imagine, from the sound of the wind, how cold it must be outside. She stopped knitting and shut her eyes, and heard, up in the roof, a muffled clatter as though something—perhaps the roof itself—were about to become detached and go winging away in the gun-metal evening-light. In her fancy she saw it go. The whole roof. It rose and went flapping off, over the pine woods, toward Bisley, a quarking pterodactyl thing of dread under the cold sky of late autumn.

"Open your eyes, child," said her father, Mr. Herbert Jarrow. "Makes me think of your mother when you do that."

Flapping and quarking . . . Black and baleful.

"I won't have you go reminding me of her."

Mrs. Jarrow, his wife, sighed, and leaning forward in her chair, trowelled up some coal from the scuttle and threw it on the fire.

The chimney seemed to resent this act, for instantly a slate-grey powder-puff of smoke billowed out of the fireplace and broke in mushroom curls over the mantelpiece, rushing up toward the cracked plaster of the ceiling. Again the demon in the wind whined its message of menace, and they heard a window in the back room rattle as if a gaunt hand had hit it.

"When you shut your eyes," said Mr. Jarrow, "you look like a ruddy martyr. I don't like ruddy martyrs about the house. That's what your mother used to look like before the Accident. Ruddy martyr."

Grace opened her eyes—not because her father had told her to do so but because she had decided that it was time to open them. She glanced furtively about the small room with its shabby furniture and shabby rugs. Her light-brown hair was parted in the middle and braided down on either side, meeting at the back of her head in a coiled knot; it gave her the look, with her long, narrow face, of a woman in a Rossetti picture. She had blue eyes, and in them, at most times, there dwelled a slightly worried, yet detached and composed, light.

Mr. Jarrow tapped his stick contemplatively on the floor, frowning at the pile of out-dated medical magazines beside his chair; they had once belonged to his wife's father, the late Doctor Chester. Without warning Mr. Jarrow uttered deep, doleful laughter.

"Haw, haw! Haw, haw, haw!"

His eyes, which were of an almost childishly clear blue, twinkled, and his lined face grew more lined, his hooked, hawk-nose more hooked and hawk-like. He shrugged himself more comfortably inside his old brown jacket and began to stroke his cheek slowly and with an air of waiting wonder, as though puzzled to know why he had laughed but expectant of being informed by a spectral voice from the void behind the sofa. He glanced up sharply as another gust of wind moaned around the cottage, and the frown that caused his shaggy eyebrows to lower was one of reproof. He began to stare reflectively at the fire.

Now, thought Grace, he must be remembering the Accident. She gave him a half-pitying glance over her knitting-needles.

Seventeen years ago Mr. Jarrow, a lorry-driver, had met with an accident which had left him with a limp and had affected his mind so that he had been unable to drive again. He feared motor traffic and never ventured near the London Road; he found har-rowing anything that hummed like the engine of a car: when an aeroplane passed overhead he wailed softly or whimpered. His wife—whose existence he persistently refused to admit—sup-ported him out of her private income, helped by Grace's sewing and knitting. Grace made children's clothes and knitted cardigans and pullovers. Her fame had spread beyond Middenshot, and sometimes a firm in Camberley gave her orders for children's summer dresses. Once she had had an order for a dozen women's cardigans to be delivered in six weeks. She had delivered them in five. A knitting-machine, Mr. Jarrow called her.

"The old buzzard."

"What did you say, Dad?" asked Grace, alert now, her fancies gone, for she thought she knew what had occasioned this comment of her father's.

"The old buzzard," repeated Mr. Jarrow. "Think I don't know it? It's she he's after," he told the fire as the fire abruptly staggered in the down-draught from the chimney, the flames doing a stunted dance dimmed by the new puff of smoke that shot phantom-like out of the fireplace.

"Must get a cowl for that chimney," said Mr. Jarrow. Every autumn he said the same thing. He coughed and tapped his stick on the floor—the room was milky with smoke—and Mrs. Jarrow took up the poker and jabbed it tentatively at the fire. She did everything tentatively, for she was, by nature, that kind of woman, and her father had been a bully; he had suppressed her whenever he could. One of the most vivid pictures that remained in her memory was of her father threatening her with a scalpel, his bald head scintillant with perspiration in minute pips, his loose denture rattling in his mouth as he shouted at her. Her cousin, too, an orphan who had lived in the same house, had from an early age harrowed her spirit and made her feel her inferiority. Her cousin, who was now Mrs. Pendlefield and lived in the big house with the cedars, had one day said to her: "Agnes my dear, you'll never marry. You're only eighteen but you're on the shelf already. An upper shelf. Well out of reach." And Ernestine, her cousin, had laughed maliciously, for she was that kind of person—a person who could do delightful water-colours and say clever things in company and cruel things to her intimates. A person who was fond of hurting weaker creatures.

Oh, the wind, thought Grace. It sounds so alarming—and yet I do like it. It gives me such a safe feeling in the house here.

"Old buzzard. As though he can fool a wasp. It's Grace he's after. My virgin daughter Grace. Sure as night is night he's after her."

"I knew it! You're referring to Mr. Holme, Dad. I don't think it's right that you should say such things."

Her mother gave her an appealing look equivalent to saying: "Don't trouble, dear. You know he can't help it. It's his Mind."

"Old runt," said Mr. Jarrow to the fire. He uttered a bark of laughter and tapped a rapid tattoo with his stick on the floor, and the sound frolicked about in the overwarm room like a lively jinnee trying to imitate the agitated groans and whisking noises of the wind outside the cottage. A door, or shutter, banged remotely down the lane with the dull note of a rotted coffin, and the pine woods hissed frenziedly like broken glass scattered on dense grass. Though the windows were shut, the exterior noises came clearly into the room. Quarrelling spirit-voices, thought Grace. That's what the wind in the pines sounds like. A smile of secret affection and content passed over her face, for despite her father and their modest circumstances, she was happy living in this cottage. She was in no way troubled because she was thirty-two and unmarried. Like her mother, she was plain looking, but she was resigned to her plainness—so she assured herself. Further, she felt that no man could ever be interested in her, therefore she had decided that men must not be thought of nor dreamt about. Since nineteen she had resolved that life for her must consist of nothing more than sewing and knitting and assisting her mother to take care of her father.

Mr. Holme, a widower of fifty-two, often stopped by the gate to talk to her, but he did it—she was certain—only because he was lonely and because he wanted to be neighbourly, though her father, mentally warped as he was, could not see it like this; he had to go imagining that Mr. Holme was after her.

"Grace."

"Yes, Dad?"

"Did you enquire at Boots if they've got that new book on Belsen yet? The one with illustrations?"

"I asked yesterday when I was in Camberley. They haven't got it yet."

"Slow coaches. Boots is on the decline. Nearly a month since we saw it reviewed in the evening paper."

"Well, you don't pay an A Class subscription. What can you expect?"

"Is the Laytons' cat dead yet?"

"I don't think so."

"Have you been across there this evening?"

"I was there late this afternoon."

Mr. Jarrow leant forward. "Was it frothing at the mouth?"

"Yes," said Grace quietly.

"H'mph! I must take a stroll across in the morning and have a look at it. Might be in time to witness the final death agonies."

"You'd better not go too early, Herbert," said Mrs. Jarrow, speaking for the first time in half an hour. "They don't chain up that dog until nine o'clock after Mr. Layton has left for London."

"Grace."

"Yes, Dad?"

"Conditions seem favourable for a séance this evening."

Grace said nothing. She knitted on as though he had not spoken.

"I heard the voice of your dead mother, child. She's in this room now, if we only had eyes to see her. The ruddy martyr. Remember what she looked like? I'm talking to you, Grace. Answer me. Remember what your mother looked like?"

"Yes, Dad," said Grace in a toneless voice. This catechism was seventeen years old. It left no impression upon her. It was one of the segments of the life she had accepted. It would have upset her vaguely had her father not asked these questions, for it would have meant that he was changing, and she distrusted change of any kind.

"Mousy hair—that's the kind of hair she had. She's still got it. I see her ghost in this room every day. Pug nose—always reddish. Round back and round shoulders. When I married her she was twenty-two, but she was an old lady already. Plain as a pebble. Woebegone. Pulled her off the shelf, I did. Dusted her and married her."

Grace was silent, knitting. Knitting relentlessly. Consuming the energy that might have gone into a bout of lovemaking had Nature and Fate conspired in more kindly fashion.

"She had her good points, I won't say not. Took good care of me. Just as you do now. Yes, she was a good soul at heart." There was sudden moisture in Mr. Jarrow's eyes. His thin lips pouted in senile grief. He tilted his head as though hearkening to a new sorrow in the wind.

Mrs. Jarrow was smiling and wagging her head. This moment gave her consolation—and contentment. Her lips moved silently, and her weak grey eyes had, like her husband's, grown moist.

"It was books that brought us together. Me a humble chauffeur. She the doctor's daughter living in the grey-brick house by the Big Pond. Yes, child. We must hold a séance before we turn in to bed. I want to communicate with my dead wife's soul."

"Very well, Dad," murmured Grace, happy, because she knew her mother would be happy. A séance made them all happy.

"May be a sight worth watching," said Mr. Jarrow.

"What did you say, Dad?"

But her father was addressing the fire again. "A sick cat dying," he told the fire. "Writhing and mewing in pain. Frothing at the mouth. Distended belly. Ten to one its belly might burst right before my eyes with a good loud squelchy pop. Who knows, by ruddy God!" He clenched his hands with a cloying ecstasy, and his wife sighed again—but this time it was a happy sigh: a muffled miniature wind, a low accompaniment to the major burden of the wind weeping over the common, soughing through the swaying trees.

"I'll have the little table ready after supper, Dad."

"Yes, my child. We must talk to your mother. A good woman, rest her dear soul."

Grace shivered, hearing the feather-like flick of a leaf against the window-panes. A pixie from the pine woods, she thought, trying to tempt me out into the cold. But I'm safe in here. Oh, I'm safe and cosy.

She snuggled herself luxuriously in her chair and knitted with renewed energy, feeling the blood tingle in her cheeks like the tickling of many tentative, tiny hatpin points.

2

Will an evil, black-and-blue ewe-lamb loom up and leap at me out of the dark if I open the window to take a look at the common? Perhaps, thought Grace, but I'll risk it and see.

Fumbling with the catch of the kitchen window, she pushed and found that the window would not yield with ease. The wind kept ramming hard against the purple frosted panes. I and only I alone, the wind seemed to tell her, have the right to reign to-night over the gorse and heather on the common. You there! Keep inside your cottage and leave me to drone my song of mourning in the moonless dark.

Will it punish me if I insist on looking?

"Grace dear! Are you getting the supper ready?"

"Yes, Mother, it will be ready in a minute or two!"

The water had begun to simmer on the gas range. A tiny leaf of steam waved mysteriously at the tip of the kettle's spout, semaphoring to an unseen presence on the dresser where the plates and pots were stacked.

As she pushed the window slightly open, Grace peeped through the aperture but could see only the black blur of two pine trees on the edge of the common. They waved strenuously in the wind, beckoning to her, she was sure, in warning not to persist in further peering. They stood like sentries guarding the view to the common. She simply had to push the window out an inch or two more to see the open expanse of the common, undulating and blobbed with clumps of gorse and tufts of heather, each clump and tuft concealing unnamable glooms, innumerable miasmas of the murdered summer.

The wind inserted icy teeth that gnashed and champed about her head, as though in remorse for many sinister sins. It whisked her hair about her face—the few straggly strands that had escaped at her temples—and made her blink, tickling her eyelashes. But all the while a cool bravery moved within her, for this was how she adventured when alone. This was her private, childish pleasure.

The kettle simmered earnestly and more earnestly, and then began to boil, and its insistent hissing filled the small kitchen and seemed to wheel round and round within the brown-painted walls, insinuating its way officiously between the plates and pots and pans on the dresser, each of which bore its elongated eye of light that shone slyly from cover, side, rim or corner. The Ideal boiler, black and greased, a blank-faced gnome, kept listening to the kettle, a secret smile within its burning midst. Sometimes Grace felt an urge to hug and kiss it—not through idiocy but because of a head-turning whirl of happiness and contentment. This cottage with its contents was her world, complete and cocooned. She had no need, while enclosed by these walls, to fear ridicule. Should she caper, should she stand on her head, who in here could wound her with a laugh? So sometimes she capered. Hummed to herself, whistled like a boy. And danced. Free, gay-hearted, undiffident. Hampered in no way by the prohibitions of Middenshot, of surrounding Surrey. This cottage—it was called Pine Tree Cottage—stood on the edge of Brameley Common, less than half a mile of lane and road from Middenshot's High Street, but, to Grace, with the doors and windows secured, Middenshot appeared a distant, a foreign, world. An arid land in which when she ventured in it to do her shopping or to deliver a dress or a cardigan—she had to be demure, prevaricative and properly English.

She whistled a tune she had heard on the wireless that afternoon and did a brief, restricted waltz around the kitchen, and ten minutes later called out to her parents that supper was ready. They came and sat with her at the small table and ate cheese and biscuits, and sipped tea, Mrs. Jarrow, as customary, in silence, Mr. Jarrow with an occasional chuckle or guffaw or comment directed at the sink or at the boiler, Grace tilting her head to listen to the wind and to smile in concert with her callow but happy fancies.

Mrs. Jarrow, too, was happy, her awareness anointed with the cool oil of anticipation at the coming séance. Once a week, perhaps twice, Mr. Jarrow called for a séance, and this event constituted the one great balm of Mrs. Jarrow's trying life, for only on the occasion of a séance would her husband speak to her or in any way become aware of her existence, and her fondness for him now in his madness, her devotion to him, was no less what it was thirty-three years ago when they were first married and he was sane.

Supper over, Grace and her father returned into the living-room to prepare for the séance. Grace cleared a small mahogany table and placed on it a large, clean, smooth stone that came from the brook that ran through the woods and across the common.

She then pulled the curtains aside, unveiling the slightly misted panes of the bay windows that looked out on the front garden (beyond the garden-fence loomed the gloomed pine woods). Had she not done this her mother's spirit—according to her father's reasoning—would have found difficulty in gaining entrance into the room, for her ghostly eyes would not have been able to discern the light in the room, the curtains being very thick.

These preparations over, Mr. Jarrow and Grace sat facing each other at the table, the old gentleman carefully adjusting his stick across his lap. Indoors or outdoors, he never moved anywhere without his stick. He slept with it. It had become a part of his personality.

In the kitchen, Mrs. Jarrow wrapped her shawl about her shoulders, switched off the light and tiptoed into the hallway. She paused at the living-room door to listen for her cue. It might come in a minute, or in ten.

Mr. Jarrow cast his glance upward as the wind caused that remote clatter in the roof heard earlier in the evening by Grace—a loose slate, perhaps, or a demon in pterodactyl shape—and his brows showed disapproval. "A night," he said, "for any kind of horror. Good mellow horror with blood and tearing flesh." He fixed his gaze on the stone on the table and scratched his left buttock contemplatively, murmuring something to himself.

"What did you say, Dad?" asked Grace.

He ignored her. A dry leaf, like a dead paw drifting in the dark, brushed against the bay windows, and Grace glanced toward the windows and shuddered with fear and security, snuggling deeper into the cosiness of her being. She wanted to smile with contentment but restrained herself. Her father did not allow smiling during a séance.

Suddenly Mr. Jarrow's back became humped. His face grew crumpled and grey. His head seemed to shrivel and retract into his jacket. A low forlorn wailing fluted forth from him. All the pugnacious arrogance vanished from his manner.

The drone of the aeroplane grew louder, coming in waves through the welter of wind outside. It groped like a hand through the room—a hand that, at length, found the poor mad gentleman, and having found him, hurt him unrelentingly, pummelled the ruined pulp of mind, ruled a finger-nail line of finality to the dreaming humanity that lingered within him.

His wife and daughter watched him and suffered with him. For his sake they deemed aeroplanes enemies—like cars, coaches, bees and all things that came into a buzzing, droning, humming category.

The agony, however, as always, was brief. The plane passed over; its droning ceased. Only the wind remained. A brume of smoke hung about the room, like ceremonial incense from a Druid mound. The fire kept wavering as the flames snarled and dwarfed.

Mr. Jarrow emerged from his trough of tribulation, felt in his lap for his stick, and after a silence, head bowed in a rigid humility, said to Grace: "Let us concentrate," saying it as he might have said: "Let us pray."

Concentrating, they heard, during a momentary lull in the gale, the sound of traffic on the London Road, but Mr. Jarrow did not mind, for this massed sound came to him here at Pine Tree Cottage as a remote rumble. He liked a rumble, remote or near. A rumble reminded him of thunder of which he was very fond, for he associated thunder with lightning. Lightning that could strike down man or beast and create havoc and horror.

"A dark night," murmured the old gentleman. He was going into a trance, his gaze on the stone.

"A dark night," echoed Grace, solemnly, also in a trance.

"A night dark like dung. As full of filth as man is full of larks and lunacy. I'm moving in it, and it's raining like misery. Road all shiny like patent leather. Lorry piled high with cases of washing blue and curry powder and Colman's mustard."

"An evil night," whispered his daughter.

"An evil night," agreed her father. "I was reading Burke before I left London. Nice Everyman edition handy and neat for my pocket. Had it beside me on the seat. God, but the rain. Rain, rain. English rain. A nasty night. I kept remembering Burke. And Agnes, my plain-faced wife. Doctor Chester's daughter whom I wooed and married. She married beneath her class, but I took her off the shelf. Dusted her and married her, I did. Rain, rain. When shall we three meet again in rain, rain, rain?"

"In rain, rain," murmured Grace.

"Swish and hum. Hum and swish," intoned Mr. Jarrow. "I dimmed my lights. A Bentley or a Rolls that was. Gone with a hum and a bumble. I mumbled a bit of Burke. Swish and hum, and the rain hitting at my wind-screen, and my wiper working like hell and high water. Nine more miles to Camberley and a cup of tea. Agnes, a cup of tea, my dear!"

Mrs. Jarrow pushed the door softly in and entered the room, making no sound. She had had her cue. Her husband was silent, staring unblinkingly at the stone on the table, a fine network of wrinkles around his infantile blue eyes.

The wind screamed round the cottage with hurricane violence so that it seemed certain the roof would be torn off and hurled into the pine woods. But, as always, the scream tailed off and the chimney moaned. The danger had side-stepped them.

"Swish and hum," whispered the old gentleman, leaning forward, his hands tight around the stick in his lap. "Swish and drone. When shall we three meet again in love and rain? In rain and love? Stone, speak to me. Tell a mad old man his ugly fate. Blow, blow, thou winter wind, thou art not so unkind as man's atomic deeds. Swish and whoosh! Oh, God! The dread doings are done! Blue and curry and mustard with Burke, all sprawled in the grass by the roadside. Agnes love, save me! Oh, Agnes beloved, where dwellest thou, simple soul? Come if thou canst hear me. Come in love and rain. In wind and love. Grace!"

"Yes, Dad?"

"The stone moved."

"Yes, it moved."

"You saw it move?"

"I saw it move."

Silence. Only the wind.

A dog barked far away. The woods rustled.

Reverently Grace stretched out and tapped her father's clasped hands which now rested on the edge of the table. "Dad," she whispered, "Mother is here. She has emerged from the Gloom."

Mr. Jarrow made no response. He sat very still, a strained look on his face. A look, too, that was sombre and tinted with sadness. In this instant there was no madness in his eyes—only a tortured quiescence, a surrender to a fate that had tracked him down, tricked him, and now stood poised to trail around him a pullulation of punishment. Punishment that he had sought. Punishment that would prove salutary.

"She is with us, Dad," whispered Grace again.

"Where?" asked her father, pale. The wind shrieked.

"She stands behind your chair."

"With a rod to beat me?"

"No, with a hand to pat you."

"Kindness. Oh, kindness," murmured Mr. Jarrow, moisture in his eyes. "She was always forgiving. Always full of kindness, my poor Agnes. Where are you, Agnes? Speak to me."

"I am here, Herbert," said Mrs. Jarrow, stroking his head.

A tear ran down Mr. Jarrow's cheek.

"I'm always near you, Herbert."

"But in a different world, my love."

"But still near to you. Always very near."

"Are you lonely without me, Agnes?"

"Very, Herbert. Very, my dear. If only you could speak to me more often." Mrs. Jarrow was crying, too—from happiness.

"How did you enter the cottage, Agnes? Through the windows?"

"Yes," answered his wife—with some reluctance.

"Did you see the light?"

"Yes, I saw the light."

"Were you in the pine woods all alone?"

"Yes," murmured Mrs. Jarrow, as though ashamed at the lie.

"One day I'll join you there, Agnes."

"You'll be welcome, Herbert."

"You were a good girl. You took good care of me when you were alive. I'm happy. Grace, our daughter, sees after me in your absence. A kind, simple-minded girl. Kind and simple-minded as you were."

"I'm glad."

"I feel your presence often in here, Agnes."

"I'm always with you."

"How the wind howls, Agnes!"

"But I'm with you, Herbert dear."

"It rained the night you died."

His wife said nothing, stroking his hair.

"All mixed up with washing blue and curry and Colman's mustard. I saw you lying there in the grass, my dear—all dead with Burke in the pouring rain."

The wind uttered a soaring whistle, and the window in the back room gave an indeterminate stammered rattle. An unseen wing seemed to flap inaudibly through the room here, fanning them with a phantom draught, chilly and touched with the scent of earth and damp pine needles.

"You died and I went mad," said Mr. Jarrow.

"Never mind, Herbert. Never mind," whispered his wife.

Grace uttered a cry. "The window! Look! Mother, look!"

Mrs. Jarrow looked and gasped—and the face vanished.

Mr. Jarrow became rigid. Jerked out of his trance.

Grace had risen. The wind screeched.

"Did you see it, Mother?"

"Yes," said Mrs. Jarrow, white.

"Who could it have been, I wonder," said Grace in a frightened voice. The séance was forgotten.

"A spirit from the other world," murmured her father. "Wandering in our front garden. It must have followed your mother, child."

"It—perhaps . . ."

"What were you going to say, Grace?" asked Mr. Jarrow.

"I wonder if it could be an escaped lunatic from Broadmoor."

"Lunatics," said Mr. Jarrow, "are all about us. Not only indoors."

"I . . ."

"What's it, Mother?"

"The face at the window, Grace. To me it looked . . ."

Grace waited.

"For a moment," said Mrs. Jarrow, "I thought it was Mr. Holme."

3

All night the wind howled, abating somewhat in the early morning, but during the day coming in fitful strong gusts from the south-east or south-west. By nightfall it was howling again, lugubriously and with the harrowed note of the lost. Toward dawn it had become a low baying and hawking, and the announcer on the wireless told his listeners (as though to give them a surprise) that before the general weather forecast there were gale warnings. Severe gales, he went on, in Rockall and Shannon and in Biscay-Wight-Dover-Thames.

Mr. Jarrow made it a habit of tuning-in every morning to the six fifty-five weather forecast. Gale warnings gave the old gentleman delight. "Think," he had once remarked, "of all the ships that might be in danger. Men being washed overboard at this very minute. Men being dashed against stanchions. Men falling into holds and breaking their necks. Cracking spines. Smashing limbs. Splitting heads. Dozens drowning. And the sharks always waiting. Yes, gives me a walloping thrill to hear about gale warnings."

Two cottages away, Mr. Holme, too, never missed the early morning forecast. An amateur gardener, he disliked gales for fear of the damage they might do to the greenhouses in which he cultivated orchids, ferns and out-of-season flowers. His was a bungalow cottage, small and cosy-safe (so Grace had once described it). It was situated in two acres of grounds every square-foot of which Mr. Holme had cultivated.

This morning, frying his bacon and listening to the voice of the announcer, who was telling about the Korean war now, Mr. Holme uttered a sustained grunting sound of gloom and told himself that he wished these high winds would stop. For the past two or three mornings he had awakened expecting to find a few panes of glass missing from one or other of the three greenhouses. Number Two greenhouse, especially, gave him deep concern, for it was in here that he was coaxing two or three rare tropical orchids. With the aid of paraffin heaters he kept the temperature in Number Two always between sixty-seven and seventy-two. Should the chilly south-westerly wind find its way into Number Two the temperature would drop and that might mean the death of his orchids.

Mr. Holme did not know it—he was not given to deep intro-spection—but without his greenhouses and his small, trimmed, brown moustache he would have felt considerably less the man he was. His greenhouses gave him hope of something big and exciting in the floricultural future, and his moustache produced in him the feeling—an entirely sub-conscious feeling, for he was an unassuming man, quite lacking in conceit—that he possessed a young and handsome, even a distinguished, air.

It was because of his greenhouses and his moustache—always without his knowing it—that he continued, day after day, to feel confident that he would achieve the three big things on which he had set his mind. One of these—and he was already succeeding in this—was to prevent a relapse of the tuberculosis from which he had recovered only after two years of a treatment involving a diet of greens, cereals and cheese and meat. He wanted, also, a woman in the house to take care of him, either in the capacity of a housekeeper or as a wife—preferably the latter; the woman he had in mind was Grace Jarrow. The third big thing he wanted was to produce an orchid of sensational yet tasteful loveliness: an orchid bearing dots and streaks of violet and cobalt stamped upon an array of frayed white petals like bridal veils melting into valley mist (this was how he had seen it, at two one morning, in a particularly vivid dream).

As he sat down to his breakfast, Mr. Holme remembered that this was his day for buying paraffin. Paraffin for the heaters in Number Two. Half his pension went on paraffin, and it was not a big pension. He was a retired police sergeant; through ill health he had had to retire at forty-five—after twenty-four years' service. He was now forty-eight, though Middenshot (including Grace Jarrow) had decided that he was fifty-two. Had he had his way he would have left the Police Force in 1944 when he was forty-two. In this year his wife had been killed, while in childbirth labour, during a heavy Vɪ raid on London; the doodlebugs were coming over regularly when pains set in, and a neighbour, who had some knowledge of midwifery, had taken on the job of assisting Millicent in the basement; a bomb had entombed them both, and their bodies had been dug out five hours later. Mr. Holme, swearing that he would get his own back on the Nazis, had put in a request to be released from the Police so that he could enlist in one of the armed forces; grief had temporarily unbalanced him. His request had been refused. Police were as necessary to the war effort, he had been informed, as soldiers, sailors and airmen, and, moreover, he was forty-two—somewhat on the old side—and had an excellent record in the Force. He was a valuable man and the Force could not afford to lose him.

After eating, Mr. Holme washed up, and leaving the plates and cup to drain on the dresser, made his way to the front door and picked up the newspaper which the newsboy had slipped in through the letter-slot about an hour earlier. Returning to the tiny kitchen, he settled down by the boiler, where it was warmest, lit his pipe and opened his paper.

Mr. Holme planned his day. He had set times for everything, and before going to bed at night sketched out in his mind the following day's routine. He read the newspaper until eight, then between eight and nine pottered about in the garden and in the greenhouses. At nine o'clock he went out to do his shopping, leaving Hyacinth Withers, the girl who came in to clean, to proceed with her chores.

Even as the clock in the living-room was striking eight—tiny pinging notes—Mr. Holme rose and folded up his paper. He took down his mackintosh from the peg behind the door and put it on. He unbolted the door, turned the key, pulled the door toward him, and was about to step outside when he was obliged to pause and utter an exclamation.

On the step where, in about two hours' time, the milk-man would place a two-pint bottle of milk, lay the body of a cat, bloated and damp and with traces of earth adhering to it. Its eyes stared, wide and slaty-glazed; its jaw hung open, rigid in a macabre grin.

"Well, of all the . . . What the devil's being going on out here during the night!"

Something caught his attention. There was a white label—

an old envelope, it seemed—attached to one of the forelegs by a string. Stooping, he examined it and saw that something was written on it in block letters. OLD RUNT. In firm, pencilled letters.

Fumbling in the pocket of his mackintosh, Mr. Holme brought out a pair of scissors, clipped the string and straightened up, the label in his hand. He turned it over and noted that the name and address originally written on it had been carefully obliterated. With the point of a pen-knife as well as with a lead pencil the perpetrator of this practical joke had made sure that no one would be able to trace the envelope back to its owner.

"Damned funny sort of joke," muttered Mr. Holme. The wind kept tugging at the envelope in his hand, flapping his mackintosh about with a sound of eggs being beaten up in a bowl. "Old runt." Could the insult be meant for him? Why, though? Who should want to call him an old runt?

With a shrug, he stepped carefully over the carcase and made his way into the back garden, the frown on his long, rather handsome face gradually fading. He was a tall man, over six feet, and walked with a springy, forward-bending motion.

So engrossed did he become in the garden that, within less than five minutes, he had forgotten the carcase. He made, as a preliminary, a tour of the whole of the area under cultivation, including the narrow strip of front garden, in order to take in the situation, so to speak, at a glance. Pine Tree Lane ran east-west, with the pine woods on the northern side and the cottages on the southern. A broken branch had fallen just inside the gateway, hurled across the lane in a freakish eddy of wind during the night. It lay humped on the crazy pavement, a furry demon harrowed into defeat while fugitive in the night.

In the back garden, the wind had beaten down two or three cauliflowers, but other than this no damage met the gaze, so Mr. Holme turned his attention to the greenhouses. He went round and round them, carefully inspecting them, the wind tossing his loose greying brown hair about and trying to tear his mackintosh open and bind his slim body with fierce ribbons of draughts. The contents of his mackintosh pockets jingled and clinked, making a continuous chilly music.

Of the three greenhouses Number One and Number Three were comparatively new, having been built within the past two years; they were low to the ground—no more than four feet from the highest point of the sloped roofs—and were fitted with roof-windows which could be lifted open or flapped shut at will. Number Two, however, had been erected long before he had bought the cottage; it was fifteen feet by eight, and seven from the highest point of the roof. Some of the panes were loose, and rattled when the wind was high. Mr. Holme was forever securing loose panes with putty and oakum; it was a task without end. But he never grew discouraged; he liked a struggle. It had been the same with his tuberculosis; the very knowledge that he had been opposed to a tough adversary had given him courage and exhilaration. The doctor who had treated him—he had been privately treated—had told him, on his recovery: "Your will to get well has been half the cure."

For Mr. Holme, it came almost as a joy to discover a loose, rattling pane. Immediately he would fumble out from his mackintosh pocket a piece of chalk and mark an X on the pane, and within an hour he would have put an end to the rattling. Sometimes, in the midst of fixing a pane, the wind, in a terrific gust, would reveal another defective pane, and with a soft sustained grunting sound Mr. Holme would mutter: "Found you out, you little devil!" and reach out to chalk the new offender. It was small things like this that gave him zest for living. Tiny victories over tiny enemies. At each day's end when smoking his pipe and thumbing through his *Book of Orchids* or one of his floricultural manuals, he would mentally add up the day's minuscule conquests, and if the sum were a big one would smile and nod to himself in satisfaction and contentment. Should the sum be small he would still smile and nod, assuring himself that tomorrow would come with its new agonies; there were always victories to be won, for no day was without its battles.

This morning Mr. Holme failed to find any rattling panes, so unlocked and entered Number Two and had a look at his orchids. One plant was contained in the shell of a coconut, exactly as it had been given to him by a seaman acquaintance. Within the four months that it had spent in the greenhouse it had grown about seven inches and had, within the past three weeks, begun to throw out thin shoots bearing tiny feathery leaves and what looked like very incipient buds. What sort of blooms it would eventually bear was as much a mystery to Mr. Holme as it had been to the seaman acquaintance who had brought it from South America. Mr. Holme lived in a state of perpetual excitement on behalf of this plant; he kept anticipating the day when the blooms would appear. Would it prove to be the orchid of his dreams?

He had noted the temperature on the thermometer—sixty-nine—and was examining the paraffin heaters when a shrill voice triumphed above the drone of the wind and made him glance toward the kitchen.

"Lord, Mr. Holme! What's this you've got here!"

"Nine o'clock already," muttered Mr. Holme. "Time. How time goes!"

He left Number Two, locking the door carefully after him.

"I'm as much in the dark as you, Hyacinth," he said to the girl who stood at the kitchen door in a pale-blue plastic raincoat, her coppery-gold hair itching to burst out from under the dark-blue, shabby felt toque pressed down on her head. "Haven't an idea where it came from. Somebody's trying to be funny, that's all I know."

"You mean you didn't put it here?"

"I didn't."

"But who would want to do a nasty thing like this!" Mr. Holme fumbled in the pocket of his mackintosh and brought out (together with a piece of string and two old nails) the tag he had detached from the carcase. "Have a look at this. I found it tied round one of its legs."

"Old runt? It's an insult." She uttered an indignant grunt. "If I was you I'd show it to the police, that's what I'd do!"

"You forget I'm an old policeman? People bother the police too much. We'll have to bury it, Hyacinth. Just bury it quietly and say nothing about it. That'll show whoever did it I don't give a damn."

"You like to take things lying down too much, you do! I'm always telling you that. What you want is somebody to look after you." As she said this Hyacinth shed her raincoat and wiggled her rump, a mannerism inelegant because studied.

Hyacinth's rump, it was agreed by nearly everyone in the neighbourhood, male and female, was the roundest and most shapely in Middenshot, and the girl was intensely aware of this. From the age of sixteen—she was now twenty-two—it had come upon her that when men looked at her rump they were inclined to scratch their chins with the back of a thumb and continue to look. Eventually her dreams had become centred around her rump. She had grown to put her faith in her rump. In the same manner that Grace Jarrow believed in the security of Pine Tree Cottage, Mr. Jarrow in the pleasures of horror, and Mr. Holme in his greenhouses and his moustache, Hyacinth believed in her rump—believed in it and had hopes for it.

For several months now—she had been cleaning for Mr. Holme for nearly a year—she had felt that to be the mistress of a handsome middle-aged widower's cottage would be far more desirable than to be the mistress of a two-roomed flat or a squatter's hut which would, inevitably, be her status were she to marry Dick Barke who worked with the village scavenging gang and who had set his mind on making her his wife. A bungalow cottage near the pine woods; in about two acres of grounds; greenhouses, cabbage and potato patches, tulips in the front garden, a crazy pavement, holly hedges; a quiet, well-behaved gentleman without any airs and with an income of his own—all this Hyacinth dreamt of; all this, she felt, could be hers—through her rump.

"Some day. Some day I'll have someone," murmured Mr. Holme, going slightly red as he always did when she indulged in such remarks. "Well, look here, I've got to run out and do some shopping. Think you could bury it for me, Hyacinth?"

" 'Course I will. Leave it to me. Near the compost heap?"

"Yes. You know where to find the shovel? Or leave it until I come back if you want. I'll dig the hole myself. It might be chilly for you with this wind blowing."

"What's a little wind! Go and hide your face," said Hyacinth, with a whinnying laugh. "I'm not so soft I can't face a little wind."

"Hardy girl."

"Hardy like you."

"You'll find the shovel in the coal-house. Not the tool-room."

"I know where you keep it. I ought to by now, don't you think? Eh?" she smiled.

Her rump.

4

"You were out very early this morning, Dad."

"Very."

"Where?"

"Everywhere."

"Common?"

"Or garden."

"What for?"

"Doings."

"The cat?"

"Or the rat."

"The cat?"

"The cat."

"But the Laytons had it buried yesterday in the woods."

"I saw it buried."

"Oh."

"A stone marked the grave," said Mr. Jarrow.

"Oh."

The wind.

"You haven't . . . ?"

"Perhaps."

"Dad!"

"Child!"

"I do hope . . ."

"You shouldn't."

"Dad!"

"All, dear child, is illusion and delusion."

"Is it in the garden here?"

"Or over there."

"Not . . . ?"

"Who knows?"

"What!"

"Old runt."

Grace said nothing more, and for a long while the meal continued in silence. Only the wind spoke—whispering and grumbling in the boiler. Whistling. Insistent but unheeded.

Grace looked upset; Mrs. Jarrow sad. The morning after the night of a séance always found Mrs. Jarrow happy, memory of the night before fresh. But the second morning after saw her sad, for memory had staled and she might have to wait a week for another séance. Dear Herbert! Would he never again be kind to her except through the medium of a séance? Would he continue like this to the end, near to her yet sulkily apart, vocal yet avoiding her? Seventeen years. Seventeen years. It was hard on a woman.

Had the past before the Accident been ugly her present plight would have been easier to bear. True, even in the days when he was her father's chauffeur he had shown a tendency toward the morbid—he had liked collecting bones and keeping medical photographs; he had once told her that he liked working for her father because it had been his boyish hope to become a doctor, a surgeon: the thought of cutting up bodies fascinated him—true that he seemed to revel in discussing gruesome events, accidents involving terrible injury, earthquakes, massacres in foreign parts, but she had put this down simply to a little oddity, for toward her he had been most gentle and considerate. In those early days no wife could have wished for a more tender and devoted husband.

They had lived in Camberley then, for it would have been awkward for a daughter of Dr. Chester to live on in Middenshot after marrying so far beneath her class. The cottage in Camberley had been her own, willed down to her by her father, like the one in which they lived now—for after the Accident they had had to come and live here; it was quiet here and the neighbours in Camberley had begun to complain about Herbert's antics: they had wanted to have him certified insane and put into an asylum. In Bisley there were three other cottages that belonged to her, too, also willed down by her father together with the old home just off the London Road—the old home which, shortly after her father's death, she had, on the advice of her solicitor, sold to a biscuit manufacturer who had later sold it to a barrister, Mr.

Gray, who lived there now with his family; he travelled to London every morning by train, always in black. Ernestine Pendlefield, her cousin, and her family were great friends of the Grays.

In the late spring and summer Ernestine and Mrs. Gray could sometimes be seen on the common or in the woods with easel and palettes, for Mrs. Gray, too, went in for painting. More than once Mrs. Jarrow had come face to face with them in the lane, and Ernestine had not even glanced at Mrs. Jarrow. Every time this happened Mrs. Jarrow would feel a twinge—not of pain at the slight, nor of envy, but of shame at the awareness of her own fragility of nature. Her father had bullied Ernestine as much as he had bullied his own child; Agnes had wilted because weak: Ernestine had survived and flowered because strong. Ernestine, Mrs. Jarrow knew, had been born with the stuff of strength; no environment could have suppressed her: had she even been plain she would have triumphed. But she herself, Mrs. Jarrow knew, had come into the world bearing the streak of the weak; the fate of people like herself was to peer forever out of their foxholes of fear and eventually to pine away and perish with squeakings and chicken-like peep-peepings.

Oh, the wind!

"Grace."

"Yes, Dad?"

"Did the wind blow away the papers as it did yesterday?"

"No, I picked them up the minute I heard the newsboy throw them inside the gate."

"We ought to get a letter-slot made in the door."

"Yes, we ought."

Actually it was Mrs. Jarrow who had hurried out of bed and picked up the newspapers, but Grace had had to claim doing it; had she told the truth her father would have called her a silly stinking young stoat and would have been angry with her for the rest of the morning. How could a ghost pick up newspapers and bring them into the house!

Now, more than ever, reasoned Grace, she must be careful not to anger him, for it was evident that he had taken it into his head that poor Mr. Holme was trying to make overtures to her; even without her angering him he would go out of his way to annoy

Mr. Holme. Heaven alone knew if he had not really thrown the Laytons' dead cat into Mr. Holme's garden, as he had hinted a few minutes ago. Later in the morning she would have to make discreet investigations. Yes, she could not afford to anger him. Poor fellow. Not his fault. It was his Mind. Before the Accident he had been an ideal father. More than once he had taken her to London in the lorry. And there was the memorable trip to Plymouth when she was fifteen. They had had a puncture on the way, and she had helped him to change the tyre; he had praised her for her aptitude, and she had been so proud of herself that she had cried softly with her face turned away. It was that same year—not two months after the Plymouth trip—that, like an angel with anvil head, the Accident had swooped smashing upon their happiness.

Sometimes, in the silence of the early morning, cosily cuddled up in bed and saturated with a shuddering ecstasy of security, she would ask herself why it had to happen. Why should their quiet, simple lives have been disrupted in the way they had? God, of course, knew best, but now and then she did wonder what his purpose, in their case, could have been. When she went to church—she went about one Sunday a month—she prayed on kneeling as she entered her pew: "Dear Almighty God, if ever you can think of a better best for us three in Pine Tree Cottage please let it come to pass soon. Through Jesus Christ Our Lord. Amen." It was a sincere prayer. Everything Grace said—and her every action—sprang from a deep sincerity.

"Grace."

"Yes, Dad?"

"After the newspapers I should like you to read me a few paragraphs from Phillips's *The Belsen Trial*."

"Very well, Dad."

This was his way of punishing her for catechizing him about his early morning escapades. He knew it disgusted her to read aloud passages containing details of horrible events. Should she defy him and refuse to be punished he would retaliate by falling ill. This was the punishment most dreaded by her mother and herself, for his illness would take the form not only of pretended physical disabilities but of new mental ones as well. Not many months ago, during one of these punitive illnesses, Grace and her mother had missed him from the house, and, after a search, had found him perched on the upper branch of a cedar tree on the fell to the east of Mr. Holme's cottage. Trousers lowered, he sat on the branch as though on the seat of a toilet. It had taken them more than an hour to persuade him to come down, and during that time twice they had had to dodge droppings from above.

Breakfast over, she accompanied her father up to his room, taking the newspapers. Two newspapers. Every morning, for an hour after breakfast, and every afternoon, for an hour after tea, it was her duty to read aloud to him items of interest from the papers.

There were two bedrooms on the first floor, one facing south—the larger—the other north. Mr. Jarrow occupied the southern one, Grace and her mother sharing the northern.

Had a stranger walked blindfold into Mr. Jarrow's room his immediate impression would have been that he had entered a hospital surgery, for he would have caught a whiff of eusol. After a moment, however, this smell would have been superseded by another: a strong tang of earth. The stranger would have felt that he could well have been standing by a freshly-ploughed field—or a newly-dug grave. Tearing the bandage from his eyes, he would have looked around him and discovered that this smell of earth came from two white-washed soapboxes that, indeed, contained freshly-dug earth and that stood one on either side of the mahogany chest of drawers. He would have noted that in each box a wooden cross had been planted so that the boxes had the look of rather odd and rudimentary tombs.

The old gentleman sniffed the air and nodded. "Good grave-yard odour, eh? I changed the earth in the boxes this morning. Had to. They were losing their funereal perfume. It was since last week I put in fresh earth."

He limped across to an easy chair near the fireplace, on the tiled hearth of which stood an electric heater already switched on; the fireplace was too small to heat the room effectively with a coal fire.

Grace seated herself nearby on an upright chair. She arranged herself so that her back was to the big double bed, for she had never been quite able to get used to the sight of the bones piled up on the bedside table; among them were the skull of a bull with horns, an almost complete skeleton of a dog, several rats' skeletons and rabbit skulls: some white and polished, some greyish-green with mould or verdigris. Nor could Grace gaze for long upon the gibbet—complete with noose—her father had rigged up at the head of the bed; she could not forget a remark of his one evening when peeved: "Who can tell? The morning may yet be when you will come into this room and find something blue and horrid hanging from that gibbet. Something with bulging eyes and lolling tongue. And who can tell if it won't resemble your poor Dad."

No matter how she arranged herself, however, she could not avoid seeing the pictures that crowded the walls. Pictures cut from medical books of her grandfather's and framed in passe-partout—pictures of tumours and ulcers and of syphilitic chancres and rashes, of cancerous breasts: one or two of these in colour. Above the chest of drawers there were four showing, respectively, a case in India of scrotal elephantiasis, one of leprosy, another of *peau d'orange* of the female breast, and one of a gangrenous hip—all these four in realistic colours. Topping these, in a position of prominence, was one of a suicide with throat hacked open by a razor, which the old gentleman had cut from a book on medical jurisprudence. This, too, was in rich, bloody colours.

Other pictures depicted scenes at Belsen and Buchenwald and Dachau cut from various periodicals; there were a great many of these: indeed, a whole wall had been devoted to the theme of the Nazi concentration camp.

Grace opened one of the two newspapers, and glanced up and down the front page. How the wind hooted round the house, scattering dry leaves against the window panes and the walls downstairs. Anyone would have thought that it was this sudden new height of fury outside that caused the worried look to appear on Grace's too narrow face with its too thin, too humped nose, though generous, almost sensual, mouth.

"Dad, I'm afraid . . ."

"Yes?"

But it was not the wind.

"Dad . . ."

"I'm waiting."

Grace searched up and down the front page.

Oh, the wind!

"Come on, come on," urged her father. "I'm waiting. Reel it out."

"Dad . . . Dad, really, there's . . . I'm afraid I can't find anything at all of interest to-day."

"Nothing interesting on the front page!"

"I'll look and see what's on the other pages."

"Are you sure there's nothing on the front page?"

"Yes, Dad. Nothing at all."

"Pah! What's been happening to the country during the past twelve hours! Not even an old lady coshed in a railway coach?"

"No, Dad, no coshings to-day," murmured Grace, searching in the middle pages.

"What about the foreign cables? No earthquakes?"

"I—no, I can't find any, I'm afraid. Oh, wait!"

"Yes?" Hands clasped around the curved top of his ash stick, Mr. Jarrow leant forward eagerly.

"There's a little paragraph here. *Racing Motorist Killed.*"

"Ah!"

"It happened in Italy. It just says: 'Benny Crowe, the well-known racing motorist, was killed during practice for the Pimini Prix to be held on the French Riviera next week.' That's all."

"H'mph! Very bare. Why couldn't they have given some details! Did he break his neck? Was he impaled on a fence after being hurled out of the car—or on very sharp iron railings? Or did the car fall on him and squash him so that his intestines gushed out in the dust? These newspapers still have a lot to learn about reporting accidents. Come on, come on! Look for something else. What about Korea? Surely there should be some ripe and stomach-turning atrocities from there!"

Grace made a search but was compelled to admit that nothing strikingly gruesome had been reported to-day about the Korean war. "They say the United Nations troops are converging on Pyongyang."

Mr. Jarrow made a puffing sound of disgust.

"Oh, here's a slight thing that might interest you," said Grace. "It's about a child that was snatched in a country lane."

"Ah! Good! Sounds promising. What did they do to her? Raped her and carved up the body? Stuffed the parts into a suit-case?"

"No. It simply says: 'A seven-year-old child, Winifred Brody, was snatched by a youth in a lonely lane near Amsbridge End. The youth put the struggling child on to the cross-bar of his bicycle and rode off, but the child's cries attracted the attention of James Mather, a farm labourer in a nearby field, and—' "

"Very well, very well! You haven't got to finish it. She was rescued and the youth rode off. Chuh! These country youths losing all their guts!"

Grace shivered as the wind inserted into the room, through some minute unknown crevice, an arctic fragment of cold: a rag torn from a blizzard that circled her neck, disintegrating into a thousand threads that scattered and glided down her bosom, glowing and tingling over the undulations of her skin from throat to navel.

"Get the Belsen book," her father ordered, after she had failed to find anything more in the newspapers to interest him. "Select two paragraphs of vivid description and read them aloud. And see you put some expression into your voice. Put the right inflections on the right words."

Grace, with a routine sigh, rose and took from a shelf near the bed a book with a buff paper jacket. It was one of eight volumes that stood stacked on the shelf. She resumed her seat and began to flick over the leaves with the certainty of long practice.

"Old Peeping Tom."

"What's that, Dad?" said Grace, glancing up quickly.

"Hurry up, hurry up! What are you going to read? Get on with it!"

"That remark you made, Dad. What did you mean by it?"

Her father began to tap with his stick on the floor, his gaze, suddenly contemplative, on the electric fire.

"Peeping into people's living-rooms at dead of night. Old stoat."

"I think you're being very unfair. Mother said she *thought* it looked like him. The windows were misted over. It could have been any of our neighbours. Somebody might have lost their bearings and entered the wrong gate. I've done it myself on a dark night."

Mr. Jarrow started. "What's happening, child? Have you gone to sleep? Read me something. Go on. That passage describing the walking human skeletons and the victims of dysentery wallowing in their filth. Let's hear that again. And mind you, put some expression into your voice. Be sure you emphasize words like 'blood' and 'stench' and 'excrement.'"

It was not difficult for her to do, for she was well inured to it. The repugnance she felt could without effort be sloughed off; it affected her only skin-deep. Always she kept remembering that he was not to be blamed but to be pitied. He was not, strictly, insane, it was true, but for him to make the demands he made of her his mind had to be warped, and it was her duty to be patient and indulgent with him. His sight was perfect and he could have read the newspapers himself—every day he did a certain amount of reading—but it gave him, ill in mind as he was, a perverse pleasure to hear her reading sordid news items aloud to him. In just the same way it gave him pleasure to surround himself in this room with all these dreadful pictures and grisly objects and relics. Yes, pity. Pity and patience he needed from people.

While she was reading—she had reached a place about people dying horribly on camp-beds—he rose and took two paces over to the bed (without the slightest trace of a limp), lifted the sheet and brought forth a tall, fat bottle containing a clear liquid. Unstoppering it, he shook a few drops of the liquid out across the bed and the room instantly fumed with the stifling, pungent odour of eusol.

"Old skunk," he told the bottle, stoppering it again and putting it back under the bed.

"Must have thought he would have seen her stretched out naked on a sacrificial altar by the mantelpiece and me cutting her throat. The old weasel!"

He returned to his chair—again, without any trace of a limp—chuckling deep down within him: a guttural, clucking sound as though he were digesting rubies and north-pole snow that the wind had culled for him and cached in his stomach.

5

On his way back from the High Street, a gallon-tin of paraffin in each hand, Mr. Holme had come within less than a hundred yards of his gateway when he saw Grace Jarrow approaching along the lane, bareheaded and in her dark-green winter coat, string-bag in hand, the wind lashing it about by her side.

In the Police Force Mr. Holme had been valued for two particular qualities: efficiency involving a thoroughness in the execution of any commission and resourcefulness in an emergency. Calculating rapidly now, he concluded that, at their present rate of progress, when he arrived at his gate she would be a clear twenty or thirty yards off and he would be called upon merely to smile and hail out a greeting as he continued his way into his home. This, he decided, did not suit his inclination, so flicking deftly with a thumb at the left pocket of his mackintosh, he dislodged a piece of waste which had been protruding slightly but which would have remained in the pocket in perfect safety had it been left alone. The waste, caught by the wind, was whisked across the lane and trapped against the holly hedge where it hovered, a cowering blue-grey victim-thing in the spider-grip of the holly leaves.

Putting down the paraffin tins, Mr. Holme made a lunge and rescued it, then took his time over tucking it back into the safety of his mackintosh pocket. As a result of this delaying interlude he and Grace met when he had got to a point about four or five yards from his gate.

"Good morning, Miss Jarrow!"

"Good morning, Mr. Holme!"

"Glad I met you," said Mr. Holme, halting. "I've been hoping I'd run into you."

"Yes?"

"A little apology to make."

"An apology?"

"About the other night. I took my usual walk on the common,

and on my way back I stupidly got mixed up and entered your gateway."

"Oh. Then it was ... Oh."

"Yes, it was me. I knew I'd left the light on in my living-room—and the blinds weren't drawn—so on my way back I came out of the woods and just saw these lighted windows and made straight for them."

"Oh."

"It wasn't until I was practically right up against the panes I found I'd made a mistake."

"It's nothing. Please don't upset yourself about it."

"Stupid of me, all the same."

"I did the same thing myself one night last winter. I went in at the Laytons' by mistake. I didn't realize it until I heard the dog bark. It was a dreadful night. So dark!"

"Afraid I was lost in thought," laughed Mr. Holme. "I get that way sometimes. Especially when I go walking on the common at night."

"Do you go walking every night?"

"Most nights, whatever the weather. It's become a habit with me. I sleep better for the fresh air and exercise."

"I used to walk on the common at night myself—when I was eighteen and nineteen."

"You did? Ah, well, sensible. Very sensible."

"I didn't do it for fresh air and exercise, though," laughed Grace. "I used to do it to frighten myself."

"To frighten yourself?"

"Yes. I would go hurrying out in the dark and pretend that some terrible monster was after me, and then I'd come hurrying back after a short walk and rush inside and slam and lock the door. I felt so safe after I'd locked the door! It was simply a silly girlish game of my own."

"We all did silly things at eighteen and nineteen."

"Mother used to be quite alarmed."

"Mothers always are."

"Yes, that's so. Well, I must be getting on. I have my shopping to go and get done."

"Always busy, eh? I like your coat, Miss Jarrow."

"Do you? Well, I must be getting on."

"Good morning, Miss Jarrow."

As he entered his gateway, Mr. Holme felt within him that lilting flow of livingness that never failed to flood through the tunnels of his being after an encounter with Grace. Thoughts moved with a rippling freedom past magically raised lock-gates in his mind, spreading runnels of sparkling limpidity over a landscape fresh again with the spring-green hopes of youth. He felt on the verge of great verse, and there was power in him—and purpose. Courage and certainty. 'Here she is,' ran a rilled thought. 'You have her here, Holme—the mistress for your house. Hold her and never let her go.'

'. . . never let her go!' He heard it again like a tinkling echo trailing far into the wind-hissing pines. 'Never let her . . .'

"Who," asked Hyacinth, glancing round her rump, "was that you were chattering with out here! I heard you two, but I couldn't see you. The hedge was in the way."

"That was Miss Jarrow," he told her, in a slightly abstracted tone, putting down the tins of paraffin in the corner of the kitchen that he had allotted to them. "Did you bury the cat for me?"

"Of course I did. Did you know me never to keep my word?"

"Good girl."

'Never let her go . . .' In the high winds. In the woods . . .

"Near the compost heap. Didn't take me long. The soil there is soft. Before you could say 'knife' I'd had a hole dug two feet deep. Then I dumped the nasty thing in and heaped back the earth on it. Must have taken me about five minutes, the whole job." As she spoke Hyacinth kept scrubbing the floor, rotating her rump the while in rapid accompaniment to every twist and flick of her hand.

"Good girl," murmured Mr. Holme, his thoughts still in the woods . . . 'Hold her . . .'

"That mad father of hers. He's a case. Should be in a home."

"Who?"

"Old Jarrow."

"Never heard that he annoys anyone," frowned Mr. Holme, the magic vanished from his mind. He heard the scrubbing-brush on the floor.

"No. He just slinks around looking for nastiness."

"What sort of nastiness?"

"Anything nasty. Dead creatures and old bones."

Mr. Holme grunted and took a step toward the door to pass into the hallway, and Hyacinth, anticipating this move, made a sudden lurch across his path as though to start with her scrubbing-brush on a new patch of floor, causing him to collide with her rump and stumble over her. To steady himself he was compelled to place his hand for an instant on the small of her back.

"Sorry, Hyacinth."

"My fault. Moved at the wrong moment."

His face was flushed.

Hyacinth giggled. "Would you have minded?"

"What? Minded what?"

"If you'd fallen on me."

"Silly girl," mumbled Mr. Holme. Guttural. Still flushed. As he moved on into the hallway, making for the living-room, she giggled again.

"Wouldn't it have been a mess," she called after him, "you and me trying to sort ourselves out on the floor here?"

The outer door of the kitchen slammed shut with a detonating bang.

"Oooh!"

In the boiler the wind squealed, too.

A plane was passing overhead, its drone coming in hoarse curled roars, as though it were a ribbon being furled and unfurled in the gale.

"Think you'll be much longer in there, Hyacinth?" called Mr. Holme from the living-room.

"No. Give me two more minutes."

Tapping.

"You know what?"

"Said something?" he asked.

"Yes, I'm just thinking. I wonder if it could have been old Jarrow."

"What about him?"

"The cat."

Hammering.

"What's that you're mending in there?"

"The sofa leg. Didn't you notice it was crooked?"

"Yes, I was to have told you about it. Didn't look too safe."

Tap, tap, then hammering.

"I do believe it's him who did it."

"Did what?"

"Old Jarrow. The cat."

"What makes you think he did it?"

"It just smells like something he might do."

She spoke in her imitation American accent; often she imagined herself the heroine in an American film drama.

Mr. Holme made no reply, and Hyacinth told herself that it looked bad, buddy. Yeah, boy, she thought, it looked as if he wanted to defend the old man because of his daughter. Then she forgot she was an American film heroine and thought seriously: Could something be up that had not come to her ears? Had that plain Jane of a Grace Jarrow been setting her cap at him? It would be cheek. As if she stood a chance!

What, Mr. Holme meanwhile was asking himself, could she be getting at? Why should she think it was old Jarrow? The old man had nothing against him. He had hardly even, in his memory, exchanged a word with him. Hyacinth was too flighty. Not a bad sort—damned attractive—but a little too frivolous for his liking.

Yet she hadn't liked the look in his eyes when he came in a few minutes ago. It wasn't an ordinary look. And though she hadn't been able to hear what they were saying near the gate she could tell that he sounded happy talking to her. Funny. Very funny. Not a bad figure, but look at her nose! And the old-fashioned way she did her hair. And the chipping, frightened way she walked along the lane. As if she thought Satan was following her with a red-hot poker.

He had dismissed the matter from his mind as soon as he had left the house to go and get the paraffin, telling himself in the back of his awareness that some mischievous urchin must have done it as a joke. After all, there was nothing to get excited about in a dead cat. No, he was sure she was wrong. Old Jarrow couldn't have any reason for doing such a thing.

No harm if she watched the position. These plain-faced halfwits could be very scheming. They had ways of turning a man's head.

From what he had heard, the old fellow made those two women of his most hellishly unhappy. Poor creature. All the more reason why he would like to get her out of that household.

He would be wasted on an insipid creature like that. He would.

She was so simple and sincere. So sweet. Almost like a child.

"Rightee-oh! I'm done. You can come in now and fuss around if you like."

"Thank you, Hyacinth."

"I'll tackle the hallway right away."

"Good girl."

"Aw! Don't go on calling me a good girl like that." She was Mae West now. "How do you know I'm good?"

An amused grunt from him as he entered the kitchen.

"I can be naughty when I want." She was herself again, and a little self-conscious. She giggled, avoiding to look at him directly.

They heard a metallic clatter in the wind.

"What's that outside?"

"Some dog foraging on the compost heap, I suppose," he said. "They're always knocking around some empty tin or the other."

"Hee, hee!" Her face gone red.

"What's the joke now?" he asked.

"I'm remembering you."

"Me?"

"How you nearly fell over me."

A grunt as he bent to open the lower part of the cupboard set in the wall.

She emptied the pail of dirty water down the sink, and turned on the tap. And as the water gushed and the wind wheezed in the boiler she hummed a tune. Moving her rump in rhythm. But self-consciously, as though deep down she knew she was making a fool of herself.

"One day you *might* fall," she said, watching the water gushing.

"What's that?" he asked, in an abstracted voice. He was measuring out some fertilizer. Clinking the tins.

"I say don't be too sure of yourself."

"About what?"

"One day you *might* fall."

He flushed. And moved toward the larder door.

Wheeze, went the boiler.

"You might, you know."

"Silly girl." Patting her rump before he passed into the larder.

Wheeze!

"Hee, hee!" Like an echo of the wheeze.

Her rump wiggled in triumph.

6

By noon it had abated to a few indeterminate puffs at long intervals, and had veered to the south-east so that the vane on the steeple of St. Philip's Church kept pointing with its scissors end toward the near-distant woods of Berkshire; toward the spot where Swithin Lake lay hidden beyond the edge of the common—an elongated crescent of water that, on fine days, looked, with the woods around it, part of the Bois de Boulogne, though the water seemed fresher and less syrupy-green than the water in the lakes of the Bois; toward the spot, too, pointed the wind-vane—the spot much further off—where a group of men with dreams and dwarfed fancies dwelt together in uneasy subjection, awaiting their day to roam the woods alone, to the terror of homes around.

A pale sun, that resembled a blob of coagulated castor oil, shone down, now and then, upon the flagged landscape whose oaks and poplars and many chestnuts had not yet shed all their leaves, though there were some—among them evergreen as well—whose shattered limbs lay shuddering in ditches and near hedges, on fells and cattle-dented fields, in lanes and by gates and stiles. The chill air held the tang of leaves and broken trees, of everything vegetable wind-violated; even the whiffs of coal-smoke from red-brick chimneys could not kill the smell of injured green, of chlorophyll spilled and sap still bleeding. Brown leaves, and some not so brown, lay in heaps against embankments, and at the base of great tree boles; some crawled and crackled along pavements like enfeebled insects fumbling toward any haven at all, however forlorn.

Many, like machine-gunned corpses, were swept together and tilted into the small grey cart managed by the small dark man who wore a dirty coat over a dull-blue pullover: a man seemingly too poor even to possess a dilapidated mackintosh. His old grey flannels were patched in the seat and at the knees, and bore innumerable stains: stains that, long ago, had merged into each other, forming a soiled map where land and sea were linked in outlines lacking all significance.

Yet he was a cheerful young man, and whistled softly to himself as he worked, expertly sweeping the leaves together and then spading them up and canting them into the cart. He had wide-apart grey-blue eyes under well-defined eyebrows, and a sharp, slightly up-tilted nose that could never hope to cast a shadow upon the perky pouted mouth beneath. His chin was clearly dimpled, and, at the moment, smooth after his morning's shave; on many another day there could be seen upon it an ample growth of beard, for he was a young man not careful of his appearance, even in his off-duty moments.

Had it not been that he happened to be taking Hyacinth to a cinema show that evening he would not have bothered to shave. "I won't be seen with you if you don't shave and look decent," Hyacinth persistently told him—though when he forgot to shave she still went out with him, for secretly she hoped he would never shave; it gave her a shivering thrill when, in the dark of the cinema, he rubbed his unshaven chin against her ear and her neck, as he was so fond of doing: it made her want to giggle luxuriously deep inside her quaking stomach, and quivers of animal delight moved all over the eager sponginess of her body.

If only, she would assure herself at such instants, it could have been Mr. Holme beside her rubbing his moustache against her ear and neck, how much greater would have been her pleasure! What did it matter that Dick was twenty-three and Mr. Holme fifty-two! A neatly trimmed moustache was far more exciting than an unshaven chin—especially when it went along with a cottage. And a garden.

Dick lived in a squatter's hut off the Barkingstoke Road, and with him lived his slovenly mother who charred for the Council School and, three times a week, for Mr. Czenty, the Polish dentist, at Purling, two miles up the Barkingstoke Road.

Hyacinth was fond of Dick and could see herself married to him and being happy, even in a squatter's hut. But there could be no happiness, she felt certain, if his mother lived with them. "That's why I can't say yes," she told Dick, whenever Dick proposed. "It's that mother of yours." She had never given Dick a hint that Mr. Holme also constituted an important factor in her refusal of his suit. Often she had naïvely spoken to him of Mr. Holme—what a nice man he was—and of his cottage—what a nice cottage it was—but Dick, as naïve as she, saw nothing to be alarmed at in this; indeed, equally as much as Hyacinth scorned the idea of Grace Jarrow being a rival to be reckoned with, Dick would have scorned the idea of Mr. Holme proving attractive to Hyacinth.

Like Hyacinth, Dick Barke had been born in Middenshot, and had attended the Village Council School until the age of fourteen. On leaving, he had worked as a gardener's assistant at Rogan Hall, the Pendlefields' place, then as a porter at Barkingstoke Station—from both jobs he had been dismissed for slacking and inefficiency—and then as dustman in Middenshot—and this job he had held for the past year and a half, and seemed likely to hold for good. "At last, Dick's found his level" had become a popular remark in Middenshot during the past few months.

It would be no disgrace, felt Hyacinth, to marry a dabbler in dust and ashes. As a child of seven, a lasting impression had been made upon her by the words of the parson at the graveside, on the occasion of her mother's funeral. "Dust to dust ... ashes to ashes." In her child's mind she had thought of her mother's corpse as being reduced, within the lowered coffin, to dust and ashes at the instant of the parson's uttering these words, and for weeks after—indeed, for months and years—she had been unable to rid herself of the image of an elongated heap of dust and ashes cached beneath the grass like a well-preserved treasure. Whenever she had seen the dustman emptying an ash-can into the refuse cart she had thought of her mother underground, a shapely pile of ashes, grisly-grey but dully shining, as might an old pewter jug. And, for her, the dustman became a man of noble doings. Think of the human dust and ashes he must handle every day! How did she know that in his cart, at the very instant she was watching, there were not several heaps representing several dead humans! People, perhaps, who had been too poor to have coffins and who had merely been laid out on their death-beds and then, at the magic words of the parson, changed into dust and ashes, and reverently—by their relatives—deposited into the ash-can! In her immature mind a dustman had taken on a sheen of glory—the reverent sheen of pewter.

Her Uncle James—after the death of her father, a year later, she had been adopted by her childless uncle and aunt—had kept two pewter jugs on the mantelpiece in the living-room; he prided them greatly—indeed revered them—and said that they were the only reminders of the days when he had owned a public house at Barkingstoke. "A man of means, me," he would say, wagging his large round head, his brick-red face sad and jovial all at once. "Big man, me, in Barkingstoke in them days, Cinthy. Now look at me. Working for the village coal merchant." And then he would wink and snap his fingers at her. "Anyway, things could be worse, eh?" And she would giggle and sit on his knee, and they would talk until they heard her aunt coming in at the gate when Hyacinth would jump down and rush into the scullery to do her neglected chores. Uncle James was a sport and did not mind her neglecting her chores, but Aunt Sylvia, who did chores for the vicar, slapped her rump and clouted her neck when Hyacinth failed to do her quota of chores in the home.

One day—she was thirteen then—after a severe slapping and clouting from her aunt who went stamping out of the home, vicarage-bound, Uncle, in a sympathetic mood, had examined her wounds. Opening his eyes wide, he remarked: "You're coming to come, my girl. With a rump like this any young maid can get far in the world." He had run his gaze down her body, from head to foot, circling her elliptically from rump to upper façade and back to rump, and nodded approval. "Don't mind if she licks you, my girl. Licks won't kill. Do you good, in fact. Licks can't take away the shape of a rump like this." She had giggled shyly, but—as on the occasion of her mother's funeral—a new image had been born in her imagination. Her rump in a glow of glory.

By evening the wind had returned, blowing monotonously once more in full gale force from the southwest, and it was a relief for Hyacinth and Dick to enter the cinema, though Dick never complained about the cold; winter or summer he wore no overcoat. This evening he was garbed in his one good suit: it was of grey serge, with pin-stripes of blue; the trousers had long lost their creases. He wore a tie—a green one with large red ovals interlocked—and he had donned a yellow pullover on top of the dull-blue one in which he was always to be seen during the day. Hyacinth wore her fawn winter coat and her plastic raincoat as well, for there was rain in the wind—stinging sprinkles of fierce drops that came in unexpected bursts.

As per routine, Dick rubbed his chin against her ear and neck during the show—though she did not experience any deep thrill because of the comparative smoothness of his chin. She let him do some vague fumbling down her bosom, but he was by no means an artist at bosom-fumbling, and before long she sniffed and re-buttoned the front of her coat. It always happened this way; he only succeeded in tickling her and making her want to giggle. Mr. Holme, she had not the slightest doubt, would have done it better; he would have known exactly what knobs, so to speak, to turn and buttons to press to achieve the desired results both for him and for herself. Look at the gentle, unobtrusive way he had patted her rump this morning—the first time she had succeeded in getting him to yield to any kind of temptation. Only a man who knew about women could have patted her like that; she was sure Mr. Holme knew a lot about women. But Dick. Dick could be exciting—especially out on the common in the summer when they played their old game, touch-and-run—but he was green. For all she knew, he was still a virgin.

After the show, when they were battling their way against the wind along the High Street, toward her home in Miller's Lane, Dick, as per routine, said: "Well, how about it, Cinthy?"

"How about what?" she rebutted—as per routine.

"When's it to be?"

As per routine, she had to pretend that she did not know what he meant. "When's what to be?" she asked.

"Our wedding."

"Oh, that. What's the hurry? Give me time to think it over."

"How about a smack?"

"Why can't you say 'kiss'? 'Smack' sounds common." This was not according to routine, and Dick looked at her and said: "Who you've been visiting to get so upper-class sudden like this?"

"Wouldn't you like to know, buddy?" she drawled, as Hedy Lamarr, she felt, might have drawled.

"How about it, Cinthy?" persisted Dick, reverting to Theme One.

"Not with that mother of yours around. No, buddy. I guess it's just nothing doing with this baby."

"Mother won't be in the way."

"Not your way but mine." She dropped Hedy Lamarr and retrieved herself; the theme was too serious for affectation.

"How's she going to be in your way?"

"In lots of ways."

Dick grunted.

"That's why I can't say yes. It's that mother of yours."

"Every time I propose you say the same thing. Over two years we've been walking out and it's always Mother preventing you from saying yes."

"Well, it is!"

"What have you got against her?"

"She keeps that hut like a pig-sty."

"That's not true."

"I've seen it myself, haven't I?"

"It's only a hut, after all."

"She could still keep it clean if she wanted."

"She's getting down—and she's not well."

"That's no excuse. And don't let's quarrel in this wind. Oooh! It's cold!"

"Give me a smack."

"Say 'kiss' or you won't get it."

"Give me a smack."

"Then you won't get it!"

So he stopped, grabbed her and kissed her—as she knew he would have done. Kissed her roughly and defiantly and without finesse. With the maximum of noise. Indeed, a smack. And she liked it. It made her shudder to the very central mystery of her body's cravings. And with a silent, baffled groan she thought: 'What a pity it isn't Mr. Holme doing it!' But Mr. Holme, a sure instinct at once informed her, would never be able to kiss like this. He was too much of a gentleman. She so wanted to marry a gentleman. And she so yearned to be made love to by a ruffian.

7

Mr. Holme, meanwhile, was moving over the common toward Swithin Lake. Stout stick in hand, at the trail, body bent forward, he had the air of a man advancing against a desperate foe, himself desperate. The gale tore past him, roaring in his ears, contesting his every step, hooting and hawking at him, and, when he entered now and then the shelter of the pines, hunting him out with sudden triumphant howls of discovery. Around him the woods were in a gnashing animated torture of motion, waving and squirming and producing an insistent and seemingly endless commotion of hissing, as if on purpose to emphasize the boisterousness of the wind. Mr. Holme's mackintosh flapped an accompaniment to this sibilance, the metallic objects in the pockets clinking and jingling at intervals, like little cool flecks of green and pink sketched against the vast sepia nocturnal background of tree-and-wind hubbub.

He had not mentioned this to Grace, but apart from his desire for fresh air and exercise, it was his ambition, whenever he went for a walk at night, to reach Swithin Lake. It was a kind of test he had set himself. The night he failed to reach Swithin Lake— the night he felt exhausted and had to turn back before he had attained his objective—he would know that a decline had set in, both in his body and in his will; the tuberculosis had launched a new offensive and his own forces were withdrawing.

He always wore wellingtons on these occasions, for the tracks that wound across the common were frequently boggy—especially after a day of rain. However, even when it was dry he wore wellingtons, for he had discovered that they helped his *morale*.

Wearing them, he felt martial: a hero journeying through the night, on the way to a battle rendez-vous—a Siegfried menaced by gods and mortals but determined to be victorious; there were nights when he thought he could hear the blare of trumpets, and horn-calls that trailed, muffled, like smoothly rounded hoops of mist, from the middle of the woods.

There was not much of the fanciful in Mr. Holme, but his Siegfried mood, as to himself he had dubbed it, was the one oasis of fantasy he had cultivated in the desert of his stolid realism, and it continued to flourish only because the fruit it produced proved a powerful antidote against his fear of a return of his illness. It was a secret garden of his mind, and he tended it no less consciously nor zealously than he did the garden of his cottage.

In the private nursing home of Doctor Raven, there had been a wireless set in the corridor, just outside Mr. Holme's room, and Doctor Raven kept it tuned-in all day; should any of his six patients find it a nuisance all that was necessary was to close the room door. Mr. Holme generally closed his door when talks were in progress and opened it when there was music. Light music entertained him; serious music left him unmoved, but he tolerated it.

One afternoon in the summer, he was in a depressed mood because the sun was shining and the countryside, through his window, looked dreamily idyllic, and he kept wondering whether he would be alive to see it like this next summer. The wireless was emitting loud orchestral music and louder vocal passages. He listened to it all without hearing it until abruptly a crescendic brassy blare shivered through his apathy and made him sit forward in his chair. He found himself sad and excited, hopeful, his heart throbbing within him like a warm woollen ball being gradually charged with an unearthly electricity. His depression disintegrated as though sucked out of him at a single puff of denigrated pollen.

About twenty minutes later, he heard it again, and this time the doctor happened to be with him. He asked the doctor what music it was, and Doctor Raven told him the story of *The Ring*. "What you heard," he said, "is the Siegfried *leitmotif*. Siegfried the hero." The doctor was a great lover of Wagner; his fervour infected Mr. Holme.

It was from that afternoon that hope took possession of him; the seeds of his fantasy-garden swelled and sprouted. From that afternoon he was sure he would recover; he almost felt superstitious about the Siegfried *leitmotif*. Whenever he hummed or whistled it it gave him courage, confidence, made him feel he could fight anything and win. What was a little tuberculosis! So he had fought and won. And henceforth he had seen himself a hero fighting back—always fighting back when he thought himself attacked by the virulent bacilli.

This evening when he rounded a bend in the track and saw Swithin Lake burnt-umber under the windy sky of shifting clouds, he found himself remembering Doctor Raven and the story of *The Ring*. And mingled with it was the memory of himself talking to Grace near his gate that morning. He knew now that it was the awareness of Grace within him that had generated the vitality that pervaded his present brooding. Had he not met her that morning his Siegfried mood would, this evening, have been less phosphorescently aglow in his fancy; he would not have looked at the water now and imagined the Rhinedaughters appearing and calling to him to yield up the ring. Nor would he have smiled and fingered the signet ring on the little finger of his right hand.

The smile was a shame-faced one. He felt—as he had felt on dozens of previous occasions—that he was making a fool of himself; he felt he was doing something out of character; all this mushy business about Siegfried and the Rhinedaughters—it was not in his line. Yet he still tilted his head and listened to the wind in the pines and the firs and the silver birches. Suppose he did hear a horn-call. Suppose he did hear the voices of Woglinde and Wellgunde and Flosshilde singing in the water, and out of the inky-ragged welkin should see Brünnhilde spring with a blaze into being, her shrieked battle-cry like a sword slashing into awed silence the very wind itself!

He lashed his trousers leg with his stick, and smiled again—this time a smile of elation. He was a hero. Siegfried on the Rhine.

Since he had come to live in Middenshot the habit of falling into reveries had grown more frequent, which was only natural, he supposed, living alone as he did. He enjoyed his reveries.

Especially when walking on the common and when, on his return home, he settled down to glance through some magazine or gardening manual and review the day's events—the day's small victories. Or defeats. Though, as a rule, he disliked admitting the defeats. A cowardly attitude, some people would say, but he preferred it so. In his way of seeing things, it was better to note one's victories and not dwell on the defeats. That, it seemed to him, was the true way to happiness. The positive, optimistic way.

Of course he needed to cultivate a certain amount of discipline in respect to these reveries of his. Look what had happened the other night. Going into the Jarrows' gateway and right up to the living-room windows before realizing he had made a mistake. That kind of thing wouldn't do at all. What had he been thinking about that night? Not about Grace. Nor about Siegfried or Brünnhilde ... No, it was the orchid ... Yes, he remembered now. The old dream. Picturing the orchid in bloom. He had seen himself entering the greenhouse one morning and discovering that a long spray of buds, appeared a few days earlier, had dramatically burst open during the previous night and the whole spray hung before him, a misty bridal veil speckled blue and green and violet ... He had been fumbling for his latch-key when he looked up and saw hazily through the misted panes old Mr. Jarrow sitting at a table with someone—Grace. With a gasp, he had turned and hurried out into the lane again, impatient with himself for having made such a blunder, hoping that he had not been seen, though he had had an uncomfortable notion that Grace had turned her face toward the window in the same instant that he recoiled. Could it be that his apology this morning had come as no surprise to her? Had she and her parents been discussing him during the past day or two—perhaps accusing him of being a Peeping Tom?

Grace ... Now, what was it about her that had struck into him that first day he had seen her in the High Street two years ago? It had not been a question of falling in love with her—no question of raised heart-beat or an urgent desire to be in her company—but he had experienced ... how could he put it? A feeling of harmony. A feeling ... No, just that. A feeling of harmony. There was no other way of expressing it.

It was only gradually, as the months had passed, that the idea of having her in his home as its mistress had taken shape in his mind. He had thought of her as a hired housekeeper, and then, in his imagination, he had decided that the housekeeper might as well be his wife. The development of his interest in her had been as prosaic as that. With his first wife—in his fancy Grace was already his second—it had been the same; they had been acquainted since schooldays, and each had become to the other a pleasant habit, so that eventually when he did propose it was as though he had merely endorsed a course of action that each had tacitly agreed upon more than a decade before. Between Millicent and himself, in all their years together, there had never been once an explosive scene of passion; theirs had been a slow, unsensational affection: except for a mild "my dear" on occasion, they had not indulged in endearments. Yet, so far as he could recall, there had never been an instant when the deep feeling between them—it somehow embarrassed him to think of it as love—had seemed threatened; perhaps for the very reason that it had never flared up it burned without wavering.

There were moments when he thought that it would be the same if he were married to Grace, and then, unawares, he would sense a hungry dungeon open inside him, and there would be a howling and a murky whirling down there, for—though he could not fathom this, lacking as he did the requisite introspective depth—there had come alive in him lately an element of insta- bility: a new demon, an unfamiliar jinx born of recent years, a dragon-jinnee with a breath that, who knew, might blow upon the staidness of his life a torrid turbulence of passion.

No, with Grace it would not be the same. With Grace—and again he could not fathom this himself—there would be fire and fanfares. Horncalls haunting his peace, and the cool fluting and tintinnabulation of many a fanciful feathered creature. Siegfried wandering in the woods.

He watched the water in Swithin Lake, letting his gaze move across to the silhouette of trees on the opposite bank, an ani- mated design against the sky with its hurrying daubs of cloud: trees like frayed wolves' heads waving without fatigue—pawns impotent in the night's pattern—their ferocious mien as meretricious as the insistence of their soughing. The dark was their dynamic—and the damp west wind. Only the wind and the black-bat shadows of night had donated them their terror. Only . . .

Mr. Holme turned.

A footstep.

And a fluting, too?

He had probably, he decided, imagined it.

He listened to the flap-flap of his mackintosh. He reflected on the miscellany in the pockets. He loved the odds and ends in them. Almost looked on them as familiars: dumb friends. Old pipe. Old penknife. Nails of all sizes, some rusty. Bits of string of various lengths. A piece of waste—very useful, that, for wiping glue from his fingers. Several coiled bits of copper wire. Buttons. Seeds. Scissors. A small file . . .

The wind was very damp. And warmish. The five-to-six forecast that afternoon had said there would be fog in the morning. Brave as the wind sounded now, its death was near; by dawn it would have faded into some northern grave, a withered mummy harmless in the isobaric heavens. By dawn the fog would be here, cold and enclosing.

Mr. Holme turned again.

He was sure of it now. A footstep. Coming from the north-west. Over there. It was very dark. He waited.

Now a figure. Approaching along the bank of the lake.

He advanced to meet it.

"Disgusting weather," remarked the overcoated man. A heavy, expensive-looking overcoat, it seemed to Mr. Holme, though it was too dark to be certain.

"Yes, disgusting," agreed Mr. Holme.

"Trying to find my way to the village. I'm from the farm over there. Ashbole." The accent was cultivated. A gentleman farmer, without doubt. Retired major or colonel, thought Mr. Holme.

"You live in Middenshot?" asked the gentleman.

"Yes," answered Mr. Holme.

"I sometimes shop there. Off and on. Not a damned post-box near our way, and there's a letter I must have posted to-night."

"Well, I could show you the way," offered Mr. Holme, "unless you'd care to entrust the letter to me. I could drop it in the box for you. There's a post-box round the corner from where I live, just opposite the church."

"Would you do that for me? Awfully nice of you. It would save me a long walk."

"It would be a pleasure," Mr. Holme told him.

"Very good of you. I'm extremely grateful."

"Don't mention it," said Mr. Holme, taking the letter.

"Well, good night. And—ah—you won't forget it in your pocket?"

"No, you can depend on me. I have a fairly good memory for such things," laughed Mr. Holme.

"Thank you. Good night!"

"Good night!"

As the stranger turned and plodded off in the direction from which he had come Mr. Holme smiled to himself, feeling a warm, enveloping love of humanity moving within him. It always affected him this way when he did anyone a favour. He found a genuine pleasure in helping others. It must be a very unhappy person, he sometimes felt, who rarely had the opportunity to do something helpful for a fellow being.

On his way back, he was in a mood of reflective contentment. He remembered the farming gentleman and the letter to post; he remembered Grace in her green coat that morning. And seeping like a little hillside spring between and through the two images was the fresh memory-mirage of Swithin Lake and the wind-troubled trees he had just left behind him. More vague—though it was in the nature of a background support to his mood—was the thought of his savings in Lloyd's Bank and the two or three pounds he made every week off the flowers he sold to a flower-shop in Camberley or Barkingstoke. Tomorrow was the day Mrs. Leete came from Barkingstoke. She would want some lupins and delphiniums and some of the tropical ferns he grew in Number Two.

The wind was behind him now, and, as always when one backs the wind, he had the illusion that it had died down. It no longer roared in his ears, though the trees still persisted in their agonized riot of noise, and now and then, monotonously, tirelessly, his mackintosh would flap and jingle.

He emerged opposite the Laytons' cottage, glanced at the Jarrows' and saw that there was light behind the curtains of the living-room windows. With his own cottage they were the only cottages in Pine Tree Lane. East of his came a fell where cedars grew; the south-eastern boundary of this fell looked down on Great Oak Road. Down an embankment bordered by a ragged holly hedge.

In the lane he stepped squelchingly into a pool, squelched his way out and plodded east past his own cottage. At the bend where the lane turned into Great Oak Road occurred the first street-lamp. The bluish gaslight gave to the holly hedges an air of sinister vigilance, as though each leaf had acquired an evil metallic eye. Glancing at his wrist-watch, he saw that the time was nearly a quarter to nine. He was lowering his wrist when he noticed that the letter in his hand lacked a stamp.

Frowning, he halted—he was about ten yards from the letter-box, a red square set into the thick grey wall that bordered the churchyard—and brought the envelope into view, letting the gaslight fall full upon it.

"Well," he muttered.

He stood there staring at it. Gave a grunt.

"Well."

A sealed envelope. And all that was written on it was: "The bearer may open this. Must."

8

"Oh!"

"Ho!"

"But . . ."

"What?"

"You didn't, Dad!"

"I did."

"No!"

"Haw, haw!"

"Oh!"

"Grace, please," implored her mother.

"I must, Mother."

"Ho!"

"It's disgusting!"

"So?"

"Shameful!"

"Please, Grace dear."

"Poor man."

"Old boar."

"Where did you put it?"

"Somewhere."

"At the back?"

"Or the front."

"The back?"

"The front."

"But really . . ."

"Wrong. All, dear child, is roguery and unreality."

"Shut up!"

"Grace dear, please!"

Whoo-whee, went the wind.

And the whisper of withered leaves.

"I'm going to tell him."

"Go."

"I will!"

"Go now."

"It's horrid."

"And hateful."

"You're a horrid old man."

"And hateful."

"I'm glad you know it."

"Hee, haw! Hee, haw!"

"You've made our home a hateful place."

"Every home to-day is a haven of hate and horror."

"Shut up!"

"Please, Grace dear!"

"Mother, I must."

"Haw haw!"

Big Ben striking nine o'clock.

Muffled clatter in the roof.

And the chimney wailing.

"I'll have to see him tomorrow morning and apologize."

"Old hawk."

"Here is the news . . ."

"He's no hawk."

"Old skunk."

"He's no skunk."

"Grace dear . . ."

"He's a quiet, charming man."

"Aha."

"He's worth ten of you."

"Oho."

". . . the North Korean armies are continuing their retreat . . ."

"You're going too far now."

"Far from the madding cow. Wish I were."

"Are you calling me a cow?"

"Virgin cow."

"Oh!"

"Ho!"

Grace left the room sobbing.

Mrs. Jarrow followed her.

The wind whooped down the chimney.

Mr. Jarrow guffawed. Abruptly stiffened in his chair at something the announcer said in his preliminary summary of the news. He rose and called out: "Come back! Come and hear the news!" He was excited.

After a minute or two, Grace and her mother came in again.

"Ho!" taunted Mr. Jarrow.

"Say nothing, Grace dear. Please."

"I don't want to, Mother."

". . . the motion was defeated by a majority of seven votes . . ."

"Go on with your knitting, dear."

"I'm too upset to knit, Mother."

"Ha!"

"Ha about what, Dad?"

"Grace dear, please! For my sake . . ."

". . . an inmate of Broadmoor Criminal Lunatic Asylum is reported to have escaped during the early hours of this morning . . ."

"Good Lord!"

"What!"

"Aha."

"... *the discovery was made only at noon to-day. He is wearing a fawn-coloured overcoat of rather expensive cut, and sometimes poses as a gentleman farmer, sometimes as a Lord High Executioner...*"

"Gracious!"

"Oh, heavens!"

"Haw."

"... *he is a homicidal maniac, and residents of Crowthorne and the surrounding district have been warned to secure their doors and windows and be careful when out-of-doors...*"

Mr. Jarrow tapped with his stick on the floor. "You've heard it!" he bellowed. "We shall all be murdered in our sleep to-night!"

"Grace, have you bolted the back door?" asked Mrs. Jarrow.

"Yes, Mother, I did. I do every night."

Grace and her mother began to speak excitedly. Mr. Jarrow rose, in an ecstasy, limped across the room and struck the wall a cracking blow with his stick. "We shall all be butchered at midnight!" he cried to the ceiling. "Cut up piece by piece, and daintily stacked in a trunk—by the Lord High Executioner."

"Dad, please be quiet."

"Ho, ho! Haw, haw, haw!" The old gentleman continued to exult. After a while he limped back to the fire, gazed down at the flames and told them: "A regular rollick of blood and bones. In Crowthorne and Middenshot—every house a charnel-house. The Lord High Executioner will get them all. Off with their legs! Off with their arms! Swipe! Off with their heads!"

"... *the forecast is that the high winds will abate before dawn. Fog is expected in most southern and eastern districts...*"

"Fog! Fog! More power to the Lord High Executioner! Off with their noses! Out with their rotted hearts! Every one of them! House-wife and whore! Pimp and parson!"

"Dad, be quiet!"

"Ho, ho! Did you hear that?" Mr. Jarrow asked the fire. "The cow is in a heat. My virgin cow of a daughter."

"This is shocking!"

"Haw, haw! The old bull!"

"Oh!"

"After my virgin cow, that's what he is. Stinking old bull!"

A knock at the front door.

Mrs. Jarrow gasped.

Grace, about to reprove her father, stopped short and paled.

The knock came again.

"Who can that be, I wonder," murmured Mrs. Jarrow.

"No one ever visits us at this time of the evening," said Grace.

"It's the Lord High Executioner!" bellowed Mr. Jarrow. "Welcome, my Lord! Welcome!"

Again the knock.

"Open the door, child," said Mr. Jarrow. "Go and let his Lordship rape you—and then carve you up. What are you waiting for? Go and open up unto the Lord!"

"Dad, be quiet! Mother, what do you think we should do?"

The knock again.

Grace made a move to leave the room, but her mother said: "No, dear, let me go."

"Mother, don't. No, please. Be careful."

"I'll ask who it is before I open."

"Go and open the door, child," said Mr. Jarrow. "You're in a heat. You'll like the raping."

"Say nothing, Grace dear."

"Can't expect an old man like me to go to the door," grumbled her father. "Only right that you should have your throat cut first. Youth before age. Go on. Open the door and get it over quick. He'll pounce on you, tear off your clothes, do a good, clean rape, then slit your throat with a razor—and it'll be all over. Neat and expert. What are you worrying for? Go and open the door."

Grace, ignoring him, moved into the hallway after her mother.

Mrs. Jarrow paused near the hat-rack and called out: "Who is there? Did someone knock?"

"Yes, Mrs. Jarrow! It's me. Holme."

Grace pushed hurriedly past her mother and opened the door. "Oh, Mr. Holme, it's you! Sorry we had to keep you waiting, but we thought . . . we didn't know . . . Oh, please come in."

"Sorry to disturb you at this time," said Mr. Holme in an uncomfortable voice. His manner was inwardly excited, Grace noted. There was a glitter in his eye she had never before seen.

"Please come in, Mr. Holme," smiled Mrs. Jarrow.

"I didn't intend to come in—but perhaps I'd better. Better close the door, too. You've heard the nine o'clock news?"

"We were listening to it when you knocked," said Grace. "You mean about the man who's escaped from Broadmoor?"

"Yes. As soon as I heard it I thought I'd rush over and warn you. He's in this neighbourhood now."

"Won't you come into the living-room?" said Mrs. Jarrow.

"Mother, do you think . . . well, perhaps . . . yes, do come into the living-room, Mr. Holme. It's rather chilly in the hallway here."

"Thank you. But—ah—I shouldn't like to disturb your father."

"Ho!" came Mr. Jarrow's voice from the living-room.

Grace, in a whisper, said: "He's—he's a little difficult sometimes, Mr. Holme, but please don't take any notice of him. Simply pretend he isn't in the room."

"I understand, Miss Jarrow," mumbled Mr. Holme.

When they entered they found Mr. Jarrow perched on the window seat. He had drawn aside the curtains, and was gazing steadfastly through the misted panes, having rubbed several patches clear with his hand.

"Horror," he murmured. "Horror on every hand. Without and within."

Mr. Holme, by no means at ease, seated himself in the chair Grace indicated. He had taken off his mackintosh in the hallway, and Mrs. Jarrow had hung it on a peg on the hat-rack. He began to fumble in his coat pocket, then started and said: "I think I left something in one of the pockets of my mackintosh. Excuse me a moment."

He rose and went into the hallway, returning after a brief interval, Grace and her mother staring curiously at him. Mrs. Jarrow stood behind Grace's chair.

"I came to warn you because of this," said Mr. Holme. He held out what looked like a letter. "It was given to me on the common."

"On the common?"

"Not the garden," murmured Mr. Jarrow.

"Yes. I went for my evening walk as usual, and a strange man gave this to me and asked me to post it for him."

"Oh."

"The Lord High Executioner," rumbled Mr. Jarrow, as though addressing a sinister someone outside.

Mr. Holme gave him an uncertain glance.

Grace took the letter.

"Read it, Miss Jarrow."

Grace extracted from the envelope a small slip of pinkish paper, and read: *Tell Middenshot I'll be there to-night and many another night to perform my duty as Lord High Executioner.* It was written in a strong, if somewhat ornate, handwriting with what might have been a Biro pen.

Grace's reaction was: "Oh."

Mrs. Jarrow, reading the message over her shoulder, also said: "Oh."

"I didn't want to alarm you," said Mr. Holme, smiling with discomfiture, his manner almost boyishly agitated. Excited. Grace saw him as a looming hero. Her heart bumped like a barrel in a cave behind her ribs. She forgot her father at the window. She had never before in her life felt like this. It was as though lights were coming on in lovely undreamed-of rooms within her.

"I think it's very kind and considerate of you to come," she said softly.

Dry leaves prattled on the back windows. Smoke puffed into the room.

"This terrible chimney. We really need a cowl for it," said Mrs. Jarrow.

"Everything," said Mr. Holme, "has fitted in perfectly."

"Fitted in?"

"What's that?" asked Grace.

"Yes," he told them. "I mean about this fellow who's escaped. This morning I was puzzled to know how that carcase came to be on my kitchen step."

"Carcase?" said Mrs. Jarrow.

Grace was silent, troubled.

"Ha!" exclaimed the old gentleman.

"Carcase of a cat," said Mr. Holme. "It must have been he who put it there."

"Oh."

No sound from Grace.

"And a few minutes ago, on coming back from my walk, would you believe I found the very same carcase on my front-door step?"

"What!"

"Ho!"

"There was a label attached to it, with two words written on it. 'Old weasel.'" Mr. Holme laughed. "This morning it was 'old runt.' The fellow seems to have a sense of humour, if nothing else."

"Yes," whispered Mrs. Jarrow.

Still no sound from Grace.

"I got Hyacinth, the girl who comes in to help, to bury it for me near the compost heap. He must have been hiding in the woods and watched her, and then later dug it up."

"Yes," whispered Mrs. Jarrow.

"Mr. Holme," said Grace, sitting erect.

"Yes, Miss Jarrow?"

"It was not the escaped lunatic who left that carcase on your door-step."

"No?"

"No. It was my father."

"Oh . . . Ah," said Mr. Holme.

"Old stoat," murmured the old gentleman to the front garden.

Mr. Holme rose. "Afraid I must be off."

Grace rose, too. "I'm sorry it happened. I do hope you'll forgive him. He's . . . he's not responsible—"

"Please don't be upset, Miss Jarrow. I understand."

"Haw, haw!"

"I . . . It's so nice of you to have come in, Mr. Holme."

"Don't mention it, Miss Jarrow. Simply had to warn you—especially as your cottage is at the end of the lane, right on the edge of the common. I'm going now to the police station to report that I met him on the common, and show them this communication. I'm sure it won't be long before they recapture him."

"You'd better not stay out too late, Mr. Holme," said Grace.

"Old fox."

Grace trembled, her face white.

"Oh . . . Ah. Well, I must be going, Miss Jarrow. Mrs. Jarrow. Good night—and lock up carefully."

"You should, too," said Grace softly. "Lock up carefully."

"Yes. Yes, I will."

"Are your orchids coming on nicely, Mr. Holme?"

They were in the hallway now, and he was putting on his mackintosh. He looked at her quickly and smiled, the blood coming to his face. "Yes. Yes, they're doing very well. One morning, if you're not too busy, I could show them to you if you care."

"Oh, I should so like to see them. I hear you have a rare one."

"Yes, but it hasn't bloomed yet. I'm waiting to see what it will be like when it does bloom."

"I'd like to see it, too. Really I would." She held out her hand as he was about to move toward the door, and he took it and said: "I keep dreaming what it will look like, Miss Jarrow. Very foolish of me, I suppose. I've always been keen on orchids." He was still holding her hand, and of a sudden became aware of this and aware, too, that she was not trying to tug it away. He released it abruptly with an inward trembling—a sense of pleasant shock. "Well, good night, Miss Jarrow. Good night."

9

For a long time after Mr. Holme had gone the three of them were without a word, gathered about the fire in the living-room, hearing the wind and the low clattering in the roof, now and then, and the patter of a leaf on the wall at the back. The old gentleman would move a foot warily along the floor and grunt or moan, far down in a tomb of contemplation, treading what weird, winding path he alone knew. And the poor elderly lady, pale, worried, would look toward the window, apprehending a whole world of terror; awaiting the moment when it would break into the room and overwhelm them. Only the younger woman appeared untroubled by the terror without; a dream-like calm had come upon her: she looked like one reclining in a valley gloomed with the green of many a leaning plant, drugged with the scent of too many sleep-giving vapours. She had a transfigured mien, as though her human frame had, within the past few minutes, grown filled with a light from the more remote and sacred alcoves of the night, transforming her into a thing of peculiar beauty; a thing of translucency, over-flooded with light rather than overflowing with shape.

Oh, the wind, whooping and whining! But dying. Every moment dying.

A door banged down the lane, and how the pines hissed! But the wild stirring was gone. The intervals of quiet grew longer.

The old gentleman of a sudden got up. He looked slowly about him, then raised his stick, swung it round and struck at the shaded electric light bulb, and the bulb went off with a loud pop, the shattered glass raining down in a tinkle on the carpeted floor.

The two women shrieked in the fire-flickering dark.

"An ill man! I'm an ill old man who won't tolerate horrible strangers in his home! Woe to all women! Woe! Woe!" howled the old gentleman.

He slammed the door after him as he left them. They heard him bellowing as he began to plod his thundering way up the stairs to his room.

"How ill I am!" he bellowed. "How horridly ill! For days and nights—for weeks—I shall be ill! Ill, ill, ill!"

Tweep, whoop, tweep! went the wind. Mocking him.

THE FOG

I

All of us ... we're all moving in it, and we never know what we'll encounter, nor what we'll behold when we emerge. If we do emerge ... Cold fog. Cold, cold ... How I do hate a fog in the late autumn. How I hate to walk on the common in the early morning. Me an ill man, too. And horror humped up hiding round the corner. Not knowing when the mallet will fall on my poor bubbling brain. Hell, hell! Whoever could have made me mad, I wonder! Whoever could have put the berry in my brain and brewed the beer that drunkened my dreams! And who could have told anybody that mine would be the wayward way and theirs the one to heaven! Oh, this wonderful, warped world that no man can nail for sure! ...

"... Mother, I'm sure, I tell you."

"You may be wrong, my girl. It could have been next-door."

"No, Mother, I'm sure it was here. I heard the door slam."

"But it's so early, Grace. Look at the time. Twenty past three."

"Shall I go into his room and see?"

"You'd better not. If he's there he'll be very angry."

"I don't care. Let him be angry. I'm getting tired of him, Mother. He's going too far. Much too far."

"Don't tire, Grace. Please don't tire, my child. It's the one thing I've always asked you to try not to do. I know how hard it must be for you, but please, for my sake, do be kind to him. Be tolerant."

"We've been too kind to him, Mother. I'm coming to see that now."

"You mustn't say that, Grace. You must be patient with him. You're not yourself. I noticed it last night. You must be run down. Perhaps you need a tonic."

"I'm not run down, Mother, but I'm ... oh, I don't know what's the matter with me, but—but I simply can't stand it when he says anything against Mr. Holme. I feel like fighting him. Like striking him. I feel really terrible."

... what can be more terrible than knowing you're normal and the crowd around you unnormal! Am I odd for wanting nothing but horror about me! Why—when the very pattern of life created by people who feel they're normal seethes with horror in every tiny creek and cranny, in every minute whorl and curve! Even compassion, a healthy orange, the loveliest human fruit, they have allowed to rot, and now its tainted, bitter juice seeps into every natural act, turning it into a putrid, sentimental cheese that stinks like July carrion on the common. Compare my garnered bones and pictures with their decayed ideals that result in how many cumulated nightmare scenes! An old lady sitting in a train at night—and whonk! Down comes the cosh, and down again! And kick, kick her in the face, kick her in the rump, kick her in the stomach. Grab her purse and leave her crumpled and nearly dead. Off, my lads! What a lark! No one will hurt you—no one will flog you—no corporal punishment. Poor lads! Blame society for your brutal, thieving pranks. Blame environment—not your filthy heredity. Oh, poor lads! Put them in approved schools so they can escape and cosh and kick more old ladies, and throw in a rape or two for good measure; then recapture them and treat them kindly so they can escape again and cosh and kick and beat more old ladies—how old ladies like being coshed and kicked! How young girls in lonely lanes like being raped! Then once more catch them and put them away to grow into fully fledged gun-men and let them loose to break shop-windows and shoot bank clerks. Only when they have done a murder in two it would be right to hang them and be rid of them. Oooh! But what have I said? Hang them? Oh, no, no, that would be most unkind. Hanging ought long ago to have been done away with. Better by far to put them in prison for life; that would be more humane, for it would give them yet another sporting chance of escaping to do just a little more frolicsome shooting and stabbing. The evening papers must be fed with sensations; what would they do without smash-and-grab raids and coshed old ladies! How would some of our Sunday papers carry on without raped young girls and good choppy, bleeding murders! Pity our poor papers! Provide them with horrors. Long live our lags and larking lads! . . .

"Oh, what a foggy morning! Haw, haw, haw! What a foggy-woggy world we live in!" . . .

". . . and it's such a dreadful, foggy morning."

"Suppose he were to fall foul of that lunatic."

"Anyway, he would deserve it, Mother. I refuse to worry."

"Are you sure he went out, Grace? Go and take a peep into his room, then, my child. Please."

"Very well, Mother . . ."

Oh, why must my life be so hard! If you could only know the grief you cause me, Herbert! Sometimes it's all I can do to believe you're the same person as that quiet, kind-hearted youngster who came to work with my father. You were so soft and shy and willing to please. I admit there were moments when I did seem to sense that behind your outward pleasantness you held some bitter thing. You have never told me, but I know that some early incident left a terrible mark on your mind. If only I knew what it was! You never liked telling me about your boyhood in Kent. The apple-picking and your old father who wanted you to go to sea because he had been a seaman himself—I know no more than that about your early days. Even your mother you have never said much about, except that she was very fond of you and took up your part against your father in not wanting you to go to sea. She may still be alive, poor thing, and wondering what became of you after you ran away from your home at seventeen . . .

". . . It's just as I thought, Mother. He's not there. His bed has not been slept in. He must have been sitting in his chair ever since rushing upstairs in a temper as he did after Mr. Holme left."

"He sometimes sleeps sitting in his chair. Perhaps he slept and then suddenly woke and decided, on a whim, to go out."

"Yes. And slammed the door on purpose to wake us, knowing we'd be worried at his going out in the fog."

"It's his Mind, Grace. We must be patient."

"He's no more mad than you or I, Mother. You know that as well as I do."

"Not mad to be locked up, dear, but still, he's not normal."

"Oh, heavens! We've gone into that so many times before. Don't let's talk about it. Please, Mother!"

"You're not yourself, my child. Something has come over you—"

"I know, I know. It's—it's—oh, I'm just tired of him. Very tired. He's gone too far now. Too far. He's a nasty-minded man . . ."

. . . Oh, this nasty white fog! How I hate fog! It's better than London fog, though. Nasty yellow fog. Oh, yes, Middenshot fog is clean and bridal-white—pure like the spittle of silk-worms climbing in the kingdom of the night. Clean and pure like that sweet little girl, my schooldays Paula, my heart's lamplight. And wasn't it by lamplight I found her in the ditch, all ragged and raped—a horror muddy and bloody and mewing. Whining to me a tale of Borstal* boys pouncing from the hedge. Parasites living on the state to harm the citizens of the state. Pampered in the name of humanity and compassion! How wrong it would be to treat them as vermin and wipe them out as they crop up. Human vermin? Whoever heard of such a thing! Sacred human life! Only fleas and bed-bugs should be stamped upon. Only lice and cock-roaches should receive no mercy. But human life! Even a rotting, drooling, syphilitic human chunk of flotsam, even a filthy, stinking, low-browed moron of a human life, should be venerated and kept in cotton wool to breed more rotting, drooling wrecks and stinking, low-browed morons. Human life! Not lice!

" . . . for the life of me I can't imagine why he should have wanted to go out on the common at this time."

"I'm not puzzled, Mother. He's vindictive, that's what it is. He has done it because he knows it will worry us."

"Don't be too hard on him, my girl. Please, Grace. After all, he's my husband, and we had some happy days together. He wasn't always like this. He has been a good husband to me—and a good father to you. You have admitted that yourself many a time."

"He's long ago cancelled out all that, Mother. Oh, he's a dirty-minded man. Look what he's done to Mr. Holme. Leaving that carcase on his door-step."

* A Borstal is an institution for refractory adolescent boys of criminal tendencies.

"Yes, I can't think why he should have wanted to do that."

"He did it because of me."

"Because of you?"

"Yes. He—he knows."

"Knows? Knows what, my child?"

"I—let's not speak of it, Mother. I'm too upset."

"What are you trying to say, Grace?"

"I—he knows. He knows that I'm fond of Mr. Holme. And he knows that Mr. Holme speaks to me—and—and—oh, I don't know what I'm saying. Please don't let's speak about it, Mother. I feel—I feel as if I'm in a fog . . ."

. . . how far, fog, to the land of limbo? How far? Tell a groping mortal the secrets of the further vale. Tell a warped and withered old waif like me how to avoid the muck and mire that lie about him, waiting to tangle his foot and draw him down, down and deeper down. If the nettle be near can the dock-leaf be far? You hear me sighing for the antidote, fog, and you won't lift a finger to point out the path. You hear me weeping for an answer and you only wreathe around me, wearing me down—down, down. I don't want to go to heaven, fog. I wouldn't know how to be happy there. To be happy you have to be trained, and I'm badly out of training. Only tell me how to get to Limbo-land where two and two equal nothing, and nothing naught or two and two plus naught . . .

"Now, there, my man!"

"What man?"

"You there, my man! Stop!"

"Who's there?"

"You hear me? Stop!"

"I've stopped."

". . . don't trouble, Grace dear. Sleep. Try to go back to sleep."

"All the sleep has gone from my eyes, Mother . . ."

. . . I remember one day he was tinkering with the car and didn't know I'd entered the garage. I wanted to give him a surprise. He was muttering to himself. Talking about his old home in Kent. I couldn't hear everything, but I caught a word or two. He was saying something about rape and putting someone quietly out of the way. It was that day I discovered there was something strange about him—some bitterness that he kept to himself. It made me feel all the more tender toward him. I just crept out of the garage without letting him know I had come in. I could sense that he would have been upset if he had known that I had overheard him muttering ... Poor Herbert. Grace is right. I shouldn't indulge him as I do. I ought to be firmer with him. But I simply can't. I can't forget those days when I was so lonely for a man's company and when he was so good to me. So tender and considerate. I remember, in particular, that summer when it was so dry and fine and we used to go after lunch into the woods to our favourite spot and read *The Golden Treasury* and Burke and Jane Austen, my head leaning against him, and he reading aloud for us both. I shall always have to be grateful to him for the happiness of those days. No matter how dreadfully he behaves now, it's he who gave me my only happy memories ...

"I see you dimly."

"I see you dimly, too."

"You know me?"

"I think I ought to."

"I'm a killer, my man."

"I know you're a killer."

"... there's nothing we can do until daylight, my child."

"I know. But I still can't sleep, Mother. I'm too upset. Too much is on my mind. Not only Dad ..."

... and Father was so hard on him. Took a pleasure in humiliating him. Just as he humiliated Ernestine and me with his bullying. I could never understand how Herbert stood it, because Herbert was a young man with fire. He seemed to hold Father in great awe. I remember him telling me one day: "I respect him. Will always respect him. He's a doctor—what I'm not. If only I could have been a doctor." He had such a strange look when he said this. His eyes got bright and he clenched his hands slowly as though he wanted to throttle some invisible creature. He seemed to forget my presence, and I saw his lips moving silently. I heard him say: "Think of what I could have done for the community if I had been a doctor. One by one. One by one. Quietly, one by one, until the whole community was clean. Pure." He spoke as if to himself, and I wouldn't ask him to explain what he meant because

I knew he would have been upset at my having overheard. Often
when we used to be alone, he would mutter to himself and then
suddenly start and say: "Was I saying something? I'm sorry." He
would look alarmed and uncomfortable as if he were afraid he
had revealed something he ought to have kept to himself . . .

"Who told you I'm a killer?"

"The wireless told me."

"And so you're seeking me, my man?"

"You *and* myself I'm seeking."

"Queer talk."

"I'm your brother, Executioner."

"You know my title, then?"

"I know it, my Lord High X."

"Who told you?"

"The wireless told me."

"And you're my brother?"

"Me."

"Name?"

"Jarrow."

"Not Barrow?"

"I'm your brother. Me Jarrow."

"Cain, remember, killed his brother."

"Are you Cain?"

"And you may soon be Abel."

"No, I'm Jarrow."

"My brother?"

"Your mental brother."

"I'm armed, Jarrow."

"Me, too. With a kitchen knife."

"And a stick."

"And a stick."

"You're hunting me, Jarrow."

"And myself as well."

"Where are you going?"

"Trying to go."

"Where's that?"

"Limbo-land."

"Queer talk, Jarrow."

"There's a berry in my brain."

. . . and a bird singing in the woods, Agnes. We two sitting in the woods, reading Burke and *Northanger Abbey*. And the thrush singing in our future. Like the one in my boyhood past . . .

"I'm beginning to believe, Jarrow."

"Believe what, my Lord?"

"That we're brotherly by brain."

"Brainy brothers both."

"What a foggy-foggy morning!"

"What a woggy-foggy life!"

"Listen, Jarrow!"

"I'm listening."

"Hear them?"

"Dogs."

"Dogs and men."

"Hunting you, Lord High X."

"Hunting me."

"Poor brother."

. . . poor fellow is what I ought to say. The state feels you're too sacred to touch, you tainted lump of turd! Poor fellow, indeed! Wait till I ram my hand down the gargling hollow of your homicidal throat . . .

"They won't get me to-day, Jarrow."

"But they'll get you in the end."

"Are you friend or enemy, Jarrow?"

"Friend and brother."

"I wonder."

"What do you wonder?"

"If you're fool or friend."

"Friend. Friend to help you."

. . . to extinction. That's where I'm going to help you. That's where the state should have helped you years ago—ever since you did your first dastardly crime of violence, you ex-Borstal bug . . .

"You really mean to help me, then?"

"I really mean to help you."

"Dear Brother Jarrow."

"Dear Brother Lord High Executioner."

"Listen!"

"I hear them, my Lord."

"They're off the scent, Jarrow."

"Ah."

"My friend has done that."

"Which friend?"

"The one who helped me escape."

"Ah."

"They had him once in there."

"Ah."

"But they let him out as cured."

"So?"

. . . just so, you rotted raper of young girls. You razor-slashing runt. You and your friend are fed and coddled by the state, and then let loose to murder the people who are paying for your upkeep. You sarcoma in the womb of the community . . .

"Tricky people, Jarrow."

"Who?"

"We with the berries in our brain."

"Too tricky, my Lord."

"We always win the rub."

"But remember, Lord."

"Yes?"

"Your coat is fawn."

"How did you know?"

"The wireless told me."

"I'm armed, though, Jarrow."

"With an axe?"

"With a gun."

"Oh, modern Executioner!"

. . . who should have been quietly given a dose of poison by the state but instead was put in Broadmoor to make your get-away one day. I hope you do a welter of good raping and killing before they get you . . .

"Jarrow, we must think."

"Think of what?"

"Our friendly moves."

"I'm ready to think."

"You live near here?"

"I live near here."

"Alone?"

"With wife and daughter."

"A complication."

"No, a consolation."

"Are they on our side?"

"Who?"

"Your wife and daughter."

"They're not for us."

"Then we must think, Jarrow."

"Let us think, High Lord X."

. . . we know not where we are, oh, Lord. The brume is everywhere, and policemen are on the move. We have halted here to think our way through the gloom, but where can we find a haven or a heaven in the wild welter wrapped like wool around us? Think, Jarrow. Plot how you'll bring him down. It was one like him that raped your Paula and bred in her the bastard she never wanted—the bastard that took her life by being born foot first. An ex-Borstal lad he is, Jarrow. Do for him! Down him! Your coat is black. Not fawn. Black like dene-hole darkness, or that other dark in the nether-where from which we never return . . .

"My Lord."

"Quiet. I'm thinking."

"I have thought."

"Well?"

"My coat is black. Not fawn."

"Well?"

"And I have a room that's black."

"You have?"

"I have."

"But I have a hut in the woods, Jarrow."

"Your own?"

"My friend's."

"Is he still helping?"

"No, he's done all he could already."

"Is it safe in the hut?"

"There's a secret cellar that's safe."

"A hut with a cellar?"

"Strange but true, Jarrow. It's a partly filled-up well over which the hut was built."

"And is the cellar safe?"

"I hid there all yesterday."

"Didn't they search the hut?"

"I heard them above me searching."

"Have you food?"

"Enough for two more days."

"Have you money?"

"About ten pounds."

"Then you have no worries, my X High Lord."

"And Jarrow is my brother?"

"And your friend."

"He had better be."

"I have a room that's black."

"Yes?"

"Called a coal-house."

"You have a wife and daughter, too."

"Who are simple Simons."

"And simple cyphers?"

"Very simple cyphers."

"Let us think, Jarrow."

"Very well. Let us think."

We stand here and hang our heads in thought, oh, Lord, hearing men and dogs departing to the north. How fares it, Herbert lad? Have you gone too far? Can it be that your virgin cow spoke true, or will the path you contemplate lead to that heavenly peak of your fleeting dreams? If only this fog could prove a friend and not a flimsy foe I would have no fear of droning fiends. Oh, for a strong friend, or a stronger foe! A strong friend curdles my fear and gives me courage; a stronger foe enflames my ego and eggs me on to flay with fury. Can I do what the state would not? Can I wipe out vermin that the state rates human and therefore holy? . . .

"My Lord, I have thought."

"So have I."

"The dogs and men have gone."

"I've eluded them."

"Clever my Lord High X."

"Hee, hee, hee!"

"Haw, haw!"

"Good fellow, Jarrow."

"Good fellow to you, too."

"Hee, hee!"

"Whoa!"

"I'm no cab-horse, Jarrow."

"But your coat is fawn."

"Yours is black, you say."

"Like the heart of a raper."

"Suppose we exchange."

"That, Lord, is what I thought."

"Two minds with one black thought."

"Like my coal-house."

"That's black, too. So I thought."

"Two minds with a cold, black thought."

"Here's my coat, Jarrow."

"Here's mine, Lord."

"Any need for further thought?"

"No need whatever, my Lord."

. . . in future I'll do the thinking for us both, you lordly louse! . . .

"And now for action, Lord."

"Action?"

"Arm in arm we go."

"Frolicking, rollicking?"

"Rollicking through the fog."

"Come, then, Jarrow. Arm in arm."

"And a song to keep us warm."

"A song?"

"Skipping and singing, Lord, to the tune of *Round the mulberry bush*."

"Hee, hee! Come on, then, Jarrow."

"Here we go, Lord. One, two. All together . . .

"Here we go gathering blood and bones!

"Blood and bones! Blood and bones!

"Here we go gathering blood and bones!

"This dark and foggy morning!"

"Hee, hee!"

"Haw, haw! Come on. All together . . .

"Oh, here we go gathering blood and bones!

"Blood and bones! Blood and bones!

"Oh, here we go gathering blood and bones . . ."

"Hee, hee . . ."

"Haw, haw . . ."

"This dark and foggy morning! . . ."

2

"They say it's going to be worse than ever to-night."

The sun, low in the south-west, looked like a blob of weak blood wallowing behind a woollen veil.

"Yes, so the forecast said at lunch-time. And if you'd take my advice, you would do well to keep indoors."

The cedars on the fell were cold phantom birds with melting feathers.

"How did you happen to come this way at this time of the afternoon, Hyacinth? Didn't you work at the Rectory?"

She looked around her at the holly hedges milky in the fading light, and after a moment said: "I've just done my work there. I wanted to talk to you. I just felt like talking to you."

They could hear the traffic on the London Road, droning with a subdued and uneven, indeterminate note, seeming every moment to move slower and slower as though being clogged and entrammelled by the thickening fog.

"Talk to me about what? You'd better come into the cottage. It's cold standing in the lane here."

She nodded and shivered, hugging herself. Even while they had talked the sun had gone. The pines beyond the cottage, palled with an evanescent frosty softness, had a half-hovering air. Within the dampness of their needled depths they seemed aware of danger ensconced in the hidden furrows of the coming night.

"You heard about old Mrs. Frank? They found her in the woods."

He held the gate open for her, and they entered the cottage through the front door. He had not, he told her, heard about old Mrs. Frank.

"They found her without anything on, and her back was raw from the lashes he gave her. He must have beaten her with a cane."

He shook his head and make clicking sounds with his tongue, slamming the door shut. The hallway smelt of the fog, and the damp gloom had a powdered quality, reeking vaguely of coal-dust and floor-polish. She said he had better bolt it, too, and when he asked her what, she said the door. Bolt it. "Don't take any chances."

"After you've gone I'll bolt it, no fear."

. . . after I've gone. If only he didn't have to say that. If only he would ask me to sleep with him here instead of talking to me about when I've gone. I don't want to go. It's cold outside, and it's comfortable in here. I wish I was his wife, and could go into the kitchen and prepare a meal for him . . . She listened to the low clucking flap-flap of his mackintosh as he took it off and hung it on a peg on the hat-rack. The hat-rack looked like a skeleton-figure in the gloom. A fog-thing, grisly like the body of Mr. Toole found on the common two days ago, his throat cut open. She heard a car in Great Oak Road. The police-car, it must be, patrolling. Police were everywhere in Middenshot, but still the mad murderer remained at large . . . How cold it was out there!

"Come into the kitchen, Hyacinth. I didn't light a fire in the living-room. I can make you a cup of tea."

"I'll make it."

. . . if I can't even make a cup of tea for him I must be a poor kind of mug. If he only knew how badly I want to run this cottage, and how badly I want to have him make up to me . . . Cold . . . She took off her coat and hung it on a peg on the hat-rack with his . . . When they were in the kitchen they heard a fluttering outside and stood still, listening. The kitchen was warm and a welcoming place to be in, not so powdery with the fog . . . The fluttering came again, and now they knew what it was. A chicken in the Laytons' poultry run. They heard the squawk of a hen, followed by the feebler pleadings of the very young birds . . . Cold . . .

"She was alive when they found her? Mrs. Frank?"

Filling the kettle, she nodded and told him yes. Alive, but by now she might be dead, cold like the water in the cold tap. The chickens fell silent and the hush closed round the cottage. It might have been a ragged blue-grey thing oozing from the woods and encircling them: tree ectoplasm with evil intent ... He was asking about the police. Was it the police who had found her? Had she heard?

"No. Her nephew and a friend. Her nephew, Raymond, came back from Camberley at eleven o'clock, and when he knocked she didn't come to the door, so he went round to the back and found the door open. The lock was smashed, and she wasn't in the kitchen. A chair was overturned."

A harsh sound, the clatter of the kettle on the gas-range. It made her shudder far away in the regions of her fear. Metal could be made into knives and hatchets, and jemmies to break into a house ... "The nephew called a friend and they went searching in the woods."

"Fifth in a week."

"Queer how they can't get him yet. Where can he be hiding, I wonder? In a small village like this. Looks very funny to me."

He made no reply, and they began to hear the traffic again—on the London Road—remote like iron men tramping into a land being telescoped further and further away. They would never get there, the iron men. After an interval came the rumble of the train. Green but no green could be seen in the cluttered damp pips in a million sheets hanging in the air and over the landscape. Green electric train—the Southern Railway—uncaring about death or rape. Metal on parallel, polished metal, rumbling toward the south, toward Frimley and Aldershot, and leaving behind it only the traffic and the new brief noise that was the low bark of a dog somewhere in Great Oak Road ... Cold ... Very cold out there.

"It must have happened early this morning."

She agreed. Early this morning. The same as with old Mr. Hibbins two days ago. Early every morning one victim. Only on two mornings there had been no victims, and on those mornings the fog had not been dense ... The dirty coward, she said, going for old people like that ...

"What's it you came to tell me, Hyacinth?"

"Am I in your way here? You want me to go?"

"Don't be foolish. Stay as long as you like. I only thought you came to tell me something. You said you wanted to talk to me, didn't you?"

... a dull man if he can't see why I've come to talk to him ... Dup, dup from next door. Mr. Layton must be hammering something. Or Mrs. Layton. Mr. Layton probably had not yet come home from work; he would be late, for certain. The fog would make the train late. Dull hammering ...

... instead of keeping herself safely at home. Suppose I'll have to see her to her gate. It will be dark by the time she's ready to go. Not a bad girl, Hyacinth, but too unstable for me. Never seen her so quiet and thoughtful as she's been these past few days. Not unnatural, though. Whole village is on the jump. I can't think why the fellow keeps only to this neighbourhood. Why doesn't he stray further afield? Almost looks as if he might have some accomplice ...

They heard the car again in Great Oak Road. The police never rested. Comforting to think that a policeman might be in the woods now, on the look out for the mad danger ... Now if I could get him to come out with me to the cinema this evening! Dick would think it odd if he heard, but what do I care? When I set my mind on anything nothing can stop me. And I'm sure now about that Miss Jarrow up the lane. She's setting her cap at him. I could tell from the look on her face when she was passing the cottage here yesterday morning and looked in. This morning, too. She was hoping to see him. I thought she would have come in. If I don't do something about it she'll be all over him before you can say knife, and I'll be out of the picture. These quiet ones have a lot of guile. A plain face won't stop them, and they can be clever if they feel they're getting left on the shelf. But she can't compete with me. I've got too much she hasn't got. Good tough flesh. It's flesh that gets the men in the end ...

Now a plane, like a lost large bee droning in the waste of grey overhead; a long sigh wandering over the sombre welkin, bemoaning the plight of poor Mrs. Frank and old Mr. Hibbins and the tramp with the bashed-in head they found by the roadside three mornings ago. Old Mrs. Browne strangled in her bed. Bemoaning them all up there . . . Mr. Toole . . .

. . . I do believe she has some notion in her head about me. I've wanted to think it's simply her high spirits that make her go in for all her little tricks and hints, but now I'm not so sure . . . Attractive young bitch in her way. Good rump and good figure and pretty face. Look what I'm letting myself think now. Bad for me. Mustn't let myself be tempted. I couldn't see myself tied up with her. I'd never feel I could depend upon her. Not like Miss Jarrow. Reminds me Hyacinth mentioned this morning she saw Miss Jarrow looking in here hard. Why hard? Imagination. Hyacinth would imagine anything. Haven't seen Miss Jarrow to speak to since that night over a week ago when I called to warn them about the escaped maniac. Might be my fancy, but I have an idea she's been avoiding me. Either because she's shy as usual, or it might be something to do with her father. Perhaps she feels ashamed about that carcase business. It must be that . . .

. . . If only I could get him to go to bed with me I believe it would do the trick. Men have a funny feeling about women when they go to bed with them. I've heard Mary Galpinger say that more than once in the Greyhound; she said they feel sentimental and protective and obligated toward their bed-companions, and only if a man is a real rat he would go to bed with a woman without getting feelings of wanting to marry her. It was true he might not marry her in the long run—that would be the woman's fault, though, Mary said—but he would have the feelings, all the same: soft, mate-like feelings.

I believe Mr. Holme is a man like that; he's no rat of a man. He would want to marry me if he went to bed with me. And they say all's fair in love, so why shouldn't I try my hardest to go to bed with him if that's the one way of getting him to feel soft about me and want to make me his wife! I'd do it to-night, I would! Really I would. Oh, boy, can you see me and him in a clinch! Yeah, buddy. A clinch? It would be a cinch . . . No, but I mean it. I'd do it to-night. I'd feel shy about taking off my clothes, but if I do it in the dark it wouldn't be so bad. I don't think he would hurt me. He's a widower; he's had experience. Dick would hurt me. Dick's green. But I believe I'd like being hurt a little. Funny about that. I like a man to be rough with me, and yet I admire a soft, gentlemanly man . . .

He rose and said he would get her the packet with the tea, but quickly she intercepted him and stood herself before the cupboard, laughing and telling him to keep himself quiet, that she would find the tea. He chuckled deeply, thinking: That's more like the old Hyacinth . . . She opened the cupboard and found the packet with the tea . . . They heard the gate click in the turgidity of the cold evening coming down outside. It was dark outside the window now . . . "Is that your gate?" she asked, but he shook his head and murmured: "I don't think so." Then with certainty: "No, it was the Laytons'."

. . . she began to tell him how she had hardly slept last night. She mumbled, and he asked her what she had said, and she repeated it. Not a wink, she told him. Well, you never knew. Perhaps toward morning time she might have dozed a bit. Every minute during the night she had kept raising her head to listen for some suspicious sound. Her aunt was old, and her uncle had to be at Barkingstoke every night to help with the coal-trucks. The Executioner seemed on the look out for all the old people. She was sure he must have his eye on their cottage. She was afraid. Suppose she slept with him here tonight . . .

"Here?" He laughed and asked her if she were dreaming. And yet he felt a little touched at the naïve way she had suggested it.

"Why couldn't I? I could sleep on the sofa in the living-room. You've mended the leg, haven't you?"

He laughed again, regarding her as he might have regarded a child of eight who had put forward a charming but absurd proposition. He even had the inclination to get up and give her a hug, but, of course, that would have been foolish. He watched her taking up things and putting them down—plates and cups; she dried a cup and a plate, avoiding to look in his direction, her whole manner shy and self-conscious. Though the look of determination remained on her face. She mumbled again that she was afraid. There would be no sleep for her at home, she told him. He could lend her a blanket, or she could go home and get one and come back. What was it? Was it that he was afraid of people gossiping? She didn't care that about gossip! Did he? Well, no—he shifted his foot about—but still, he replied, one had to be careful. Couldn't go getting himself a bad name in the place. He tried to sound amused, but her instinct probed through him and discovered a patch of weakness. Only a weak man was afraid of people's opinions of his reputation; a strong man snapped his fingers at people's chatter. He might be strong in other ways, but here he showed weakness, she decided.

He sat at the table, cross-legged, still watching her as she got the tea ready. Telling himself what a queer girl she was but feeling an ache of desire swirling like a mist-cloud within the opacity of his fancy. Cloud within a cloud, chilly. Chilly as the vaster cloud breathing on the window panes from without, whispering of dead summer bliss amid the gorse and the heather and the cowering clover. The dead years. No breath of wreathing brume could bring life again to dead years ... He wondered what Miss Jarrow was doing now. Knitting in the living-room? Or making tea in the kitchen? She had held out her hand and he had taken it and gripped it tight, forgetting to release it, and she had not pulled it away. Lovely soul in a body that daily seemed lovelier to him ... Moved him. No explaining it. Simply moved him. Made him feel unimportant and at the same time big and prepared to do giant deeds ... Siegfried on the common ... He had promised to show her the orchids one morning. Since that evening it had been foggy every morning but two. No chance at all during the past week. But never mind. Soon. There would be a morning soon when it would be bright and clear, and if he met her in the lane on that morning he would remind her. Come with me, he would say, into my garden—and he felt she would come ... It was as though it were happening at this very minute. He heard the click of the lock as he opened the door of Number Two. And here she was moving past him as he waved his hand toward the interior, and here was he merging after and through her ... Green. Green coat, grey mackintosh. Green matching the greens glassed in around her ...

He started and began to pay attention to what Hyacinth was saying. The kettle was simmering softly, and Hyacinth was saying why it was they had to let such beasts of men go on living to be a danger to ordinary people? He asked her what she meant, and she replied that it was a shame to let maniacs get out of asylums to harm innocent people. Left to her, there would be no criminals and maniacs in the country ... She was leaning against the sink, shapely in her dark-grey frock ... What, he asked her, would she have done about it? How rid the country of maniacs and criminals? She sniffed and tossed her head, fire in her eyes ... What would she have done, eh? She knew what she would have done, no fear! ... Well, tell him, he urged. Go on. What would she have done?

What? She would tell him. She'd have had them all killed off from the moment they showed signs of being that way. That was what she would have done ... Surely, he laughed, she didn't mean that! Kill them off! Of course she meant that. Kill them off. Not cruelly, but quietly, with some kind of sleeping drug—she forgot the name of it. Mor-something. Morphia? Yes, morphia, that was it. It was no laughing matter, she insisted. She meant it. Kill them off from the start. Wasn't it sensible to kill off criminals and lunatics rather than let them go around maiming and murdering other people who were normal and unoffending? ... Well, he said, imagine her having such ideas! He wouldn't have thought it of her. In a way, he could see what she meant, but one couldn't be as inhumane as she advocated. Our business, he said, was to do what we could to help these mental cases—criminal and lunatic. We had to try to better conditions of living so as to wipe out criminal habits, and medical science must do its best to discover means of curing lunacy and mental troubles—

She interrupted him impatiently, saying that she had heard a lot of that kind of talk in the Ram and Cross. Talk. Nice high-falutin' talk. What was the use of that? People who talked about bettering conditions of living and wiping out criminal habits were only dreamers. How long hadn't people been trying to better conditions of living! But in the meantime criminals and sex maniacs were going their sweet way robbing and murdering and raping. *They* weren't waiting for conditions to change. Oh, it was so stupid to say we should do this and should do that to make better living conditions for people and not face what was actually happening around us right at the moment. Criminals and maniacs every day were spoiling somebody's happiness, and all the men with the high-falutin' brains could do was to coddle the wrongdoers and talk about being humane! You must wipe out the wrong-doers and the mad people *first,* and *then* try to do something to help normal people to keep normal and sane. What was the sense, she said, in having all these hardened house-breakers and cosh-boys and smash-and-grab men locked up in prison. They either escaped or they served their time and were released to do more burglaries and smash-and-grabs and murders. Wouldn't it be more sensible and money-saving to put them all quietly out of the way? Stick them with a needle and inject the drug—porphia—morphia—and kill them off painlessly—*that* would be the humane thing to do.

He watched her and felt an admiration for her coming alive in him. He would never have thought her capable of arguing a point like this. She had never seemed to him the sort who could be interested in any serious topic. Only showed you that you must never take people for granted, or dump them into broad types or categories and expect them to behave according to pattern. People were individuals, each with his or her own range of intelligence, each with his or her own set of ideas and quirks and fancies. Hyacinth, the girl who came in to clean for him, who cleaned at the Rectory after lunch, who frequented the Greyhound and the Ram and Cross to laugh with the men and cadge an ale, who was friendly with the village dustman—look what a completely new side of her personality she was revealing to him. She could argue. He didn't agree with her views—even considered her views obnoxious—but what did that matter? It was the discovery that delighted him—the finding of an unsuspected depth in her character; after concluding that she was a shallow, flighty creature, here he was finding that under her seeming shallowness and her flirtatiousness and silly airs she had a natural intelligence, and convictions of her own.

He reminded her about the Nazis. The gas-chambers, he said, had she forgotten how the Nazis got rid of the people they considered undesirable? Was that the system she was advocating for this country? She told him not to be foolish. You couldn't open your mouth nowadays to suggest anything full-blooded and with real guts in it but people had to compare you to the Fascists and

Nazis. The Fascists and Nazis had been criminals and lunatics themselves who ought to have been put out of the way when they were harmless. If Hitler and his crew, before they had got into power, had been quietly arrested and put to sleep for good nobody would have had to hurt their heads about the Nazis, and there would have been no war to bring misery and horror to millions. But suppose she had suggested to the governments of France and this country in 1932 that they should go into Germany, seize all the political troublemakers and dose them to death what would have happened? They would have done just what he was doing now. Laughed at her. Either that or they would have called her callous and inhuman. Yet look at it in a plain and sensible way. If they had killed off Hitler and every man who looked like being a troublemaker in Germany there would have been no Nazi party—and no world war. We would never have known of any gas chambers or Dachaus or Buchenwalds. All the horror that happened would have been avoided if the Allied governments had been sensible instead of sentimental and stupid. Hitler wasn't sentimental and stupid. "Being a criminal lunatic, he didn't care a hoot whether people called him names or not. He just went ahead killing and brutalizing right and left until he got into power. How else can you deal with such people except by treating them as vermin and stamping them out? Try to treat them soft and as if they are human beings and it will be *you* who are going to get hurt. While you're spouting your nice pretty-pretty words about humanity and goodwill and Christian compassion they're just laughing at you and hitting you one on the head!"

The water was boiling now, and she took off the kettle and filled the tea-pot. She said that, for her, there was no right and wrong of a thing; for her, a thing was sensible or stupid, or it was nice or ugly. It was ugly to let criminals and lunatics ravage the community, and it was stupid to imprison them so as to give them the chance to be set free, or escape, to continue their ugly work; the sensible thing was to kill them off as you would kill off fleas and bed-bugs. For that, she said, was what they were. Why didn't we try to be humane to fleas and bed-bugs, too? Why not try to convert lice and cockroaches from their verminous ways and make them into decent insects? If a creature was a pest it was a pest, human or insect, and must be stamped out without mercy; coddle it and it would bite you and injure you. Did you ever hear of a burglar or a maniac stopping to think whether it would be humane or not to rob or strangle one of his fellow beings? Did he ever stop to wonder how the poor fellow behind the bank counter, or the girl in the park, would feel when he pounced? Did he stop to think whether the old lady would be hurt, and would feel pain for days, before he attacked and coshed her? Did he ever stop to consider the welfare of the community or think whether he should have mercy on his victims? No, his brain was twisted, and he just went ahead and struck down the jeweller and robbed him. Or the maniac snatched your seven-year-old daughter in a lonely park or in a lonely lane and raped and strangled her.

"How would you feel if a maniac raped a seven-year-old daughter of yours! You're going to tell me you'd feel humane and kindly toward maniacs and criminals?"

If he had caught such a man would he feel like being soft with him and just handing him over to the police to be tucked comfortably away in an institution, or wouldn't he kick him in his guts until the last breath had blown out of his filthy lungs! Humane! Humane to lice! What was wrong with people nowadays was that they had grown soft and over-ripe. She had heard a chap in the Greyhound say so, and he was right. Over-ripe and rotten. What passed for humanity and Christian feeling nowadays was simply people's feelings gone soft and over-ripe. Look at all these societies for the prevention of cruelty to animals and society for this and against that. Why not a society for the protection of people against the criminal and insane! Instead of drooling over dogs and cats why didn't they do something to get rid of the muck in the community! Nobody said that dogs and cats must be ill-treated, but why get sentimental over all these animals when human beings, who were supposed to be more important, were not properly protected! Softness, that was what it was. If you spanked a child on its bottom for misbehaving some gooey-eyed social worker came along and scolded you. It was bad psychology, they said. Think of the damage you might do to its poor little mind! Damage! As if you could damage a really healthy mind!

"If a child is born with a crooked mind all the spanking or not spanking won't stop it from being a pest to the community when it grows up. It's what you're born with that makes you a criminal or an ordinary person, or a maniac or a normal person. Treating you kindly won't make any difference. A good home won't help. If you're a bad egg all the kind treatment and mollycoddling won't stop you from being a beast. But people can't see that. All these shits of psychologists have got them dazzled and dazed. And they're just getting softer and softer towards everything. Pampering delinquent boys by putting them in Borstals, spending money on housing up criminal maniacs. If that isn't rotten, stinking softness!"

She had worked herself into a passion of indignation, and he smiled, fascinated. It was as though he were listening to a passage from *The Ring*. A blare of trumpets, heroic and sword-like, hurtling through his heart. In his fancy she had become Brünnhilde. Only a few months ago he had seen *Die Walküre* at Covent Garden, and it was exactly like this he had felt when Flagstad, as Brünnhilde, appeared on the wild, rocky landscape and uttered her war-cry. He felt the crackle of a new fire within him. A new vision of heroism took form in his fancy. Foolish, very foolish of him, but there it was. How could he help being himself!

She poured out the tea and handed him a cup, her cheeks red, her eyes still aflame. She gave him a brief, shyish smile, the belligerency fading from her manner. He told her to sit down, and she joined him at the little table, but as they sipped their tea a shyness seemed to have showered down upon her. After a long silence, during which they were both awkward, he gave a grunt and said: "What's happened to you, Hyacinth? Lost your tongue all of a sudden?" She made no reply, her gaze lowered, sulky and fog-powdered, as though tentacles had reached in at her from outside. She mumbled something about having to go home. Time she made a move. He put out his hand and patted her wrist, chuckling, and she scowled and shrank away quickly, rose with her empty cup and moved over to the sink where she put down the cup with a brittle clatter. She looked round and asked him if he wanted another cup, and he said no, uncomfortable, too, the smile on his face not natural. He got up and took his cup over to the sink. She was rinsing her own, and turned slightly and took his and began to rinse it. He murmured thanks, and felt in his pocket for his pipe and tobacco. She said she must be going home, and he said yes. Yes, he would see her home if she liked.

3

Ho, ho! Stand at the window and take a look at it out there. A white murrain upon Middenshot, by Almighty Lord! Spreading slowly through the trees and over the ground, thick and furry. A germ culture gone haywire in the laboratory of the night. Ho, ho! Oh, mad Jehovah wandering on the wet, cold common, stretch forth thy black arm and smite all helpless old ladies and drooling old men cowering in fusty parlours. Play on your pipe, Jehovah, and lure all the lovely little lasses within the compass of your raping loins. Rape and strangle, Lord. Spare not one. No blame on you. Blame it on your parents who whipped you when you broke a window pane with a cricket ball. Blame your awful deeds on the doings of your poor delicate mind. It was your schoolmaster who caned you for neglecting your Latin verbs who must be blamed for warping your outlook for all time to come. That thump your old Dad gave you when you twisted the cat's tail is the direct cause of your thumping old man Hibbins on the head. And when you cut the poor tramp's throat the other night you were only reacting to the frustration fermented in you by all the anonymous father-symbols in the evil society that begat you. It was society's sin, not yours. Poor poorly invalid you! Why don't you call a halt and go back to your room in dear old Broad-moor! They'll give you nourishing soups and tasty porridges and nurse you through the winter. Wherefore the hurry, my Lord High Executioner! You'll get out another day to play more grisly pranks, no fear! You may even find it feasible to help a fellow thug to frolic with you when next you sally forth, my Lord. Even as your former friend, now free and certified cured, is giving you a hand to liven events in uneventful Middenshot. Oh, ho, ho, ho! ... Even as old Jarrow is giving you a hand under the very noses of the seeking police. But old Jarrow has his own motives, my

Lord. Oh, ho, ho, ho! Let's do a dance in the dark, my devils! . . .

"Oh, here we go gathering blood and bones!

"Blood and bones! Blood and bones! . . ."

". . . very well, Mother. Be calm, please. Be calm. Wait here. I'll wait in the kitchen. He may not go out right away."

"Yes, Grace, I'm sure he's going out now. He always does as soon as he begins to sing that awful song. For the past few nights it's been the same. Haven't you noticed? Every time he sings that song it's a sign he's ready to go out. Oh, it's dreadful. Dreadful. I can't understand why he should sing like that. He's never done it before."

. . . my poor Herbert. News of an escaped lunatic from Broadmoor generally makes him restless, but I've never seen him quite as bad as this. Not even last year when the one who called himself Marco Polo was seen actually in the lane out there . . .

"It's not his singing that worries me, Mother. It's his going to the coal-house. Every night he goes to the coal-house before he wanders off on to the common. I kept an eye on him last night and the night before last. I've heard him speaking in a low voice to someone out there. And I heard another voice, too."

"Yes, it's very strange. And he won't let me have the key for the coal-house, Grace. I wonder why. Oh, why won't he? What is he doing in there? What mischief could he be up to?"

"Anyway, to-night I mean to have it out with him. I'm going to stand before the kitchen door and prevent him from going out. Please don't interfere, Mother. Leave him to me. My nerves are going to pieces."

. . . mine, too. Mine. I'm not sleeping well. Some terrible thing is going to happen. I can feel it coming . . .

"Quick! He's stopped singing, Grace. He must be preparing to go out."

"Yes. I hear him. He's coming down. You wait in the living room here, Mother. Don't come into the kitchen. Please."

. . . and now for another night of horrible hunting. Ho, ho! And when I kill how I'll howl and hump my back. How I'll puke up with relief the purulent bile I've carried in me ever since the death of my dear sweet heart's spring bloom; the petals, and even the honey and perfume, of my flowered boyhood dreams; my lamplight in fog-gloom. If only it could be to-night, the kill! But I must be patient. I must await my moment. If not to-night then tomorrow night. Or the night after. Oh-ho, my merry Lord High X, I'll hunt you and your friend to the end of my warped old span. No let up. No let off. The state will let you off but not old man Jarrow. And now to give you your nightly fodder. Fodder to fatten you up for the kill, my merry man. Lead me—oh, lead me to your friend. You must both go down together. Not one without the other. No, no. That won't suit me, High Almighty Lord. Both, both. Both together. When shall we three meet in thunder, lightning and in fog! Oh, when! . . .

"Aha."

"Yes, it's me."

. . . so I see. An ambush, by St. Ambrose! A plot to keep me in the house. She and her mother have been conspiring against me . . .

"Haw, haw! Now, there, my child! Stand away from that door!"

"I won't."

"You won't?"

"No, you're not going out."

"Haw, haw! Come, stand away from the door, my young brown cow. Your old father has business outdoors."

"You're not going out, I say."

"So? But I must, little cow. I must go out. Out into the fearful, feathery night. Out into the drifting dungeon dark where the crabs of death are crouched up waiting. Waiting with eager claws to clutch your old dad's throat."

. . . he must be really mad now. Look at the wild light in his eyes. I've never seen him look like this. Mother would be scared if she saw him. I'm glad I warned her not to come in . . .

"I want the key, Dad. Please let me have the key."

"Key? What key? The key to Hell? I haven't it, my child—not yet. Give me more time."

. . . and yet in a way he seems quite sane. Perhaps even saner than usual. I mustn't let him intimidate me . . .

"The coal-house key. You know very well what key I mean. I won't move from here until you give me the key."

"Ho, ho! Haw, haw! Threatening your old sire, eh? My sweet

young cow waking up, at last, and showing some spirit, is she? Well, well! At this rate she'll soon be mooing for a bull. Eh? Haw, haw, haw!"

. . . how angry he would be if he knew I was in the hallway here peeping at him! My poor Herbert. I wonder where you got that fawn coat from. You didn't have it before that night you behaved so badly . . .

"I don't care how obscene you are, Dad. I want the key, I say. I've got to go into the coal-house to get some coal."

"Why, my child? When the scuttle is full in the living-room! Look. The scuttle in here, too, is full. Didn't you see me bring in fresh coal some hour or two ago? Come, come, my young moo-cow. Don't let the old bull down the lane turn your head. He's already got a fat fruity cow to service. She goes in every morning to service and be serviced. Soon she'll be with calf, you hear my word. Haw, haw!"

"You're filthy! Filthy! Give me the key for the coal-house, Dad! Give it to me. I'm determined to find out what you're hiding in there."

"Ah! A slight clearing of the fog. A small patch of sky and a moonbeam playing on the happy family. So that's it, eh? You're anxious to discover your old dad's naughty secrets. Tut, tut! Curious child. Oh, no. The old man forbids you to go into the coal-house. The devil is in there. A solemn Satan with horns and tail who likes to lift young ladies' frocks. Do you want him to hold you in his horrible hairy arms? Has the heat got you so lost to all sense of discrimination that you'll submit to being tickled by Old Nick himself! Oh, fie! Fie, my child!"

. . . has he given me away to the police, or what? Why the damned bloody devil doesn't he come with the parcel of food! Brrr. It's cold in this coal-house. At least I had some warmth in the hut . . .

"It's time all this nonsense ceased. Mother and I have hardly had any sleep this past week or so. Where do you go every night? And whose coat is that you're wearing? Where is your own black coat?"

"Curious. Curious child. Why must you ask so many ques-tions! Don't you like my new fawn coat? My beautiful, distinguished fawn coat? Satan gave it to me. I've given him my old black coat. Black matches evil. Now, does that satisfy you? Or must I take you out to him and have him baptize you with the blood of a bumptious bull? Eh? Is it only bulls you're interested in these days? Tell your old dad. Come."

. . . oh, Herbert, if only you could see yourself smiling! Oh, it makes me want to cry. You used to smile like that at nineteen. Your eyes are still so blue, my dear. They haven't aged at all . . .

. . . I wonder why he should be so down on Mr. Holme. And how absurd of him to have mentioned that silly creature who goes in to clean! As if Mr. Holme would think of giving her a second glance! . . .

"What have you got in that parcel, Dad? I *must* know something. If—if you go on like this any longer I'll have to go to the—I'll have to go and get help from the neighbours."

"Help from the neighbours? Take care. If you do that I'll send Satan seeking. Satan will get them with his horns and his hirsute claws. Have a care, my cow. Why let my parcel trouble you! There's only food in it. Bread and butter and sardines and one or two little things like that. Food I bought myself to-day—except for the butter. I got that from our own larder. Hee, hee! Satan must be fed, my child. Now, get out of my way and let me go out. We can't keep Satan waiting. Our Lord High Devil might be offended."

. . . as though I care if he's offended. Let him wait. I'm not sorry for this delay . . . Agnes must think I don't know she's peeping at me . . .

. . . this is terrible. It's the lunatic he's harbouring, I'm sure . . .

. . . I remember the day Father shouted at you, Herbert, and how you looked at him and smiled. With such restraint. But your eyes gleamed. Oh, you were always so manly. My heart shrank in me from love for you . . .

"I'm not moving from this door until you give me some explanation of your behaviour."

"Ah. An explanation. Now, what do you want to know, my girl?"

"Who is it you're feeding in the coal-house? For the past week you've kept the key. And every night you go out and we don't see you until morning. What's happening, Dad? We *must* know something."

"Now I'm really going to get angry. I'm going to dance and gnash my teeth and be really terrifying. Hee, hee! How would you like that?"

"I don't want to hear any silly threats. Give me an explanation."

"Very well. Then I must do my little tricks. Look. See my over-coat pocket here bulging? Know what's in it? Ha! Oh, yes. I keep things in my overcoat pockets, too. Just as someone else we know keeps odds and ends in his mackintosh pockets. Haw, haw! I knew you wouldn't guess who *that* was. But I'm telling you. See my coat pocket bulging? There are deadly things within! Aha. Things like hypodermic needles, chloroform, cyanide and morphia. They once belonged to your dear granddad. I've had them safely stored away all these years. Like the medical books and his surgi-cal instruments. Very useful things to have about one's person on a foggy night. Never know when they might be needed."

... yes, poor dear. He insisted that he should have Father's instruments and drugs. I didn't mind. I let him have them. He keeps them in that old iron canister under his bed. I have never feared that he would put them to any ill use. I don't think he means to do any harm with them to-night. He's only trying to frighten Grace. It's like the bottle of eusol he keeps in his room under the bed and sprinkles about the walls. Oh, Herbert, if only this fog could clear from your poor mind ...

"What do you want with such things on your person, Dad? What do you mean to do with them?"

"Do you want to know? Really want to know?"

"Yes, I want to know."

... if he doesn't hurry up and come with the food I'll break into that cottage and strangle him and his wife and daughter. Wonder how old the daughter can be. I don't mind daughters about seven or eight. Even nine. But this old fellow's daughter must be a starchy forty-year-old spinster. I won't be seen dead raping a forty-year-old spinster. Simply not done! ...

... how the Lord High must be fuming in the coal-house! Let him fume. I don't mind one jot. If only that friend of his could join him in there! If only I could catch them both together ...

"You really, really want to know?"

"Yes. Tell me."

"Very well. I'll tell you. Before I came down from my room I said something to myself. This is what I said: 'That young cow of mine is sure to try to stop me from going out. She's in a bad mood. So the best thing will be for me to arm myself with a good strong dose of morphia and a hypodermic needle, and if she won't move from the door I'll jab the needle softly into that half-shrivelled pudendum of hers. Choop! And whoop! Whisk her outside to my Lord High Satan. And then scoop! Old Satan grabs her and shoots off a quick, hot rape. But no pain. No pain at all. All done neatly, kindly and with morphia.' That's what I said to myself, and that's why I brought all these little things—"

Tap, tap, tap.

"Oooh!"

"Ah!"

"Oh, gracious!"

Tap, tap, tap.

"Grace, who is that knocking?"

"Ah! Hee, hee!"

"Oh, heavens!"

"Warned you, didn't I? It's Satan."

"Oooh!"

"Grace dear, come! Come away quickly!"

"That's it. Run off to the living-room. Hee, hee. Told you it would be risky to try to stop me going out. See you in the morning, my cow! I'm off to do my foggy-woggy work. Coming, Satan! Coming, my Lord! *Here we go gathering blood and bones! Blood and bones!* . . ." Tap, tap, tap.

"*. . . blood and bones!* . . ."

4

"*. . . and bones! This dark and foggy eve-ning!*" . . . she was sure of it now, she told her mother, who replied that we must never be sure of anything . . . He offered her his arm . . . Sure of it. It was

the lunatic. He was harbouring the lunatic in the coal-house ...
He was aware of her breathing. She said nothing as they walked,
and he, too, was silent. They were approaching Great Oak Road
... In the coal-house. Giving him food. Aiding and abetting him
in his terrible deeds. Oh, heavens! ... They nearly walked into
the hedge, and she uttered a soft whining laugh and held his arm
tighter ... "... I can't stand this, Mother. I can't stand it, I tell you.
I'm going to the police! ..." "... *blood and bones! Blood and bones!
Oh, here we go gathering—*" "... That will do! That will do! Why
were you so long in coming? What were you talking about with
your wife and daughter in the kitchen? I heard you ..." "... hear
him? Old Jarrow singing *Round the mulberry bush*. Every evening
he sings it. Walks all over the common singing it ..." "... try to
be calm, my child. You really shouldn't say such things. He's not
as bad as all that ..." "... I must say them, Mother! I must! He's
helping that murderer ..." "... *blood and bones! Blood and bones!*"
... "Shut up, do you hear me? You want to attract the attention
of the whole neighbourhood?" ... "*Oh, here we go gathering ...*"
He felt protective toward her but knew that more than that
was involved. It was the softness of her body that moved him.
The woman nearness of her body and the feel of her arm ..."
"... how can I go on living in a house with a monster like that,
Mother! How!" ... "Please, Grace! You're getting hysterical, my
child. Try to be controlled ..." ... and the new vision that had
taken shape in him. The new Brünnhilde. It complicated matters
considerably. He could feel a tug within him. In actuality, he was
a romantic fool and didn't know it ... "... I'll sing if I want to
sing. Who can stop me?" ... "I can. I can stop you by cutting your
throat ..." "... And who'll feed you if you cut my throat!" "... it
may be simply another of his pranks, my child. You know how
fond he is of playing pranks on us ..." "And what of the fawn
coat? How do you explain that, Mother? And what's happened
to his own black coat?" ... "... we used to sing it at school. I can
remember one day how Dick went sprawling ..." "... let's have
the food and not so much jabber. I'm famished. And don't get
so cocky because you're helping me out. I don't like cocky old
men ..." "... but for you, Mother, I'd go at once. I wouldn't mind
what sort of scandal it caused ..." "... yes, for my sake, Grace

THE WEATHER IN MIDDENSHOT

dear. Please don't do such a thing, my child. I beseech you ..."
"... I believe you must give this fellow Dick a rough deal, Hyacinth..." "... Dick? I've told him already I won't marry him. That
mother of his is a devil. And besides, I feel different about you ..."
"... I'll be back in the coal-house tomorrow evening. And be sure
you're here on time with the food. Here's a pound. Get me some
more cigarettes. Mind, be on time or I'll smash down that bloody
kitchen door ..."

... bones and blood murmuring in the soil ...

... if only I could understand what's at the back of all your
moods, Herbert. If only I could discover what happened to you
as a boy ...

... like fire skipping from ledge to ledge in my imagination. I
see her to-night in a glow. I can't laugh at her ...

... bones and blood ruminating with tangled roots of trees,
unseen dead streams that held life in time long gone, now mud
or simply sap in branches or slime in earthworms, some turned
leaf-juice. Chlorophyll-blood green and vegetable as once it was
red and human; static as once it stirred dynamic in battle-locked
limbs—limbs all pollen or powder now and soil-tainted. Partners
of pebbles and sandstone, gritty under seasons of fallen leaves
and twigs and acorns. The unending autumns of human endeav-
our and human vanity. The leaves of failure piling, going to
dust, but piling still ... Oh, man, wandering like me on a dreary
common in a dreary pall, hoping for the One Mountain Moment,
reaching for the Golden Cloud that remains a cloud. Wanting to
be kindly but kindled from birth with brutality. Wanting lucidity
but befogged in the paler shade, watching for the deeper shadow:
the profounder gloom ... Is it a deeper shadow I see? Wait. Move
soft. Watch. Yes—a deeper shadow. Reach. Reach for it ... Oh,
to strike at a shadow and feel *substance* shudder. To hear it shriek
and become matter twisting in the toils of torture. Knife sink-
ing into soft bladders of blood and tissue. Boot swinging—and
buried hard in a yielding body—the rubber muscles of a belly.
And to hear the panting and the rasping that pain brings forth.
So sweet to attain it, to subdue it ... Wait. Watch the shadow on
the ground. Move soft. Walk soft. Walk ... Walking home with
him, his arm and mine in one. Who would have thought it! Life

can be so sudden and funny . . . Gives me a tickling soft feeling in the slippery centre of me. Oil on water and with water lapping in the tunnel of my middle, sucking-eager for the launching of the great big craft. The hard, long, slowly-coming craft to part the warm, still water lapping in the oily, pained sweetness of my loins. Come, dream, end. Dream, stop and let it be real, real. Let the big, lonely craft loom big, big and bigger still and cleave open the pleading centre of me. Come. Welcome, burrowing bow. From bow to stern, slip right in and my waters will lure you further and further in to more and more feathered lairs where all is lovely and lazy and oiled and limpid . . . Further. Come further . . . oh, no further in the long blank night of unfulfilled half-wishes. I should have wished longer and harder, and perhaps the fairies in the fallow fields would have heard me and brought my prince before—ten years before. For I am over thirty now, and he may never come. He with his flapping coat and his orchid lore. Can he hear me sighing through the murk that makes a mat to keep us apart though only yards away? Can he hear me in the evening quiet wishing and half-wishing for the fulfilment I want but fear? For the new haven dream-gilded yet dreaded by my maiden cold? Let my peace not be disturbed, yet bring me fire and thunder, oh, Lord! I see my death in too much peace; I see life in thy leaping flames. Give me peace, though, and the safety of locked doors and the bird-warmth of my bed, the sweet cuddling calm of multitudinous feathers surrounding me. Let me be invaded, yet postpone invasion. I am a coward. I fear the unaccustomed, and the pain of parturition is a spectre in my fore-dawn fantasies. I am old and cold and want some heat. Please give me heat, oh, Lord! Oh, Lord, protect me from heat. Protect me . . . No, protection is not enough. I must see it without pretence. It's my young blood answering the horn-summons I hear echoing in the hedge, and I want to hold her to me not in paternal quiescence but with a struggle and in earthquake fury. Let me be honest and say how much I would like to penetrate the rich round flesh and weld it into me. Out and in and around me. Out and in, in delicious rhythm that only the earthy few can know. In and out and around her and within me. Oh, to let my hands lap like waves along the slope of fleshy hillocks and slither low down past woods that are silky overgrowth concealing sands that tremulously melt. Can such delight be mine? . . . I don't believe so. Oh, no. Not that for me. At my age there must be discipline. Better discipline than too much unrestrained delight . . . The coy creature, my near neighbour—it's there I must seek my bliss. Bliss befitting my sober frame and routined days. The cool-smile flower bliss, fluttering and fading but always softly adrift on the smooth waters of affection. No trumpet blaring there, no cymbals clashing and no disturbing drums. No seething heights of pain and joy and pleasure tuned to unendurable peaks of anguish. Only blossom quiet and the drone of monotony. Two bees working in a hive of tranquil and harmonious and perpetual summer. That's the bliss for me. I'm too old for the other kind . . . Much too old . . . None too old for me. None too old to be cracked on the cranium. Wait for them, and watch. Yes, watch. It is a darker shadow I see. Deeper, darker than the paler on which I stand. Two, three more paces and he'll be within reach . . . Wait . . . Watch . . . Watch and pray. I do it all day for you, Herbert. That's my trouble. I can't wipe from my memory the boy of nineteen. The image you drew on my mind is there forever. The boy of nineteen, and the young man of twenty, twenty-one, twenty-two leaning all awry on my shoulder and reading to me in the shade of the summer trees. How can I drain out of me the gorse-and-heather scenes and the bracken grazing our knees as we wandered in the woods—the scent of rosemary and lavender, and the thrush in the back garden that used to sprinkle us with melody sweetly perfumed yet with Peruvian balsam—cruel ingredient to remind us of our separate places in the world of people. People. People. If only we could have left all people in a grey limbo of their own and made our own world of green and lapislazuli, of trees and summer skies, of delphiniums and deep oceans of bracken to drift in forever . . . If this walk could last forever. What is a little fog to fuddle us when I have him near me like this, long and slim and man-hard, his arm so firm and protective against my side. Some days he would protect me, and some days he might beat me with his hard hand and I'd squeal with delight and call him my lord and master, and ask him not to beat me, pretending it hurt me. People won't understand how a woman likes being lorded over by her man, how she melts like a sugar-lump with secret bliss when he thumps her on her rump and hits her about a bit. Not too much, of course; only a bit. Especially if he's sorry after and takes his same hard hand that he hit her with and smooths down her hair and caresses her face and loves her on a couch with a crooked leg he's mended . . . Tap, tap, tap . . . What're you doing in there hammering like that? . . . Mending the sofa leg, he says . . . I feel like letting you fall on me . . .

"Oh, God, what's that?"

A scream. Not far.

"It's he! It's he!"

"Help!" Beyond the trees. The hedge.

A scream.

"Quick! Help!"

"Oh, God, I'm afraid."

A scream.

Footsteps running.

"It sounds like the Binneys' place."

"Don't get excited."

Pressed against the hedge, the two of them, waiting.

Footsteps running.

"It's him!"

"Yes, it's 'im!"

"It's he!"

Police whistle.

Figure coming running. A tallish man.

Me lurched away from her and put out his foot, and there was a crash and scramble of bodies and boots on the pavement. A grunting, male and deep. Rasping. And I curse. She saw the gas-lamp at the corner of Great Oak Road, a fuzzy will o' the wisp in the fog. A scrambling and struggling and she breathing fast. Police whistle. Bang and flash and a gasp, deafening her and sending her pressing deeper into the tickling hedge. She screamed and whimpered. And gave another whimper. "He's got you? He's hurt you?" He said his arm. Nothing much. Shriek of brakes. Police car. White ray of a flash-lamp in their faces . . . "That way. He's gone that way! Up the lane! Making for the woods!" . . . They asked about the revolver report. Did he fire a shot? . . . "Yes.

Tried to stop him. Nearly got him. He fired on me and ran." She told them to look, he was bleeding. Didn't they see? His sleeve was wet with blood. Just a slight wound, he admitted. Forearm. Quick. Nothing to worry about. Get after him. The car droned off up the lane. Distant whistles. Bay of a dog . . . And the fog, oh the fog white and woolly and wreathing its spider-web shroud over the trees and the hedges and the cottage-tops. Enfolding all. Men and men's thoughts and women's memories of gorse and heather on the common. Look, another car. Orange orbs and brakes applied, and two uniformed men quick talking but softly, fog-muffled, their flash-lamps bright on them. Questioning. First-aid for that arm. Into the car. Come . . . Miss Withers? Yes, come in, too . . . Distant whistle. And the bay of a dog. And the fog, everywhere and cold and caressing the cheek and the breast and not caring how many screams and whistles the night culled from the woods and lanes or from the closed, cowering cottages. For it was only fog.

5

The following morning, as though at the miraculous signal of little flutes and concealed tin trumpets, the sun appeared in a sky blue and clear, all the fog gone. Though the wireless warned that the fog would return at nightfall. Roofs and pavements and meadows glistened with a white coating of rime that melted reluctantly in the sun, for the air was cuttingly cold. The invigorating smell of moisture in trees and in fields drifted on the quiet north-easterly breeze.

Mr. Holme inhaled deeply of it as he emerged from his kitchen and moved into the back garden to begin his morning tour of inspection. Despite the excitement of the night before, he had slept very well, but, as he had dreaded, the newspapers had printed the full story of last evening's events, and he was perturbed. They had mentioned that he was in the company of Hyacinth in the lane, that she had had tea with him and that he had been taking her home. What would the village think when they read that? What was Miss Jarrow going to conclude? People were going to say that he was more friendly with the girl than was proper. Most unfortunate that Hyacinth should have taken it into her head to visit him yesterday. Though he did not regret it. Indeed, this morning he felt quite softly disposed toward her. In his fancy she seemed more solid, less trivial, than he had deemed her a day or two ago. Yet there was Miss Jarrow. It was important that she did not get a mistaken impression about his relations with the girl. It might prejudice his chances . . . His chances? He reproved himself. Let him not be an idiot. Anyone would imagine he was seriously contemplating proposing marriage to her. Foolish of him to let his romantic fancies get entangled with his practical situation. And yet . . . Well, was it really such a romantic fancy? Why couldn't he make it an actuality? Why couldn't he plan seriously to turn it from fancy into accomplished fact?

His discovery that the temperature in Number Two Greenhouse was two degrees below what he deemed safe diverted his thoughts from the theme of marriage. He concentrated his attention on the task of adjusting the wicks of the two heaters, and had hardly completed this operation when he heard footsteps and a voice calling his name. He emerged to discover that it was a newspaper man with a camera. His picture was wanted for one of the evening papers. He had been dreading this, too, but had to be obliging. For newspaper men he had a great deal of sympathy. It was the third time within the past eight or nine days that he had allowed his photograph to be taken for the newspapers. Middenshot was front-page news.

The newspaper man had just gone and he was pottering about in Number Three when he heard the front gate click and slam. This time he gave a gasp of surprise and pleasure, for it was Grace Jarrow he saw appear around the kitchen, her gaze moving searchingly about the garden.

He hurried out of Number Three, trowel in hand, and approached her. "Good morning, Miss Jarrow. How very nice to see you—especially on a morning like this."

"Good morning, Mr. Holme." She blushed, smiling hesitantly, her manner agitated. "Yes, it is a lovely morning. We deserve it, too, don't we, after all that fog?"

"I should say we do."

"I was reading—I just felt I had to drop in to—to sympathize and ask after your arm. I read in the papers about your encounter last night. Such a terrible thing."

"Oh, it was nothing much, Miss Jarrow. Almost like old times, in fact."

"Old times? Oh. Yes, of course. You used to be—a policeman."

"Won't you come into the house?"

"Thanks, but—no, I don't think I'll bother. I was passing. How is your arm? Was it very badly hurt? He fired a shot at you, didn't he?"

"Only a flesh wound. Just grazed me." He tapped his left forearm. "It's all been dressed and bandaged. The police took me to Barkingstoke Hospital last night. Told them it wasn't necessary but they insisted. What upset me more than anything," he laughed, "was the rent the bullet made in the sleeve of my mack. See? I had to sit down before going to bed and mend it. This mack is like an old friend to me."

"How terrible. That such things should happen in Middenshot. I really don't know what to say." She spoke in bursts, and glanced furtively, almost guiltily, about her. "How are your greenhouses getting along?"

"Splendidly, Miss Jarrow. Wouldn't you like to have a look at my orchids? I promised you I'd let you see them one morning."

"Yes. Yes, I should like to very much. I've always wanted to see what they looked like."

So he took her into Number Two, almost as nervous and agitated as she. He nearly dropped the trowel, kicked an empty biscuit tin, stooped to put it out of the way, changed his mind, flushed and apologized for his clumsiness. "Quite a relief to see the sun again, isn't it?"

"Yes. Yes, it is. But the wireless says it's going to be bad again this evening. Did you hear the forecast this morning?"

"Yes. No sense in complaining, I suppose. After all, it's November. Look, here's the one I'm really interested in. Putting great hopes in it. It was given to me by a seaman acquaintance. It comes from South America."

She bent forward to examine the slim, curved shoots that

protruded from the coconut shell that contained the plant, and he smiled to himself, recalling his fantasies about her. The green coat matching the greens in here. She looked very pale and worried-looking; not at all well, it must be that old father of hers. Heard he was giving a lot of trouble. Singing that song of his about blood and bones to the tune of *Round the mulberry bush,* and walking about on the common at all hours of the night. The police had more than once advised him to keep indoors, but he had told them that he was entitled to walk on the common if he wanted. Said he was hunting hobgoblins. There could be no doubt that he was mad. Nobody took him seriously. Great pity that he should make himself a nuisance to his family.

"You have no idea at all what sort of flower it bears?"

"No idea at all. The chap who gave it to me didn't know himself. He got it in Brazil, he said. Pernambuco. On the wharf. There was a native fellow cadging cigarettes. Trying to exchange curios and plants for them. Meadows—that's my friend—felt sorry for him and gave him a packet of cigarettes, and the fellow insisted he should take this orchid. Said it came from the depths of the Amazon and was very rare."

"The Amazon. To think of its coming from so far away. I remember reading about the Amazon when I was a girl."

"You went to school in Middenshot here?"

"Yes, but not to the Council school. I attended a small private school. Do you know Miss Pettridge in Miller's Lane? She used to hold a small private school in those days. Mother couldn't afford to send me to a good school in Camberley so she compromised by sending me to Miss Pettridge's. A very kind person, Miss Pettridge. I always liked her."

"Look, here's another one that might interest you. An ordinary Cattleya, but very pretty in its way."

"I'm sure it must be." She glanced round and smiled. "And those are your heaters. It's so delightfully warm in here. But surely it must cost you a good bit to keep these heaters going all the time."

"Eats up paraffin." He laughed. "I spend about half my pension on paraffin. Fortunately I don't depend upon my pension alone to live. I have a little money invested. We were very thrifty, the wife and myself, and we had no children. We managed to save quite a decent sum altogether."

"Yes. Oh, yes." She moved nervously away from him toward a box of seedlings. Her hair gleamed palely in the sunshine that struck through the panes of glass above them. "These are just coming up, I see."

"Carnations. Some special varieties I'm trying out," he told her. "Do you like carnations? I have some blooming now in Number One. I'll cut a few for you to take away."

"Oh, no, please! It's so kind of you, but—"

"No trouble at all, Miss Jarrow. It's a pleasure." Self-conscious and awkward, he hurried on: "See my chimneys there? I don't let any of the paraffin fumes escape inside here. I built those home-made chimneys myself. They help the heaters to burn better, too."

"Very ingenious. You take a great deal of pains over your greenhouses, I see."

"Only way to get good results is to be thorough. I believe in being thorough."

"Yes. Yes, that's so. I like—I believe in thoroughness myself."

A silence. She moved over to another box of seedlings, and he followed her. "Your mother keeping well, Miss Jarrow?"

"Yes, thanks. She was—she's well."

They heard an aeroplane passing. Small single-engined plane.

"These newspaper men—so persistent. One came a few minutes ago. To take my photograph for his paper. Never like turning them away. They have a tough life, poor fellows."

She gave a quavering laugh. "I saw a picture of you in one of the morning papers. Not very long ago. In connection with this terrible business."

"Yes, I remember that one. All because of that letter I was handed on the night I called on you." He adjusted one of the seed-boxes. It did not need adjusting. He grunted and mumbled: "Wonder if they've been bothering Hyacinth, too, for a picture of herself. Won't be surprised."

"Oh. You mean—the girl who cleans for you. She was with you last evening, I noticed in the paper."

"Yes. She was on her way home from the Rectory, and dropped

in for something she'd left here, and I offered her a cup of tea. Then it got so dark all of a sudden she said she was scared to go home alone, so I said I'd take her as far as her gate."

"Oh, what a lovely chrysanthemum! Is it a special variety?"

"That? No, nothing special. It's the soil that's made it so big. I've been experimenting with various kinds of fertilizers."

"Oh, I see. Yes, fertilizers." He noted that her cheeks were very pink. She kept bending too avidly over the box with the chrysanthemum, and he could sense that a certain relief had come into her manner. She was trying to hide it, and he felt suddenly sorry for her.

"I'm very fond of experimenting," he laughed.

"It's good to experiment sometimes," she smiled.

Turning aside slightly as though to examine a box of young plants, he looked at his watch. Twenty to nine. It would not be so good, he thought, if Hyacinth were to come and find her here. Hyacinth was such an indiscreet girl. Never could tell what she might say to embarrass them all. A feeling of falseness came upon him. He felt double-faced, and it troubled him. Let him be honest about it. It was not that he was afraid of Hyacinth saying or doing anything indiscreet but that he knew she would be jealous if she found him in here with Miss Jarrow, and he didn't want her to feel he was interested in Miss Jarrow. He knew that Hyacinth, since last night, had become as important a factor in his scheme of living as Miss Jarrow. He felt baffled and disturbed—and guilty.

"Let me show you through the other two," he said. "No orchids in there, and no continuous heating, but you'll see some roses and carnations I'm trying my hand at. The carnations I've just been telling you about."

She followed him out with docility. Trustingly, he thought— and he felt more guilty and perturbed. The sun struck through the hair straggling at her temples. The few frayed, wispy grains that could not be brushed down. She had a haloed look, but he noticed the crow's feet around her eyes. She looked older in the glare of the sun. But pathetic. Pity and tenderness moved in him.

It was ten to nine when she left. He cut the carnations for her, despite her protests, and made her take them. She blushed a great deal, almost tearful with gratitude and pleasure. "Oh, I shall treasure them. They're so lovely. So lovely. I shall put them in water as soon as I get home."

"Very nice of you to have called, Miss Jarrow. Please look in again any time you like. You're always welcome."

"Thank you. You will take care of your arm, won't you?"

"Yes. Nothing to worry over. Just a flesh wound."

"Well, good morning."

"Good morning, Miss Jarrow."

At a few minutes past nine Hyacinth arrived, shining-eyed and concerned for his wound, and indignant, too. "I wanted to come back last night and see how badly hurt you were, but I was afraid to venture out. If I'd thought of it, I'd have asked the police to let me come with you in the car to the hospital instead of having them drop me home."

"Just as well you didn't think of it, then."

"Why? Wouldn't you have liked me to come with you, honey?" She spoke in a crooning American voice, head lowered and eyes mischievous-looking. She was a film star in Hollywood. She touched his arm, giggled and said in her normal voice and manner: "Anyway, I'm glad it's not serious. The dirty old criminal!" Her eyes began to gleam. "See what I was telling you last evening! What else does a creature like that deserve except to be put out of the way! Who is going to convince me that the right thing to do with a beast like that is to house him up in an asylum! Dispose of him as you'd dispose of a rat or a snake—that's how they should deal with him when they catch him. And to think of the hundreds—thousands— more like him locked up in asylums, living on the state. Of what use to the country are such people! We may as well go out and catch all the rats and insect-pests and start an institution for them. Why not collect all the lice and bed-bugs and cockroaches and start a campaign to reform them. Put them in a comfortable asylum and hope that one day they'll become clean and decent insects!"

"All right, calm down. Calm down." But, to himself, he was delighted. He felt the fire of her moving in him, and something far back in him, something primeval, responded. He wanted to despise himself for feeling like this but the feeling persisted and held him entranced. It was as though the deeper parts of him knew that there was truth in what she said. There could be human vermin as well as insect vermin, and to wipe out such vermin was the only way to avoid being plagued by it.

She calmed down at once and said: "Have you heard anything about Mrs. Binney? Did he succeed in coshing her?"

"No. Her daughter-in-law and a neighbour screamed and he ran. She had just ventured outside her kitchen for a minute to fetch in a bucket of coke."

"I can't understand how they didn't catch him."

"The fog was pretty thick."

"In spite of that they should have caught him. He didn't have such a long start as all that."

"It's my opinion there's someone in the district helping him."

"Who do you think?"

"Haven't the slightest idea. Only a theory of mine. I may be wrong. How did you sleep last night?" he smiled.

"Not too bad, but I dreamt all sorts of stupid things, I dreamt I was sleeping in the kitchen here and two mad men were trying to break in at the window, and I kept calling for you but you wouldn't come. And I couldn't get the door open to get into the hallway. No matter how hard I tried I couldn't get it open."

"Perhaps you were trying too hard."

She gave him a quick look.

He flushed and smiled and turned off, saying: "Must be going out to do my morning's shopping, Hyacinth."

6

The sun, that morning, was still shining—though already there was a thin haze over it—when, at about eleven o'clock, a knock came at the front door of Pine Tree Cottage.

"Grace," said Mrs. Jarrow, peeping at the bay window in the living room, "it's a policeman, dear."

"A policeman?"

"Yes. I wonder what he can want."

Grace lowered her knitting. "They must have found out something. Oh, heavens, this is terrible. Terrible."

"I'll go to the door."

"No, Mother, I'll go."

"Very well, dear. But please don't say anything indiscreet."

"Yes?" said Grace to the policeman.

"Miss Jarrow?"

"Yes."

"I'm Inspector Longman. Hope I'm not disturbing you too much, but I was wondering if your father could help us. Is he at home?"

"Oh. Yes. Yes, he's at home. But he's asleep."

"Asleep? I see. Is he generally asleep at this time of the morning?"

"He sleeps all day. I mean—no, only for the past week or so. He's a little eccentric, Inspector. He—he's been going out every night and coming in early in the morning."

"How long has he been doing that? For the past week, you say?"

"Yes. A week or nine or ten days, perhaps."

"You mean since the fog began?"

"Yes."

There was a loud knocking within.

"Oh," said Grace.

"Grace!"

"Yes, Dad?"

"Who knocked on the door? What strange voice is that down there? Is it the old bull again?"

"Oh," said Grace.

"Come here rousing an ill old man out of his sleep! Confounded impudence! Tell him to go, do you hear me? I won't have any nasty old bulls smelling round my cow-pen."

"Dad, there's someone here to see you."

"What's that? Someone to see *me?*"

"Yes, Dad."

"Who can that be? The Lord Chamberlain? Has he come to censor my language? Come on. Speak up, child!"

"It's a police inspector, Dad."

"A police inspector! What's he want with me? What does he want to inspect? The corpses piled up under my poor old bed?"

"He wants to ask you a few questions that—that might be of help to the police, Dad."

"Is that all? Why an inspector, then? Why not a sergeant? Very well, tell him to come up to my room and make a quick, neat inspection. I refuse to bring my corpses down!"

The inspector smiled. "I think I'll go up, Miss Jarrow, if you don't mind."

"Not at all, Inspector. I'll show you up. This way, please."

Mr. Jarrow, in a white nightshirt, a blue-green knitted woollen shawl around his shoulders, had evidently just got out of bed. Standing in the middle of the room, bottle of eusol in hand, he glowered at Grace and the inspector as they entered. "Well, what's it you've come to inspect, Inspector. The dead bodies you've heard I brought into this house during the past week or two?"

The inspector looked round the room with frowning dismay.

"Yes, that's it. Do a good job of inspection. See the gibbet there! One morning my maiden daughter will send for you, and you'll come and find something blue and goggling hanging from that gibbet—and who knows if it won't resemble this poor old man standing before you? Who knows, I say?"

Mr. Jarrow unstoppered the bottle and sent a few drops of eusol drizzling across the room, and the room immediately smelt like a hospital surgery.

The inspector, trying to wrinkle his nose and smile at the same time, said: "Mr. Jarrow, there are a few things I'd like to ask you. It's about your going out at night."

"About my going out at night? I've been asked about that before by one or two of your bloodhounds. They've stopped me on the common at midnight and asked me what I wanted to be out in the fog for at such an hour."

"Yes, and I think you said you were just taking a walk. Taking a walk and—ah—hunting horrible hobgoblins."

"Perfectly correct. Just taking a walk and hunting horrible hobgoblins. And they advised me to keep indoors, and I told them if I wanted to walk all night on the common and hunt my hobgoblins I had a right to do so, because I'm living in a democracy where a man is free to roam where he wants to roam—free even to do acts of sabotage and undermine his own country. He's even free to sing, and I sing every night. You've never heard me, Inspector?"

"Yes, I've heard you," smiled the inspector. "But why do you do it? Why do you go walking and singing at night? Why not by day instead?"

"Why? I'll tell you. Just give me a moment." The old gentleman sprinkled a few more drops of eusol across the room, stoppered the bottle and put it back under the bed. "You know why? It's because I'm a murderer, Inspector. I have a passion for cutting old gentlemen's throats and coshing old ladies on the head, and night is the best time for doing it. Now, how do you like that, Inspector? Suppose I reveal to you that I'm the Lord High Executioner in disguise! Look here, tell you what! You'd better not lift that bed-sheet and look under the bed. You'll see a grisly sight if you do. I've got a tidy pile of human corpses under that bed. Blood and bones. Blood and bones. And stinking horror. That's my special-ity, Inspector. That's what takes me out every night in the fog. And who is to say me nay? Am I the only horror-monger in the world? Read your newspaper and you'll be able to judge. Why shouldn't I go round in the fog looking for old ladies to cosh and old gentle-men's throats to cut? Suppose that's what I have a mind to do who can say I'm wrong? If you don't like it the most you can do is to have me put comfortably away in Broadmoor. You dare not hang me. I'm a poor, delicate old mad man whose mind was soured by society. I'm a twisted old stick, and it's my environment—oooh!" Mr. Jarrow bent in two and began to wail piteously.

A jet plane was whining past overhead.

The inspector shook his head slightly and Grace murmured to him: "It's a phobia of his. He can't stand buzzing or droning noises."

When the plane had passed, the old gentleman straightened up and said: "See for yourself what society has done to me? I can't tol-erate the sound of aeroplanes or cars or big black bumble bees."

"Mr. Jarrow, tell me. When you go for these walks at night don't you ever meet anyone except policemen? I mean, you've never spoken to anyone besides policemen?"

"Of course I have."

"Who?"

"A man in a black overcoat stops me every night and speaks to me."

"Yes? And what does he say to you?"

"He says to me: 'Lo and behold! I am Lord Almighty Satan!' And when I tell him I don't believe him he promptly flashes an electric torch on his behind, and there before my eyes I see his barbed tail protruding from under his evil, sin-black overcoat. Nasty, squirming thing."

"Please be serious, if you don't mind, Mr. Jarrow."

"Then you think I'm spinning you a fairy tale! What sort of inspector are you? I tell you I meet Satan every night on the common, and you ask me to be serious. Isn't that a serious enough matter?"

"I'm afraid I'll have to take you with me to the police-station if you persist in not answering my questions satisfactorily."

"Well, then, you'll have to take me. I can't help it. If you take me to Scotland Yard I'll tell them the same thing. I meet Lord Satan on the common at midnight every night and we do a song and dance together and go a-hunting old gentlemen and old ladies, not to mention little girls in the seven to eleven age-group. I've got a pile of raped and strangled young girls in my chest of drawers in here. Packed neatly and economically away with my linens. If you care to take a peep at any time you're at liberty to do so. You're an inspector. You have to do your duty and inspect."

"Very well. I won't trouble you any longer, Mr. Jarrow, but before I go I think I ought to repeat the warning my men have given you. Keep indoors after dark. It isn't safe to wander about on the common as you do."

"Thank you for your warning, Inspector, but I'm a most dis-obedient old lunatic. Don't be surprised if your men see me again to-night. By the way," added the old gentleman, waving his stick around, "how do you like my bedroom, Inspector? Ever seen a more cosy and horrible little den? Next time you visit me you're sure to find something hanging from that gibbet—something blue and grimacing. And who knows if it won't resemble that poor old man who goes limping all over the common on a dark and foggy night?"

The inspector gave a slight smile and bade the old gentleman good morning. At the front door, he said to Grace: "I suppose there is nothing you and Mrs. Jarrow can do to persuade him to remain indoors after dark, Miss Jarrow?"

"I'm afraid not, Inspector. Oh, he's terrible, terrible. You have no idea. Oh, you don't know what we have to endure."

"I think I can guess. By the way, you have never noticed any odd characters hanging about the lane here, Miss Jarrow?"

"Odd characters? No. No, I've seen no one, Inspector." She went very pale and glanced agitatedly about her. The inspector watched her.

After a brief silence, the inspector said: "I didn't intend to alarm you, Miss Jarrow, but I may tell you this. We've discovered some rather peculiar footprints in your back garden. Footprints we believe might have been made by the man we're looking for."

"Oh."

Mrs. Jarrow appeared from the living-room. "Inspector, did I hear you say that someone suspicious was seen in our back garden?"

"Good morning, Mrs. Jarrow. No, no one has been seen, but in the course of our investigations we found some footprints in your back garden. I'm not trying to alarm you or anything of the sort, but we have to make exhaustive enquiries."

"Naturally, Inspector. Well, now you've mentioned it, I don't know if this will be of any use to you, but last evening we distinctly heard someone running past the kitchen in the back garden. It was soon after we had heard that revolver shot in the lane."

"You did hear the revolver shot, then, Mrs. Jarrow?"

"Oh, yes. Quite clearly, Inspector. And the screams, too—just as the newspapers said. We all heard them."

He glanced at her quickly. "Was your husband at home at that time?"

"My husb—oh. Yes. Yes, Inspector. Of course. He was—he was in the kitchen eating."

"But, Mother—"

"Isn't that so, Grace dear? Wasn't your father in the kitchen with us eating when we heard the screams in Great Oak Road and the pistol shot out in the lane here?"

"I—oop! Yes, yes. We were eating," mumbled Grace, gaze lowered, face very pink.

"And you heard footsteps running past outside the kitchen?"

"That's right, Inspector. Oh, it was dreadful. I warned Herbert to remain at home. I remember saying to him—I said: 'Do you hear that, Herbert? I'm sure it's the Executioner out there. Oh, please do remain at home this evening.' Didn't I tell him that, Grace dear?"

"Yes," whispered Grace, her face turned away.

The inspector grunted softly and asked: "Can you say in what direction the footsteps seemed to run, Mrs. Jarrow?"

"Towards the woods, it seemed, but I couldn't be sure."

"I see. And at what time did your husband go out?"

"Some time long after, Inspector. About an hour later, I should say."

"Are you sure about that, Mrs. Jarrow?"

"Well, not absolutely sure, of course. I didn't take note of the exact time. But I'm certain it must have been about an hour later. He sleeps from early morning until about eleven or twelve and then goes out to—to do a bit of shopping of his own. And then he has something to eat and goes back to bed and sleeps until the evening, then eats again. Isn't that so, Grace dear?"

"Yes, Mother," murmured Grace, a sob in her voice.

The inspector grunted again. "About what time would you say your husband awoke, Mrs. Jarrow—I mean after his second bout of sleep?"

"Well, it's difficult—oh, I should say about six or half past, Inspector. Not earlier than that."

The inspector shook his head. "That doesn't quite fit in with what my men have reported. The incident in the lane took place at shortly before seven o'clock, and your husband was seen out on the common as early as a quarter to six. And he's reported not to have entered this cottage until four-seventeen this morning."

"Oh, but that couldn't be so, Inspector. At least, about his going out last evening." Mrs. Jarrow's hands trembled slightly, her face pale. Abruptly, however, her eyes gleamed with a light of hauteur. "Unless you think I'm telling an untruth. My daughter is here to bear out what I say. At six o'clock yesterday my husband was upstairs sleeping. Isn't that so, Grace? Wasn't your father sleeping at six o'clock?"

"Oooh," said Grace. "Oooh-hoo!"

"Grace dear, isn't that so?"

"Oooh-hoo-hoo! Yes, Mother," said Grace. "Oooh-hoo-hoo!"

A loud knocking within.

"What's going on down there? Grace, are you rehearsing for some theatrical performance, child? Could it be one of Shakespeare's tragedies?" asked the old gentleman.

"Please don't upset yourself, Miss Jarrow," soothed the inspector.

Footsteps thumped on the stairs, and Mr. Jarrow, still in nightshirt and shawl, appeared, a heavy frown on his face, ash stick in hand.

"So you're still here, Inspector, are you? I have a good mind to give you a whack with my stick, or cut your wheezing throat with my razor. What have you done to reduce my daughter to tears like this? Have you been making indecent advances to her? As a high-ranking police officer, you should be downright ashamed of yourself."

The inspector smiled. "I'm glad you've come downstairs, Mr. Jarrow. You may be able to clear up this little point for us. Your wife has just told me that you were at home at seven o'clock last evening. Can you throw your mind back and say whether you really were at home at that hour? Just a matter of being accurate."

The old gentleman limped a pace forward. "Inspector, what's it I've heard you say? My *wife* told you I was home here at seven o'clock yesterday evening?"

"Yes, that's what I said."

"Then you mean you're psychic, Inspector."

"What do you mean psychic?"

"My wife died seventeen years ago. When I want to communicate anything to the dear soul I have to hold a séance. Yes, a séance. And here it is you can calmly inform me that she told you something about me. You *must* be psychic, Inspector."

"Very well, we won't argue over that. But can you tell me if you were at home at seven o'clock yesterday evening?"

"Of course I wasn't. If Agnes told you that it means they're still on double summer time in heaven. Slack sort of government they must have up there not to have had their clocks put back yet."

"Do you mean you were not at home at seven o'clock?"

"Of course I wasn't. I went out at about half past five. I spoke to one of your young sleuths. He asked me what I was doing out on the common on such an evening—the same friendly question—and I told him I was hunting horrible hobgoblins—the same friendly old answer."

"Oh, Herbert! I'm sure you didn't go out at half past five," said Mrs. Jarrow, on the point of sobbing. "You were upstairs sleeping. *Say* you were upstairs sleeping."

Mr. Jarrow began to look from side to side in an inquiring manner. "Peculiar. Most peculiar. I could have sworn I heard my dead wife's voice. Inspector, I'm convinced you *are* psychic."

The inspector, a short, thin man with reddish eyebrows and reddish freckles, green, rather fatherly eyes, muttered a resigned: "Oh, well," and said that he must be going. He nodded and smiled at Mrs. Jarrow, touched his peaked cap at Grace and said: "Good morning," in a pleasant voice. And went.

7

And went.

"Mother, he's gone."

"Yes, my child, he's gone."

"What do you think will come of all this?"

"I don't know, Grace dear. I don't like to conjecture."

Silence for a while, Grace knitting, her mother mending socks.

Suddenly: "What time is it, I wonder? Switch on the wireless. We may be able to hear the weather forecast," said Mrs. Jarrow.

"Yes, it shouldn't be more than a quarter to six. Oh, and look at the fog again! Getting denser and denser. It seems as if it will be worse than it was last evening."

"I don't think it could be, dear. I wonder where he's making for. Grace, do you think it could be that horrible man, the Executioner, he meets when he goes out in the evening?"

"I couldn't say, Mother. I'm afraid to guess. But that fawn coat—wherever could he have got it from? The wireless said, that first evening, that the Executioner was wearing a fawn coat of expensive cut. It's just such a coat Dad wears now."

"There's more than one fawn coat of expensive cut in the country, dear. It may be a coincidence, that's all. Oh, I simply couldn't believe that Herbert, my dear Herbert, would give aid to a murderer. Much as his mind is affected, he wouldn't do it. At heart, he's so kind and gentle."

"And all those drugs he goes around with. I wonder why."

I wonder, thought her mother.

Well, well, I wonder, thought Mr. Jarrow.

Morphia and chloroform and cyanide and a hypodermic needle, mused Grace, fiddling with the wireless knobs.

A square of paper pinned to the door of the coal-house, noted her father, flashlamp in hand.

None of the murders done within the past few days were poison cases.

Oh, Herbert, Herbert!

Then why must he go about with all those dangerous drugs stuffed in his coat pocket? Could it simply be, as Mother thinks, his Mind?

I'm lying low to-night and perhaps for a night or two to come. Police too active. Bring the food to the hut about midnight. Not before. Police usually smell around early in evening. Tomorrow night my friend will bring you a parcel for me. Paid him a call last night and had a hurried word with him. He'll leave the parcel near the door of coal-house. Bring it to the hut at about midnight. Am asking him to pin this note to coal-house door. Don't fail me or I'll rip the guts out of you and your frigging family. The Lord High Executioner.

Ho, ho! Oh, so? Oh, ho, ho, ho!

Oh, I do wonder.

Tomorrow night, my devils, seems as if it will be my big night.

If only I knew for certain. All those lies I had to tell the inspector. And he was such a nice man.

Oh, Lord, save us! My father was a parson.

I can feel it in me, by Almighty Satan! Tomorrow night will be my night. My sweet Paula.

Oh, Lord, it's cold in this hut. I'm cold and hungry, Lord.
Oh, I do wonder.

My honey-sweet spring sprig of blossoms. My Paula.

I went to Eton, but I wasn't cold there. Why should I be cold
in a damned silly hut in the Berkshire woods! Bring me oil for the
heater in the cellar, Alfred. Bring me food, Jarrow. You surly old
fool, fail me and I'll maul you with my last ounce of strength.
Mean to murder you in any event before I complete my campaign. See if I don't settle with you, you old song-singing shit! Oh,
I'll settle with you as I'll settle with the whole world. Alfred, my
old school chum, bring me oil for the heater. I'm cold in this hut.
My father was a parson. The miserable bounder. Preached piss
and pus from the pulpit. Rotten like all the rest. Oh, Lord, save us!
The world is full of maggots. Maggots have eaten the strength of
the world, and men are but shells of weakness. Mere wood-rot.
Oh, sweet Christ, it's cold, cold, cold in this hut. My father was
a parson. Alfred, you were at Eton with me. Bring me oil for my
heater. I'm shivering in this old black overcoat. Oh, Lord, save
us from the weakness of the world. The Germans, Lord. Look
how we've treated the Germans. Pampered them and made them
forget themselves. They're shouting at us again, snarling at us,
threatening us. And we the victors—do we behave like victors?
We don't. We don't because we're maggoty and weak at the core.
Effeteness masquerading as humanity and liberality. Lack of
vitality wearing the robes of kindliness and civilized enlighten-
ment. We're weak. By God, let's face it and do something about
it. We should have treated the Germans as defeated serfs. We
should have let them feel the weight of our victorious wrath. But
no. We treat them kindly. We treat them with Humanity, Kindliness, Civility. Would they have treated us so if they had been the
victors? They would have booted us, humiliated us. No wonder
they laugh at us. Scoff at us. Sneer and snarl at us. Soon new
Hitlers will arise. Soon they'll be powerful again, for they have
virility. A strong people, the Germans. A strong people love and
respect strength. And despise and hate weakness. So they despise
and hate us for being kind to them, because they know intuitively
that what we deem kindness and humaneness is really weakness.
If we treated them harshly they would love and respect us and

co-operate with us. Strength loves strength. Strength reveres strength. Strength loathes weakness. Oh, Lord, save us from the weak people of this world. Oh, Lord, convince our moralists and politicians of the necessity of strength with discipline. Teach us, oh, Lord, that we can be free from war and disillusion only when we realize that order and discipline are the corner-stones of a successful civilized community. The animal seeks to be untrammelled. Man seeks to be civilized. In untrammelled freedom lies chaos. In ordered freedom lie peace and dignity and true human happiness. But ordered freedom can result only from strength. Unwavering strength. Unwavering alertness. The vigilance of stern minds. The cold, reasoned discipline of the healthy and strong. I'm cold and shivering and hungry in this hut. Why must I be cold and hungry? I went to Eton. I was an Oxford blue. My father was a cultured Church of England cleric. Oh, Lord, save us from the superstitious, sentimental piss that's spouted from pulpits everywhere. I'm cold and hungry in a lonely hut in the woods, and there's fog, fog, fog wherever you look. Oh, ho, ho, ho!

Oh, Herbert, I lied for you.

Ho, ho! A note for the old man. And he sent it by his friend. The nerve! Coming here and pinning it to the coal-house door. If only I'd known he was coming. If only I'd known. But never mind. I'll be on the watch from early tomorrow evening.

"Oh."

"Oh, Dad! Are you back already?"

"Yes, I'm back already. Haven't been further than the coal-house. Didn't the inspector advise me to stay in to-night? Well, I'm taking his advice. I'm going nowhere. No roaming in the fog to-night for your poor limping old father."

"Oh, Herbert, I'm so glad."

"Grace?"

"Yes, Dad?"

"I thought I heard the voice of my poor dead Agnes."

"Yes, Dad?"

"Grace?"

"Yes, Dad?"

"I'm inclined to think conditions are favourable for a séance."

"Oh."

"What do you say, my child? Shall we hold a séance?"

"Yes, Dad. By all means—if you'd like to hold one."

Not so tight, she told him, shivering with delight. Don't hold her so tight. He held her tighter and said he wanted a smack. If he said kiss, she said, he could have it. Smack sounded so common. He repeated he wanted a smack—and he gave her a smack. Loud and lacking finesse. Shuddering with bliss, she said it was getting late; he had better hurry up and let them be going on. The show must have started already, and, in any case, he knew it wasn't safe to loiter in the lane like this. Remember the Executioner. They moved on, but he said what had she been doing last evening? Hadn't she been loitering in Pine Tree Lane with that old rove, Holme? Bet she hadn't minded loitering then? She tugged free from him and replied that if he dared call the gentleman an old rove she wouldn't put her foot in any cinema with him. Well, if that didn't look funny, he sneered. Why should she take on like this over old Holme? Was there something up between her and him? She told him to shut his blooming trap and mind his own business. And suppose, she added, there was something up between her and Mr. Holme, what about it? He was a gentleman—and a fine gentleman, too. In fact, she said, sniggering, who knew if something *wasn't* up between him and her! He laughed. That old codger! What could he hope to do with a girl! If she slept with him a month of nights she'd be the same as she was before. For that reason, she flared, she would go and see him this very evening and spend the night with him. How would he like that! Oh, go on! he sneered. That old codger! He wouldn't be one bit of good with any girl in bed. He'd turn his back on her and go to sleep as peaceful as any babe. Very well, then, she wasn't going to the cinema with him. She was going to spend the evening with Mr. Holme. Oh, come on and let them go. They would be late for the show. She stamped. She was not going, she said. She tugged her arm away when he held her. He grabbed her again. Roughly. She resisted. He tugged her to him again. Roughly. Gave her a slap on her fleshy rump and told her a bad word, and she stopped resisting and let him take her to the cinema, shuddering with content in the depths of her female flesh. They could see hardly ten yards in front of them, and they heard the traffic on the London Road droning slowly in funereal tone. The night was cold like metal pressed on the forearm, or wet leaves on bare buttocks. And the fog entered their lungs with the smooth chill of early morning damask rising ghost-wise off a breakfast table ... From early morning. Oh, from early morning until night she thought of no one but him. Sobbing. And all the lies she had told the inspector this morning. All to protect him. Sobbing. Was it cold in the hawthorn hedges, Agnes? Tell him. Was it lonely on the heavenly common where her soul wandered day and night? Could she guess why he wandered on the common? She shouldn't try. He had his reasons that could not be told. Reasons that had their roots in boyhood echoes. Some echoes were sacred and solemn and must not be told. They could only be let alone to toll and toll through the secret places of the mourning soul. But she was afraid for him, so afraid, she said. Let her not be, he told her. Let her not be afraid. He was mad but mellow in his madness, and the law of the land was lame. Oh, let her not be troubled. He could limp much faster than the law. The law was no match for his poor mad brain ...

... poor mad friend. Oh, come with oil for the heater, Alfred. My old school chum. I'm cold, cold. If only you could bring me a crumb, too, Alfred, but you're afraid to bring me food. Fuel oil but no food. Afraid they'll find out. Oh, they! They! It's always *they!* But they are rotted in the centre, my friend. Look how they let you out of Broadmoor. They said you were cured and a fit person to take your place once more in the world. What poor fools! A criminal lunatic is never fit. Never! To his grave he's a threat to his fellows. Oh, Lord, my father was a parson. Oh, Lord, save us from the hollow compassion of our fellowmen. Save us from psychologists and sentimental social workers.

Tip, tap.

Oh, hell! Oh, Christ! What was that? Wait. Don't move.

Tip, tap.

The silver bird branch brushing against the roof. Good. It's all right. Must be on the alert. Vigilance. Vigilance, oh, Lord. Let us always be wary of the foe. No slacking. Hand on the gun, hand on the knife. The strong are vigilant; the weak are lax. Oh,

Lord, I was a captain in the Army. Save us, oh, Lord, from pacifists and all pusillanimous people. If Stalin sent us an ultimatum tomorrow our pacifists would reply: "So sorry we don't fight, Mr. Stalin. Please walk in and take over." We're as supine as all that, Lord. Pacifists and preachers of love and kindness. Communists working like wood-ants in our midst, and we let them. Freedom of speech and freedom of beliefs. Democracy. Synonyms all for Weakness. The strong can be kind and loving and democratic—but with reason and discipline, without sentimentality. Permit freedom of speech and freedom of beliefs, but not to your *known* enemies. Not to your *openly* declared enemies. Stamp on these hard, or they'll wipe you out. *They* have no sentimentality. *They* aren't pacifists. *They* are armed to the teeth. Waiting to pounce. Waiting to crush us underfoot and *keep* us underfoot. Once in power, our enemies won't weep tears of sympathy for the lot of mankind, or coo idealistic cant about freedom of speech and freedom of beliefs. Do they let us speak freely in their own domains? Do they let us move freely about in their lands? No. But we—oh, so Good and Sweet and Charitable are we!—we let them speak their minds and act freely among us. Betray our military secrets like Fuchs. Do little odd jobs of sabotage. Ferment the yeast of trouble among our labour organisations. Bring off clock strikes. Slow down our industry. And, of course, we must let them, because we're a kind, loving, democratic people. Oh, Lord, my father was a parson. Save us, oh, Lord, from democratic idealists! Save us from parsons and all religious pamphleteers! Give us sanity—the sanity that comes of strength and discipline—that we may make the best of a bewildering world. It *is* a bewildering world, Lord, and will never be perfect so long as men and women are born of the womb and not of test-tubes, but we *can* make a better best of it than we have so far. Only rid us of religion and teach us discipline. Teach us to live with the ease of animals and the dignity of humans. Teach us to be elastic in our outlook as civilized people should be, but to be disciplined in our habits. Discipline, discipline. A word we should repeat a hundred, a thousand, times a day. Oh, Lord, how cold I am in this hut! Cold, cold, cold. It's dark and cold, and all about me is the dismal, dense and enfolding fog. Will I ever escape this fog? I wonder. Will I?

Oh, Alfred, hurry up and bring me oil for the heater. Bring me food, Jarrow. I'm cold and hungry.

8

It still clogged, when morning broke, the dark spaces amidst foliage, and still moved, a clammy shroud, through the chilly air—but Grace did not mind. Her father had not wandered abroad last night, and he had made her mother happy with the séance in the evening—and for herself she had her carnations to make her happy. Her precious carnations. Never before had any man made her a gift of flowers—nor given to her even as much as a hair-pin.

She had put them in a pale blue vase and left them downstairs in the back room, and this morning they were as fresh as when she had brought them home yesterday morning. She looked at them, clasped her hands and looked at them, retreated a step and looked at them. She did a waltz around the small room—looking at them. Paused and uttered a whining sound of delight, still looking at them.

If, she thought, he was not a little fond of me he wouldn't have given them to me. He insisted I should have them. Oh, he insisted. He must be a little fond of me. He must, he must.

She waltzed again, nearly colliding with the ironing board. She stopped by the window, and looked out at the back garden. The window panes were of plain glass, not purple and opaque like those in the kitchen. She could see the apple tree. It stood veiled with fog, a leafless thing that lifted its knobby limbs toward the sky—toward the white waste above; it might have been an octopus whose tentacles had frozen overnight. But she knew that it was the old familiar apple tree; it did not seem frightening. It was a segment of the general security and cosiness of her home.

Then her gaze moved toward where the door of the coal-house loomed in the milky air, and a shudder went through her. Who knew what horror might not have been harboured in the coal-house during the night! How often, throughout the past week or two, had her security and cosiness not been severely threatened!

That terrible man wandering about in the fog. And her father . . . Oh, let her not think about it. Unpleasant things should be shut out from one's thoughts. Horrible things only happened to other people . . . Let her think, rather, of her carnations, and of Mr. Holme. Soon she might be faced with an Important Decision. Soon. Oooh!

She hugged herself deliciously. Little blissful, yearning worms of excitement wriggled delightfully behind her ribs, tingling within the hungry vacuum behind her breasts. To think of his hands resting upon her breasts. Oooh! A lightning fork of fear sizzled through her bliss. Oh, not that! Not that! . . . Suppose, she thought. If, she thought. Perhaps, she thought . . . "Oooh!" This time the squeal was audible.

She paced about, her hands clasping and unclasping. What a big decision to make! To leave her cosy home or not to leave.

She stopped and tapped her palms on the ironing board. Frowned and thought: I'm being silly. How absurd of me to imagine he would . . . Oh, but he might, he might. He gave me carnations. He's fond of me. I ought to give the matter thought. It's not so absurd as I'd thought at first. Suppose . . . If . . . Perhaps . . . She shut her eyes and let herself dream.

She was walking along the lane on a sunny morning in late December. A cold, crisp, frosty morning—a jewel-day scintillant amidst the dross of winter's dreary waste. She was about to pass his gate when . . . "Good morning, Miss Jarrow!" . . . "Oh. Good morning, Mr. Holme! What a fine morning, isn't it?" . . . "Yes, Miss Jarrow. A really fine morning. Going shopping as usual?" . . . "Oh. No. No, Mr. Holme. I'm going to catch the bus for Camberley. I have to take some of my work there." . . . "Ah. Yes, of course. Your knitting and sewing. Well, it's odd, but I happen to be going to Camberley myself. Going to my bank." . . . "Oh. Then—then perhaps we can catch the same bus?" . . . "Yes. Yes, by all means, Miss Jarrow. Yes." . . . Silence for a moment, then: "You have no objection to my walking with you to the bus stop, Miss Jarrow?" . . . "Not at all, Mr. Holme. Not at all." . . . And so they walk. Chatting and walking. Turn into Great Oak Road. Into the London Road. Cross. Into the High Street. And now here they are in Middenshot Square. The bus-stop . . . Chatting, chatting.

Then: "Ah, here's our bus, Miss Jarrow." And they get into the
green two-decker bus, and go upstairs and seat themselves. Side
by side. Oh, lovely, lovely! Sitting actually *beside* him.

Silence as they go past the drinking trough. And the Ram and
Cross. And Rogan Hall . . . Miller's Lane . . . Then: "Miss Jarrow,
you know . . ." "Yes, Mr. Holme?" . . . "You know, Miss Jarrow,
there's a little matter I've been considering." . . . "Yes, Mr. Holme?"
. . . "I don't know what you'd say, but I was thinking . . ." "Thinking?" . . . "Yes, I was thinking, thinking of asking you something."
. . . "Oh, yes." . . . "You know, I live all alone, Miss Jarrow, and I
feel that some day—yes, some day I ought to get someone—ask
someone to share my home with me." . . . "Oh, yes, Mr. Holme.
Yes, I think you ought." . . . "Well, Miss Jarrow, I don't know how
you feel about it, but I was wondering—it occurred to me that I
might ask you to consider perhaps—one day—one day soon—if
you couldn't think of marrying me . . ."

"Oooh!" It was too much. She had to squeal and hug herself
and do a waltz around the room.

She paused again by the ironing board and shut her eyes once
more. Now what must I tell him? Oh, what can I say? . . . "Oh, Mr.
Holme, it's so kind of you . . ." No, no . . . "Oh, Mr. Holme, you're
so kind and sweet to ask me such a thing. I just don't know what
to say. Couldn't you—oh, please, you must give me some time to
think it over." . . . "Oh, certainly, Miss Jarrow. There's no hurry.
You must take your time over it. I know I've been very sudden,
and—and it's only fair you should have some time to think it
over." . . . "Oh, Mr. Holme, I've always been so—so fond of you. I
. . . Oh, I don't know what to say . . ."

"Oooh!" She waltzed again, drawing the shawl tighter about
her shoulders. Her mother's shawl which she had picked up in
the living-room a few minutes ago. She paused, feeling the cold.
It was unheated, this back room. Always, she thought, there is
the cold. And the fog. If only life could have been warm, cosy
things and no cold, harsh, exposed things to make one pause . . .
Pause. She must pause and think. It was such an Important Decision. Could she ever leave this cottage, every corner and crevice
of which was familiar to her; this cottage to which she was as
attached as though it were a person? And to leave her mother and

her father, could she do that? Yes, she could. Let her be honest. She would feel no regrets at that. Deep inside her she had always felt that her mother deserved to live with her father. Mother had pampered him abominably. If she were left alone with him it would be her own fault. Though, really, she would like it. Oh, Mother wouldn't mind being left alone with him. She wouldn't mind his walking on her all the days of her life. She was like that. Born to be walked on by someone.

She went to the window at the sound of footsteps. It was the coal-man, a bag of coal on his back. Oh, dear! She would have to tell him, as she had told him a day or two ago, to leave the coal near the coal-house door. Hurrying out through the kitchen door, she told him: "Please leave it near the coal-house door, Albert, and call back later for the sack. My father will come downstairs in a little while and empty it into the coal-house. He—he likes doing it himself nowadays."

Albert smiled whitely out of his begrimed face and said very well, he would do that. No trouble, Miss. He would call back tomorrow.

She watched him go, not knowing that her father had watched them both from his bedroom window, smiling to himself, ash stick in hand, medical book open on the window sill before him, wagging his head and murmuring: "The coal-man cometh, the coal-man goeth. Like the seconds that come, pip by pip, out of the void that is Time, and return, pip by pip. To-night always comes. And this to-night will come. To-night which is the Night. And when it's gone . . . ha! Who knows what will have happened, my devils! Who knows what will lie in waiting to be found!"

. . . to-night. If only I could be with him to-night. Why couldn't I go to him to-night and say: "I've come, take me. Dick is nothing to me. It's you I want, tall man. Can't you see? Take me. I'll never have to scrub this Rectory again if you take me. My aunt scrubbed it in her day, and now I scrub it, but only your house I'll scrub if you take me. It'll be my house and yours. Ours to sleep in and to eat in. Mine to clean." Oh, if he will only take me. I'm wishing and working for it. Wishing and working every minute, every hour . . .

. . . to-night. If you could only take it into your head to hold another séance to-night, Herbert. But that is too much to hope for, I suppose. You'll go out again and wander on the common, and I'll grieve for you. And look at the fog. Only two o'clock and it's as thick as ever. But not thicker than the warm blood of love in my heart for you . . .

. . . to-night. A knock . . . "What! I can't believe it. You again, Hyacinth!" . . . "Yes, me again. Aren't you glad to see me? You want me to go?" . . . "No. No, I don't. But the fog. Why did you venture out?" . . . "Because I wanted to come to you. Isn't that a good enough reason? Let me make you a cup of tea. Have you had your supper already?" . . . "Not yet. Yes, I'd like a cup of tea." . . . "Let me get your supper." . . . "You'd like to do that for me?" . . . "I'd like to do it for you every night of my life. I mean it I would." . . . And when they're at the table eating: "You don't believe me, but I want to. I wish I could do this for you every night." He puts out his hand and touches her arm and says: "I wish you could," feeling a shiver go through him and knowing it is the feel of her flesh that makes him shiver, not the cold, repetitious fog outside. Not the cold, monotonous fog. He can sense her watching him, though his gaze is lowered shyly. He can hear her breathing. Foolish of me to go thinking what I'm thinking. But he knows as he eats that the femaleness of her is enveloping him like a small fog in the kitchen here—unseen but powerful. I'm too old to go feeling like this, he tells himself, but he is one with the fog. A warm fog, soft and animal, binding him with caressing tendrils . . . Clink, goes metal against metal in the sink as she washes up, and he prepares to light his pipe, but can feel his hand in his pocket trembling as it fumbles for pouch and pipe. I'm behaving like a boy of nineteen, he thinks, but what is a sober thought against the warm urge misty in the vital interstices of his body! Ought to be ashamed of myself. At my age . . . "You're going to see me home?" She breaks a long silence, speaking without turning her head. He replies: "Yes, I'll see you home." Clink of metal against metal and plate against plate. And tinkle of water. Water splashing and gushing . . . "You'd like me to stay the night?" . . . He stirs in the chair, toying with his pipe not yet filled. He mumbles, trying to chuckle: "Don't be a silly girl." But he knows that he sounds unconvincing, and knows she is aware of the tension in him, the wreathing urge that holds him . . . "I'm staying," she says. And he says nothing. Fills his pipe mechanically. Fumbles in his pocket for matches. She is drying the plates. He listens to the sound of the plates as she puts them down—click-clatter—one by one. Silence. She has put down all the plates. Silence still. The hum of a car in Great Oak Road. The monotonous, persistent rumble of traffic in the London Road. Slow. Snails in iron armour. Lorries and vans and cars in a snail-slow pageant on the road. Flares at the cross-roads. Warmth in the midst of cold. A soft warmth at the back of his head. Pressing gently . . . "Don't be a silly girl." But his voice sounds like a croak, because he knows it is the soft warmth of her breasts he can feel pressed against the back of his head. And now it is the cool smoothness of her arms sliding past his cheeks, rubbing briefly against his shaven chin, touching his moustache. Hands squeezing his wrists . . . "Hyacinth, don't be foolish." She not saying a word. Only pressing against him and squeezing his wrists so that he has to put down his pipe and turn and hold her, breathing as fast as she is breathing . . . "Just for that I'm going to make you stay." . . . "I want to stay. So long I've been wanting to stay." She sits in his lap and lets him fondle her . . . At my age I ought to know better . . . But he still fondles her. Helps her to open her bodice. Later tells her in a whisper: "Come into the bedroom."

. . . to-night. Who would have thought he would have let me go to bed with him to-night? she thinks in the darkness. And he didn't hurt me as much as I expected he would have. Dick would have hurt me like hell. Dick is no gentleman; he's crude. Oh, it's good to be in bed with him like this. He'll have to ask me to marry him after this. I know he's going to. He's going to want me more and more, and he won't want to have me again without marrying me. Oh, my wish has come true. I so wanted to be mistress of this cottage and be his wife, and now I've almost got it already. People who work for things get them. That Jarrow creature, she is no match for me. Weak. No guts. I'm half Irish—that's what's given me my fire and push. Oh, I love him. He's a good man, and a gentleman. In time to come I might teach him to rough-handle me the way I like—the way Dick can rough-handle me. I'll teach him how to thrill me . . . Oh, but it's delicious being in bed with him ... Delicious. I'm going to sleep. Let me sleep. Who cares about any fog now? ... Delicious ...

... the awakening ... "Hyacinth, what are they going to say? Your uncle and aunt—they're going to imagine you've met with foul play or something, not seeing you home this morning." ... She cuddles up against him and says: "Don't worry. I told them I was going to sleep with Mary Galpinger. I sometimes spend the night at Mary's place." ... He breathes in relief. "Then you'll be able to have some breakfast with me?" ... "Of course. Kiss me." ... "Hyacinth." ... "Yes?" ... "If I ask you to marry me how— what would you say?" ... "Are you asking me?" ... "Yes." ... She is silent a moment, then: "You're such a good man. You make me feel like a bad girl who's led you astray." ... "Don't be silly. What do you say? I'm very fond of you, Hyacinth." ... "You know my answer already. I've always wanted to marry you. Kiss me. Oh, kiss me." ... and after breakfast: "I feel happy this morning." ... They stand at the kitchen door looking out on a perfect morning. No fog. Bright sunshine ... "I feel happy, too," he mumbles ... "Look. The sun's shining specially for us." ... He nods, very happy ... "Come with me into Number Two. Let's take a look at the orchids. My children." Something troubles him remotely. Not so remotely. But he puts it aside. Don't let him think about that. Queer, though, how only a day or two ago he was dreaming of that green coat. Green coat merging with the green in Number Two. Didn't think I was so inconstant ...

... They enter Number Two, and he looks at the thermometer. The old routine. Sixty-nine point five. Good. Temperature as it should be ...

"Oh, no! Look! Look at this! And you never told me!"

"Told you what?" He turns ... "Hyacinth!"

"Oh, what a sweet, beautiful thing!"

"The orchid! My dream orchid!"

"Oh, but isn't it smashing!"

"Oh, Hyacinth! My dream orchid!"

A misty bridal veil, with specks of blue and green and mauve ...

"Oh, my dream orchid!" ...

Ah, well ... Chuckling to himself, he shut his *Book of Orchids* and stretched. At my age, to go indulging in all these idle fancies. Anyone would think I was nineteen. All the same, that girl has done something to me. Damned tempting little wench. Got fire, too. Brünnhilde . . . Ugh. Smell the fog in the air. Another nasty night. Wonder when I'll be able to take my evening walks again. I miss them . . . He yawned and prepared to go to bed. Suddenly chuckled again at the memory of his fantasies of a moment ago. Told himself it wouldn't be so bad if he did have Hyacinth to go to bed with tonight. He wanted a woman to-night . . .

. . . to-night. It could happen like that to-night, thought Hyacinth at the rectory that afternoon. I'm going to win him, sure as I'm mopping this floor. As sure as day is day and night is night . . .

. . . oh, to-night. All is ready for the big moment tonight, my devils. The stage is set and the actors are ghosts in the misty wings . . . Yes, watch how the fog thickens. Thicker and thicker it grows. All in a milky tangle, cold and evil like you, my demons. Cold and conspiring. Repetitious and monotonous. Oh, how repetitious and monotonous. Cold and white, and always cold and white. And conspiring. But not more conspiring than old man Jarrow. Pst! What's the time? Three o'clock. Three o'clock in the afternoon, and all's set. Morphia and cyanide and hypodermic needle—all safely stowed away in the pocket of my new fawn coat of expensive cut. In one pocket—drugs and appliance; in the other pocket—gloves and odds and ends. Ha! What odds and ends, too! Odds death! Yours, God—not mine. Old Jarrow won't make any mistake, my Lord High Executioner. First, out by the kitchen door at half past five and take up my post under the apple tree. From there I can watch your friend as he approaches the coal-house door, because he'll be silhouetted against the lighted kitchen window. I must remember to warn my young cow not to monkey about with the kitchen light. It must burn from half past five until whatever hour I come in. If she disobeys I'll put her across my knee, lift her skirt and spank her . . . "Young cow," I'll say to her, "you see the light burns in the kitchen until I come home, or else . . ." She'll probably whine at me: "But, Dad, why should we waste the current unnecessarily?" . . . "Why?" I'll reply. "I'll tell you why. Because Satan hateth light. Satan loveth the dark, and if you put out the light Satan will break into the kitchen, hunt you down wherever you may be in the house. And having found you, he'll lift your frock and—guess what he'll do. He'll spank you soundly on your buttocks. Ho, ho, ho!" . . . "Oh, you're dreadful, dreadful! I wish you'd stay out of the house and never come back. I do wish you would!" . . . "Aha. Wishing your old sire evil, eh? Take care. Take care he won't answer your shrieks and come to the rescue when Satan holds you in a spanking clinch!" . . . "Grace dear, please do as he says. Leave the light burning in the kitchen. Please, dear." . . . "Hark! I could have sworn I heard your dead mother advising you to be sensible. I believe you're psychic, child. Now, you take her advice and leave that light burning for me. I'm going out. Going out to do fell and final deeds. I'll take the key, as usual, and lock the door from outside, and you see that that light keeps burning. Ho! Haw! Oh, what a cold and foggy-woggy night! What a night for bloody doings! *Oh, here we go gathering blood and bones! Blood and bones! Blood and bones! . . .*"

. . . but they won't be my bones, fog. Not mine. Odds death! Oh, watch it around me. Fog, fog, fog. An ectoplasmic leucorrhoea oozing in clammy silence from the vagina of the English earth. Teeming with who knows what autochthonous creatures of the soil. Infinitesimal lice unknown to man's sight or touch, all poised around me wheezing, unheard, a blanket chorus of ridicule. Laughing their lungs loose at us, poor caricatures who call ourselves human and civilized and dignified. Poor giant-fool me, lumbering in the gloom, object of their primeval scorn. No fog can touch their souls; no fog can fog their dusty eyes, or keep out the light from their translucent one-cell bodies. And where's the police force that can intimidate their mossy minds! Oh, to be a pip-like creature of the soil, undreaming, unscheming, unwanting social order and social reform, unhating, without hope or despair. Just a pip floating in the fog, really free, really happy . . . But here's the apple tree. Let me halt my fancies and adjust my gloves. Let me settle down to watch the square of pale light that is the kitchen window. Yes, Jarrow, this is the big night . . . To-night. The night to end all nights.

Pip, pip, go the seconds in the goblet of time. Pop, pop, go the minutes. Time passing. Time always passing . . .

Did I hear a step?

In the woods. Someone coming. They've stopped. They're walking again—slowly, stealthily. Going away. Receding. Some police sleuth, perhaps. I don't believe my bird would come from that way. Nor so early. Too sly, my bird. The Borstal mentality. Practised at creeping about the countryside on foggy nights. Expert at finding the police. Come, my fat, pampered bird. Jarrow's waiting for you with phial and needle. Jarrow won't pamper you . . . He'll pepper you, instead. Neatly, swiftly, lethally . . .

. . . oh, to-night. Not yester-night but to-night. The liquidity of Time. Time going. The seconds melting into the minutes and the mellow minutes welding themselves into the languishing core of the hours. Six o'clock . . . Seven o'clock . . . Eight o'clock, and all's well under the apple tree. Old Jarrow's still waiting, my Paula. I'd wait till the end of the world. I would, my heart's soft candle-light . . . Half past eight . . . Ah! A footstep. Wait. Yes, a footstep. A shape. It's he. It's him . . .

I see him going past the window . . . Now advance . . .

"Who's that?"

"Jarrow."

"Oh, that you, Jarrow?"

"Have you brought the parcel for your friend?"

"Yes. Here it is."

"And here's something for you. You miserable parasite coddled by an effete state! Take this! And this!" . . .

Hee, hee. That's it. Cough and splutter, my friend. It's only cyanide. Easy end for you, my lump of filth. In a few more seconds you'll be far away in Satanland—your soul, I mean. Your body will stay in my coal-house until such time as I can carve it up for disposal. That's it. Struggle. You're lapsing into a coma. General paralysis. First fit has passed. In the dark your eyes are staring wide, aghast at the vastness of eternity . . .

Plan One. Will Plan One succeed as my fancy sees it? Or will Plan Two merge with Plan One in one big whole? Shall I stand by the hut and view two corpses neatly needled? Oh, how nice it is to scheme and to dream at three in the afternoon . . . To dream. To act in actuality. Will to-night be like this afternoon? Or will reality be clogged and tainted with the sinews of disillusioning fog? . . . Fog of actuality. Mist of fantasy. Oh, to dream. Reality and

dream. Where does one end and the other carry on? Oh, Time . . .
Three o'clock. And after three o'clock comes four o'clock. Then
five o'clock. Then . . . Oh, fog, fog! All is hidden and hurrying and
struggling. All is illusion and delusion . . .

THE SNOW

I

Tick, plick, went the flakes softly against the panes. Click, went the front gate, and the tread of quick, clipping footsteps came on the crazy pavement. A brisk tap on the door. Mr. Holme rose at once and went to the door. He had been half-expecting the call.

"Come in," he said.

Tick, plick, went the flakes on the doorstep.

"Come right in," he invited the two men.

"Sure? Sure you don't mind? It's latish. After seven."

"No, no. Come in."

North came in—and Southerby. "North," said North. "I'm Albert North, and he's Southerby—first name John. You've seen us before in the village. Greeted you this morning in the High Street, remember? Our card!" Mr. Holme took it and read: *We cover the country—North and Southerby—Busy as bees.*

"That's it," smiled North. "Busy as bees—Southerby and me. Poof! Tch, tch. What weather!" He brushed the few flakes of snow from his shoulder. A short, dark, fortyish man with heavy, frowning eyebrows, but hazel eyes that twinkled persistently, he had a head of hair like a storm-tossed sea sprinkled with ciga-rette ash. "Unusual for early December, this snow." Flicking with his fingers at his lapels. "Up north—yes. We're accustomed to it up north at this time of the year. I'm a Yorkshire man." Wiping his feet briskly on the mat. He winked at Mr. Holme. "Tell you a secret. Only professional—our names. Fit in with our slogan. Helps business. Yours Holme, eh? Geoffrey Holme?"

"Yes. Can I help you? Come into the living-room."

"Warm in there, eh? Saw your fire from out in the lane. This weather! Whoof! Tch, tch! Believe we'll have heavier falls during the night. Wind dead north-west."

"Yes, so the five to six forecast said. Come in, come in. This way." He led them into the living-room. Fire flickered in the fireplace, making a prickly crackle-crackle, warming, ruddily cheerful. Cheering. Contrasting with the tick-plick of the light flakes against the cold panes.

"I'm at the Ram and Cross. Southerby at the Greyhound. But ssh! Hush-hush. Everything strictly under the hat. We're on a job, you see. Know what I mean? A few enquiries here and there. Cautious. Discreet. Don't even let ourselves be seen together in the village. These people talk so. Old policeman, eh? Well, you know what I'm driving at. Me? Used to be in the Force myself. Detective-inspector. Southerby—like you—a sergeant." He poked Southerby in the ribs, winking. "Eh, Southy old bun?"

Southerby smiled. Nodded faintly. A short man, too, thick-set, with a bald patch on top his large, globe-like head, the hair around this patch a reddish gold. He had shyish, merry green eyes, looked fifty-one and a family man. "Only sensible way to handle the problem. Only one way," he said, as if continuing a conversation he had broken off a minute ago. He spoke in a husky, but very distinct, voice, and evidently suffered from some permanent laryngeal trouble. He lit a cigarette as they settled into chairs. Mr. Holme sat on the sofa. "Only one effective way. Wipe them out. Treat them as pests. Sorry. Cigarette? Mine are mentholated. Good for my throat." He held out his open case, but North and Mr. Holme both refused. "We have to clean them out," he said hoarsely, leaning forward, eyes gleaming—not twinkling—merrily, his manner in no way earnest. His voice blended with the snow falling—tick-plicking against the window panes. An indoors whispering, his. An outdoor whispering, the flakes'.

North tittered. "See? Chip on the shoulder, Southerby. Means no harm, but there it is. Good fellow, believe me. One of the best. But chip on his shoulder. Got to humour him."

"I suppose it's something to do with the recent happenings in the district—your investigations?" asked Mr. Holme.

North nodded. "Hush-hush. Sssh! We'll tell you all about it in time. We're ex-policemen together. Thought it only right we should call on you."

"Yes, I was somehow expecting you to call on me."

"There you are! Policeman. Can't help it. Always expecting the thing that comes off. Accurate deductions. Holme. Holmes. Sexton Blake and so forth." North leaned forward confidentially. "It's about Major Rudstow's disappearance two or three weeks ago. Remember? Vanished from his farm over at Ashbole. Vanished at about the same time that escaped lunatic, the Executioner, stopped terrorizing the village. Both gone. Gone with the fog. Phlut! Like that! Well, our business is to trace the Major. Got to find out what happened—and if there's really any connection between the sudden cessation of the murders done by the Executioner and the old Major's disappearance. The Major's relatives have engaged us to look into things, and we're doing our best. We're progressing. Oh, we're progressing, I can tell you." He looked at Southerby and winked. "Eh, Southy?"

Southerby nodded. "Our duty is to get rid of them," he said hoarsely. "Every one of them. One by one as they crop up. It must be a deliberate, planned and disciplined programme."

North winked at Mr. Holme. "Hear him? Bee in the bonnet. But we're progressing, you take it from me. Before long we'll have got everything into shape and dug out the whole nasty business."

"Yes, it's very strange about Major Rudstow's disappearance. I've been reading about it in the papers. Looks suspiciously as if there must be some connection between his vanishing and the Executioner murders. He was once an inmate of Broadmoor, the Major. You know that, don't you?"

"We know, we know," said North. "Released a year or two ago as a person fit and proper to take his place in the community. In other words, they considered him cured. Anyway—ssh! Hush-hush! We mustn't say too much. Bad tactics. Caution and persistence are our watchwords, Southy and me. Hoof! Look at the weather! Going to hinder us a good bit. Eh, Southy?"

Southerby nodded and shook some ash in the direction of the fire. It fell on the rug. "We'll never have a satisfactory civilization until we have perfected a thorough and unsentimental system of ridding the community of dangerous individuals—thugs, thieves who resort to violence, sex criminals, homicidal lunatics."

North stretched out and tapped Mr. Holme's shoulder with a forefinger. "See what I've been telling you. Chip. Square on his shoulder. Good old Southy. Humour the old bun. Humour him."

"People with twisted brains who show violence toward the human person and who violently rifle property—we must erase these. These are on a par with vermin. We must clean them out or be prepared to continue suffering rape and murder and theft and, worst of all, war. It's a criminal or lunatic or fanatical mentality that conceives and plans a war. No healthy, civilized—note, civilized—individual wants war, nor desires in any way to do physical violence to the person of another, nor, if he is a statesman, will sanction a conflict between his country and another. Only the mentally warped—the mentally ill—have such urges. And such mentalities result not from environmental causes but from bad heredity. Such people are integrally diseased, hence unfit to live among ordered, civilized beings—so our only expedient is to eradicate them as they crop up, even from childhood, and persist in doing so until we have purged the species finally of the mentally unwholesome. It would be a long and difficult task but it could be done."

"But what about the people who will actually have to do the nasty job of eradicating them, Southy? Won't their occupation eventually turn them, too, into brutes and sadists? Won't they learn to hate humanity? Remember the Nazi beasts who ran places like Belsen and Buchenwald. They had twisted minds, Southy old cake."

"Precisely. They had twisted minds. But they didn't *acquire* twisted minds. Their work didn't give them twisted minds. They were *born with twisted minds*." Southerby leaned forward, casual and merry-eyed, no more in earnest than the flakes trivially tickplicking against the misted panes. "Had they not," he continued huskily, "been *innately* cruel they could not have perpetrated the deeds they did. No environmental causes, no ill-treatment at the hands of society, could have warped their minds to that extent. They were born that way, North. They were hereditary criminals and sadists employed—chosen and employed—by the criminals and sadists who ran the German government, themselves also *born* criminals and sadists. No, North. If the men in any government are sincerely compassionate and humane, and are sincere in their desire to better the lot of mankind, the people they employ to do the work of elimination I'm suggesting won't necessarily have to turn into brutes. Do surgeons eventually degenerate into sadists, do they eventually hate humanity because their job is to lop off diseased limbs and cut out malignant tumours? Look at it that way. The task is one which would call for a clinically detached outlook. Here's a distasteful job to be done; nobody likes doing a distasteful job, but it's for the good of the great mass of people, so let's get down to it and stop being squeamish. See the spirit? If we *know* it's for the good of mankind we do it without hatred."

North nodded and shrugged. Glanced at his host. "See what I mean? See how he argues? No use. Chip."

"Hyacinth holds the same views."

"She does, eh?"

"Do you know her?"

"That's the girl who comes to clean for you."

"Yes. This past week or two she's been coming in of an afternoon, too, to make me a cup of tea. Good girl, Hyacinth."

"Mm. We've seen her about the village. Hyacinth Withers. I've even observed her once or twice in the Ram and Cross. Southerby likes her rump. Don't you, Southy old pin?"

Southerby nodded. "We might even," he said merrily, "look at the matter in this way: Men are really only self-tamed beasts, but beasts remain beasts, whatever coating of civility and culture is laid over them. It's inevitable that savage urges and instincts will, at times, threaten to burst through this coating. But the majority of us humans possess highly developed brains, and with these brains we preserve our coating of civility and culture; with these brains we keep down the beast-urges and instincts that persistently attempt to burst forth and create chaos and damage among us. But—note this carefully—some of us, a small percentage of us, have not-so-highly-developed brains, or brains that are specifically defective, and these brains are inadequate to the task of curbing the beast-urges and instincts. The result is that the people with such brains continually menace the safety of those with the better-developed brains. Our business, therefore, is to eliminate these inferior brains, wherever they may occur, and they occur in people of all races and nationalities. In this respect, no one race or nation can claim to be better than another. Men, accordingly, in being assessed in the scale of living, behaving earthly creatures ought to be measured by this specific quality of their brains. A brain that makes for constructive, peaceful living is a good brain; a brain that militates for chaos and destruction is a bad brain."

North rubbed his hands together gleefully. "Just you watch how I'm going to trip him up! Look here, Southy old bud, tell me this. Suppose I come upon a brain that militates for chaos and destruction but I discover that this same brain is a highly brilliant one—a genius-brain in economics or a genius-brain in music— must I eradicate it?"

"Yes. Eradicate it. The world may have lost a brilliant economist or soul-moving symphonies, but the world may have been spared a welter of horror that may have brought suffering to millions of people. The loss would have been worth while."

"And what brains will be the criterion brains, Southy? In framing our laws how are we going to define exactly what is the standard good brain? Who will *decide* what is a standard good brain? Don't you think the 'good' brains might disagree as to what is exactly a good brain? Or isn't it likely that a few bad brains may be involved in the business of deciding, the result being that the finally accepted pattern-brain may not be so flawless as we had hoped?" North shook with chuckles, slapping his leg. "See how I draw him out, Holme? Oh, Southy and I have some rollicking times debating vital questions of the day."

Tick-plick, went the flakes outside. Relentlessly. Detachedly. Piling up on pavements and in lanes and in fields, on window sills and on roofs.

Southerby flicked his cigarette end into the fire. "Violence and the intent to do violence are all we need in deciding our pattern brains, North. There is no difficulty. Here is a man who has embezzled the funds of a company. He may have a warped brain—or he may not. Pay heed. In his case he might have been tempted; a thousand different circumstances might have combined to cause him to commit the crime; in short, *he* might be a case of environmental influences: too much trust put in him by his superiors; a gambler in bad water; somebody blackmailing him, perhaps. Note, however, that he has committed a crime but *he has not resorted to violence,* hence he must have our sympathetic consideration. For him we must hold out hope. His may not be a bad brain. But the man who points a pistol at the bank clerk and demands money—*that* man has a bad brain. *He* must be wiped out."

"Phlut! See? He's got me. I give up," sighed North. "Oh, I surrender. He's too good for me. Master debater, old Southy. But look here, while we're about it, let's see how good a brain you have, Holme. Kind of test."

"Test?"

"Yes. You sometimes take walks of an evening on the common, don't you? Regular little sorties, so to speak. Nocturnal sallies into the dark. Isn't that right? Eh?"

Mr. Holme fidgeted. "Yes. Yes, I go for walks—most evenings —when it's fine, preferably."

"When it's fine. Note that, Southy. Holme, did you take any walks during those two or three weeks in November when we had all that fog?"

"No. I never went out at all during that time. It would have been no fun."

"Heard that, Southy? Didn't I guess it? He didn't go out at all on those evenings. Yet someone used to wander about on the common. And I don't mean that eccentric old man, Jarrow. We've heard it on good authority about this other chap. Who could he have been, I wonder?"

Mr. Holme glanced swiftly from one to the other of them. Southerby was staring at the fire, a calm, pleasant look on his round, pink face. He seemed to be reflecting sentimentally on matters related to the happy family he had left at home. North, hands clasped lightly together, stared quizzically at Southerby, his air that of a bland spider who had no doubt that the hovering fly would anon become enmeshed in the scintillant web. Just a matter of minutes . . . Tick, plick. Plick, tick . . .

"Southy, who do you think it could have been? Holme doesn't seem to know. Holme has a good brain. Holme was a policeman like us. He *must* have a good brain. Not the kind of brain you would want to eradicate."

Mr. Holme sat very still, watching them.

"We can't look upon Holme as vermin, so we must seek elsewhere. Either elsewhere—or right here." He flashed round upon Mr. Holme. "Didn't you meet a man near Swithin Lake, Mr. Holme—on the night before the series of murders occurred in this village?"

"That's right. And what of it?"

"He was supposed to have given you a letter to post, but when you looked at it by the street light you found that it was addressed to the bearer. That right?"

"That's right," said their host.

North leaned forward, hands still lightly clasped together. "Tell me, Holme, was that the first and last time you saw that man?"

Mr. Holme looked at him and smiled. And in the silence that came upon them they heard the snow. Tick, plick, it went. Light and casual against the chilly panes. Plick, tick . . .

2

Softly and with a soothing insistence, rather than sinisterly, it fell. A quilt, up above, shedding its delicate insides, thought Grace, squinting through the blurred glass. Yes, she couldn't think of it as sinister. Tick, plick. Little pixie limbs in disintegration, peacefully settling on everything out there. A quilt split in the sides and shedding pixie feet and pixie fingers that turned to bits and pieces as they drifted down. Or insects. Yes, let her think of them as insects instead. Pip-like insects, the flakes, without purpose, with no evil intent. Just flicking the eaves and the sills and the roof as they aimlessly trailed through the dark. She could see the coal-house door. That looked purposeful, evil, in the reflected light from the window. The kitchen window. Something terrible, she felt certain, lurked in the coal-house. A frigid thing of death. A frigid, rigid thing with grey limbs, still and chilly. More chilly than the polka dots, the mystic insects, tick-plicking on the window sill, each a speck out of the Infinite, whispering infinitely. It was a solid thing in the coal-house. Still but solid, possessing tactility. To touch it would make her blood tingle. She would gasp, whimper.

She shivered. She hugged herself.

"Grace!" called her father from the living-room. And she answered: "Yes, Dad! I'm coming." And as she entered the living-room: "It's snowing, Dad." He nodded and smiled at the fire. "It's snowing. Yes, my child. I suspected it was. Get the stone. We're going to hold a séance."

"Yes, Dad. I'll get it now."

And a few minutes later as they sat opposite each other at the table: "I can hear the snow, child. Christmas is coming. Peace and goodwill to my dear dead wife, Agnes, please make me a cup of tea. It's snowing."

The door opened and Mrs. Jarrow made her entrance, shawl about her shoulder, a smile on her face. For the past two or three weeks, every other night her husband had held a séance. These days there was a softness in his manner. He seemed to have achieved a new peace. He never went out of the house, and he was affectionate during séances. His wife was happy. She wandered about the house in a dream of purring rapture. Within her breast she seemed to carry a feline ball of trembling fur. Her eyes were almost continuously moist. With happiness. Grace, too, was happy, but not as happy as her mother. For there was the coal-house . . .

The old gentleman stared at the stone on the table. The fire clicked and crackled in the grate. In the silence—the cessation of voices—they heard, too, the snow. Always tick-plicking outside. Softly. Unobtrusively. Meaning no harm. Too trivial to hurt. Too virgin-white with purity to be baleful. It was only snow. Cold but casual. Tick, plick. Plick, tick . . . Sometimes you had to listen hard to hear it.

"Oh, Agnes beloved, where dwellest thou, simple soul? Come if thou canst hear me. Come in love and snow. In snow and love. Grace!"

"Yes, Dad?"

"The stone moved."

"Yes, it seemed to move."

"Seemed?"

"I mean, it moved. Yes, it moved."

"You saw it move?"

"I saw it move."

Silence. Only the snow. Plick, tick . . .

Not even a dog barking. The woods not breathing.

Reverently Grace stretched out. She tapped her father's clasped hands. His hands rested on the edge of the table. "Dad," she whispered. "Mother is here. She has come. She's emerged from the snow."

The old gentleman made no response. On his face was a look of peace. The peace of fulfilment. The peace of deeds achieved. A dream distilled. A dream once vapour, now visible spirit. Spirit to soothe. Volatile and inebriating but always peace-giving. There was no torture in his eyes. Only soft quietude. A breathing ease dwelt in his whole poise.

"I said she's with us, Dad."

"So you said. But where?"

"She stands behind your chair."

"With a cushion to comfort me?"

"Yes. And a hand to pat you."

"Kindness. Oh, kindness. She's so forgiving, Agnes. Where are you, Agnes my love? In the ditch awaiting me with Burke and *The Golden Treasury?* Impatient for my kisses behind the rosemary copse?"

"I'm here, Herbert," said Mrs. Jarrow, stroking his head.

The old gentleman smiled. Adjusted his ash stick beside him.

"I'm always with you, Herbert."

"It's snowing, Agnes. It's early December."

"Yes, it's quite seasonal, isn't it, Herbert?"

"It wasn't snowing three weeks ago, Agnes."

"No. No, it was nasty and foggy then, dear."

"And the night was desperate. Desperate men moved in the fog, my love. But now they're gone. Gone for ever. Now the gentle snow is here."

Silence. His wife stroked his head.

"The Executioner and his friend. They're no more, Agnes."

"Herbert dear, couldn't you give Grace the key for the coal-house? She's so worried, poor child. Just to put her mind at ease."

"I must keep the key, Agnes. No one must go into the coal-house, my dear. Only this poor soul, your Herbert. He's at peace. At great peace."

"I'm glad, Herbert. But sometimes I feel puzzled."

"About me or about the coal-house, Agnes?"

"About everything, dear. It all seems so bewildering. Now the papers tell us about Major Rudstow—his disappearance a few weeks ago. They haven't found him yet. Where could he be, Herbert? Was he killed? Murdered by the Executioner? It's so disturbing, my dear."

"So disturbing. He vanished that Tuesday night, didn't he? Nearly three weeks ago. Since then we've had no more trouble from the Lord High Executioner. Middenshot is safe these days. The old ladies and old gentlemen and the children sleep in peace, don't they, my dear?"

"I thought they might have found the corpse in Swithin Lake when they dragged it, but the papers say nothing has been found, and it's several days now since they've been dragging the lake. Do you think the Major's body was hidden by the murderer in the woods, Herbert?"

"Yes, in the woods, Agnes. Or in somebody's coal-house, perchance. Major Alfred Rudstow, cold and stiff in the coal-house—not ours, of course. Oh, not ours, my dear. At least, I should hope not. He was once in Broadmoor, did you know, Agnes? He was sent there for raping and strangling a ten-year-old girl—and before that he committed other offences. Yet they released him as cured, Agnes. A person fit and proper to take his place in the community. Listen to the flakes against the window panes. What did the forecast say at five to six?"

"Heavy falls are predicted, Herbert. In all districts."

"So comforting to watch snow falling. It's so covering. Piling up and piling up—and covering all. All it settles upon. Grass and dead leaves and twigs and corpses. Odd corpses lying in the open, that is."

"Oh, Herbert, I'm so happy to hear you speak to me. You seem softer this past week or two. I wish you could always be like this."

"Who can say, my dear? I may remain like this. I've done what I've wanted to do—wanted to do since I was a young man. I'm at peace. Peace."

"I wish I knew what was troubling you all along, Herbert. I might have been able to help you, my dear. But you never would tell me."

"It's not everything you could be told, Agnes. This is something you would never have understood. You're too sentimental, my dear. You are not one who can identify yourself with a situation of horror. There are many like you. People who can only read of horrible happenings in a newspaper and exclaim: 'How horrible!' But such people can't imagine themselves into what they read. Our sentimental theorists and progressive psychologists are like that. They can theorize and tell you what should and should not be done if we want to better conditions for the mass of people, but they themselves live sheltered, easy lives. They tell us no corporal punishment for criminals, no capital punishment for murderers, no canings for badly behaved schoolboys. We must be soft and sweet and understanding toward our mentally twisted. But you'll discover, my dear, if you put it to the test, that these people lack imaginations. They can *read* of rapes and murders in the papers, but they can't actively *live* the part of the injured or bereaved. They shudder delicately and then shut their minds against the horror of the deed, and then proceed to talk in high-flown language of the state of society and of what reforms should be instituted—all gentle, loving, compassionate, humane reforms. These people can't sit down after reading of the rape of a seven-year-old girl and *feel* themselves the child's parent who hears a knock on the door and goes to the door to see a policeman. 'I'm sorry, ma'am, I have some bad news for you. Your little girl was found—dead, ma'am.' . . . Raped and strangled. It's only when you have imagination, Agnes, that you can *know* how it feels to have a child of yours raped and strangled. People who call themselves humane and compassionate crusaders in the cause of better social living standards don't always *know* how a mother or father feels when the policeman brings the news about the raped and strangled daughter. That's why they can coddle criminals and mental cases, that's why they can make prison conditions better and better—and more attractive. Nowadays which criminal can complain about the way he's treated in prison? It's like a pleasant holiday for him. Why should he be afraid of going to prison? He's well fed on a scientifically balanced diet, he enjoys perhaps more comfortable accommodation than he did when he was out of prison, the state gives his wife and family a generous weekly allowance for the time he's in prison, so why should he worry? When he's out he has every right to cosh somebody again or burgle a house, for isn't prison always there waiting for him— prison with its regular meals and its comforts and recreations— not to mention occasional concerts and entertainments! In fact, it's most encouraging to a poor criminal. On with the coshings! On with the smash-and-grabs! On with the purse-snatchings! On with the burglings!

"See what I mean, Agnes love? You're one of these people, my dear. The people who coddle the vermin of our species. People weak, sentimental, over-mellow with false compassion. That's why I couldn't have told you anything—and that's why I can't tell you anything, my love."

Grace kept glancing toward the windows, disturbed. She was not accustomed to hearing her father make such long speeches, and in such a calm, reasoned manner. This was something new; he was changing. Change always upset her. She distrusted change of any kind—even a change for the good. Oh, and listen to the soft tick of the snow. So insistent, so persistent, so aloof, chilly. Almost as aloof and chilly as the words her father had uttered. She stirred in her chair.

Her mother, meanwhile, had stroked her father's head and murmured: "I know what you mean, Herbert dear, but—but surely you don't expect us all to be perfect."

Her father replied, with a smile, so calm, so aloof: "Admitted, dear Agnes. I'm not telling you I expect perfection—or even uniformity of outlook. There must be cranks and oddities or life would be intolerably drab. What would the world do without its variety of cranks and faddists—even its pimps and prostitutes! I have no quarrel with any of these, my dear. Odd people—and pimps and prostitutes—give humanity its spice. Think, for instance, what a terribly insipid life your daughter Grace and you, in your ghostly attendance, would lead but for my upsetting presence in here. But pause. There's this about me. I'm odd—a regular nuisance at times—but I don't threaten your safety. I don't show violence toward your persons. Do I go around the neighbourhood cutting old gentlemen's throats or bashing old ladies on the head? Do I go around breaking into people's cottages or snatching purses—or raping seven-year-old girls? When I begin to show signs of doing such things, then it will be time to get rid of me, for then I will have qualified as a specimen of human vermin."

"But, Herbert dear, why should you think of such horrible things? Why not think instead of pleasant things? Why harp on what's dreadful?"

"You are not singular, Agnes. Most people, in fact, think as you do. Avoid the dreadful. Think only of what's pleasant. But the dreadful is always there, that's the trouble. Always simmering behind our backs, or beyond our blinkers. Always waiting to surge into view. When we think of it we're on guard against it, and we can check it, defeat it. Remember the last war? We could have checked that, stopped it from happening. But we preferred to wear blinkers, or turn our backs on the menacing horrors. The weak way. The way of the overripe, the too-sentimental. Hitler flouted the Versailles Peace Treaty and began to rearm, but what did the League of Nations do? Did it march straightway into Germany, seize Hitler and have him shot? Did it immediately take action and smash the Nazi Party? No, it let Hitler go on rearming. And even when he sent troops into the Rhineland zone, again against the Versailles treaty, did any of the other nations move against him? No, they let him stay, let him get stronger and stronger while we remained weak, while we shut our eyes to the threatening horrors, while we talked sweet and gooey things about our righteousness and our humaneness and our free and peace-loving ways, our wonderful democratic virtues. While we talked and wallowed in our cosy luxuries and sang hymns to our Loving God and coaxed ourselves into the belief that we were all such good and well-behaved little boys and girls, Hitler and Mussolini were arming and acting; they didn't mind being bad boys, you see. So there was war. That was what we got for being virtuous. No, Agnes. It's strength or weakness that counts in this life of ours. If you act with strength you win out—and you achieve worthwhile states of being. If you act with weakness you lose—and you suffer chaos and defeat. If we recognize that certain humans are instigators of violence and agents of violence, wipe them out—quietly, without malice. If you discern that certain humans have minds that can only conceive and carry out schemes of violence and you try to compromise with these individuals, or weakly imagine you can change them in their ways, *you* are going to be the sufferer, and you're going to bring suffering to others. You're going to—"

Grace uttered a shriek, rising. "The window! Look! Mother, look!"

Mrs. Jarrow looked. Looked and gasped.

"What is it, Grace?" asked Mr. Jarrow.

"A face. A face at the window."

"Two faces," murmured Mrs. Jarrow.

"Aha," said the old gentleman. "Two faces."

Plick, tick, went the snow against the window panes. Softly. Unremittingly. Without sentiment.

"Who could it have been, I wonder," said Grace. The séance was forgotten. Tick, plick, went the flakes outside.

"Two faces from the Other World," murmured the old gentleman. "We think we're safe in here, but Horror watches us from outside."

"I wonder—perhaps . . ."

"What do you want to say, Grace?" asked Mr. Jarrow.

"I wonder—do you think it could have been the Executioner?"

"And Major Alfred Rudstow? Possible, my child. Quite possible—providing ye believe in the resurrection of the dead."

"Oh, but this is horrible! Horrible!"

"Horror," said Mr. Jarrow, "is all about us. Indoors and outdoors."

Grace was trembling.

Mrs. Jarrow drew her shawl tight about her shoulders. The snow.

"Only the strong are safe against horror," said Mr. Jarrow. "Only the alert and disciplined need not fear horror."

Plick, tick . . . Click.

"The gate. Someone has just come in."

"Or gone out," murmured her father.

Plick, tick . . .

"Who could it have been?"

Tick, plick . . .

3

"Did you see us? We saw you."

"Saw me?"

"With our little eyes we saw you."

"Your little eyes?"

"Standing outside your window in the cold, white snow."

All night it had snowed.

"But I don't—"

"And we heard you shriek."

"You heard me shriek?"

"With our little ears we heard you."

"Your little ears?"

All night the little flakes, in dense flurries, had fallen.

"You were sitting at a table."

"You mean last night?"

All last night the little flakes, like the flotsam of fissioned fairies, had flung themselves against walls and roofs and hedges. Piling in ditches.

"I mean last night. Yes, last night, I mean."

"But I—I—I'm afraid I don't follow. Who are you?"

"We're strangers here," smiled North. "Only arrived a few days ago. I'm North—Albert. He's Southerby—John. Our card!" Grace took the card and read what was printed on it. She said: "Oh." And North said: "Ah. See what I mean! Busy as bees—Southerby and me. Here, there, everywhere. East, west, north and Southerby—Southerby and me—always on the spot. Pelting here, halting there. Peeping in at windows, winking at the women—that's Southy. Great lad with the ladies. May we step in, Miss Jarrow?"

"Oh. Yes. Yes, please step in. Can I—could I—?"

"You could—if you would. Just a few questions from us—a few answers from you. Won't keep you long, Southy and me. Too busy. Busy as bees."

The door of the living-room opened and Mr. Jarrow looked out into the hall-way. "Who's that, Grace child?" he asked. "Is it Mr. Attlee—or just a committee from the Ministry of Fuel and Power? Do they want to look in the coal-house to see if we're economizing on coal and corpses?"

"Good morning, Mr. Jarrow. North addressing you. And this is Southerby. May we trouble you for a spot of information?"

"Information? What are you? Police inspectors in full disguise? Or police sergeants posing as MI-5? I'm a peaceful, peaceable man. And it's a cold morning. Snow piled up three or four inches on the ground. I won't be pestered by corpse-hunting policemen in disguise."

North tittered. "We agree, we agree. Can't stand policemen ourselves, Southy and me. Last night we were over there to see your neighbour, Holme. *Ex*-policeman like ourselves. Nice fellow, Holme. We learnt a lot of useful things from him—and about him. Ha! A dark horse, that, your neighbour. He's going to give the village a shock before long. Take my word for it!"

"He's after my virgin daughter, did you know?"

"Dad, how dare you say such a thing! And—and before strangers! Oh!"

"Always smelling round my virgin cow, Mr. North."

"Sssh! Hush-hush. Not so loud. Southy might hear you and go after her, too. Fatal with the ladies, Southy old knob!"

"Come along, anyhow. Into the living-room, since it's information you want. I'm always ready to give information to private detectives."

"How did you know we were private detectives?"

"You couldn't be anything but private detectives since you're not policemen—or from the Ministry of Fuel and Power."

North uttered a shrill crowing of delight. "Oh, good deduction! Correct! Ask Miss Jarrow to show you our card. Private detectives, Southy and me. Holmes and Watson. Sexton Blake and Tinker. In the same tradition. Nothing ever misses our eagle eyes, Mr. Jarrow. Not even elephant tracks in the snow. Not even egg-sized warts on a bulbous nose. Everything, everything we note. From cottages to cabbages."

"That's it. That's the talk I like to hear. Lunatics are all about us—not only out of doors. Come in. Make yourselves comfortable by the fire. I have hundreds of clues for you. From elephant tracks to frozen majors. It's a hobby of mine, collecting clues for private detectives."

North and Southerby seated themselves, Southerby on the sofa, North on an upright chair near Mr. Jarrow's easy chair. The old gentleman had sunk into his easy chair before either of his guests could even contemplate taking it. Grace, very perturbed, went off to the kitchen where her mother was busy preparing lunch.

Outside the sky was an unbroken greyish white, heavy with more snow soon to fall. All night, like diced fragments of the woods' phantom denizens, the flakes had floated down from the drab wintry sky to the drab wintry earth. This morning roofs and roads, fells and fields, and the evergreen dark-green pines bore their thick quota of snow. The whole world seemed muffled in a shawl of icy air, and now and then, with a sound like the feather-bed cough of a smothered bride, a clump of snow would fall from roof to ground, or from overladen tree-limb to burdened hedge.

All night the flakes, in cotton-wool calm, without fury but without fatigue, had flecked the grey countryside until now there was no grey to be seen. Only white everywhere. White of unprinted-on paper. Of arsenic on chocolates. White of snow-white birds specked on next spring's meadowed distance. White of eyes turned up in death.

"You said something about corpses," smiled North briskly, sitting forward. "Southy and me—we're interested in corpses. Happen to know of any odd ones lying about in the neighbour-hood? We want help from anyone who can give it. Not so, Southy old turnip?"

Southerby nodded. "Take euthanasia," he wheezed. "You would have thought that, in an age as advanced as ours is supposed to be, euthanasia would have been taken for granted—that every man and woman would have had the liberty of dying a painless death if such were his or her will; that medical men would have been given the privilege of putting an end to the sufferings of a man or woman hopelessly ill and in agony. But no. So bogged down are we in our silt of sentiment and superstition that we prefer to see some unfortunate languish in bed for weeks, for months, enduring excruciating pain, rather than lift a finger to put an end to the poor wretch's suffering. To do that would be considered murder. See to what lengths of absurdity we have taken our compassion and sentimentality and religious superstition! See where our alleged humanity leads us? Here we have a woman dying of cancer—no hope of recovery; wishing for death, pleading for death—but why should we heed her wishes, her pleadings? Oh, no. Only Almighty God can take a life. Human life is precious. So we let her moan in agony day after tortured day, week after week, month after nightmare month, harrowed—and harrowing those around her. And this is called being humane; this is called being ethical—and godly. This is how a *civilized* community treats its *human* creatures in pain."

Southerby smiled. "But a *horse*. If a horse breaks its leg in a race the lucky creature is immediately shot in order to put it out of its pain."

North shrugged. "See for yourself! That's Southy." He winked at the old gentleman. "Never means any harm. Family man. Wife and four children. And a spaniel. But there you are! Oh, by the way, Mr. Jarrow, you've heard of a Major Alfred Rudstow?"

"Salvation Army major?"

"British Army, retired. Gentleman of sixty-two. Served in First Great War. Convicted in 1921 of larceny. Put on bond. Convicted in 1922 of robbery with violence—sentenced to three years penal servitude. Convicted in 1927 of rape and murder of a ten-year-old girl—guilty but insane; detained in Broadmoor Criminal Lunatic Asylum; released in 1948 as a person fit and proper to take his place in the community. Until his disappearance nineteen days ago, a farmer at Ashbole, small hamlet to north of Middenshot."

"Well, now you've enlarged on it like that, I can tell you this— but strictly in confidence, mind: I have heard of the gentleman. He left his home at seven o'clock one evening to post a letter and has not been heard of since. So his wife told the police. But mind you! It's in strict confidence. I only read it in my newspapers."

"Excellent, excellent! I'm delighted to hear you read your newspapers."

"Wrong. My daughter reads them. She reads me the news I

like best—like murders, rapes, coshings, suicides, accidents, disappearances. I'm a horror-monger of an old man—now at peace, however. Oh, so much at peace these days. Unimaginable peace." The old gentleman smiled and sighed and tapped his stick on the floor as though out of sheer happiness, unutterable contentment.

North glanced at Southerby. Southerby glanced at North.

"Cigarette?" smiled Southerby, holding out his open case. "Mine are mentholated. Good for my throat."

North and Mr. Jarrow refused, and Southerby lit one himself. "Look at it this way," he said huskily. "The tissues of our civilization have undergone a process of degeneration; they have grown soft, flabby, unhealthy. And as not uncommon in such conditions, a tumour has developed—a tumour which we can now diagnose beyond any doubt as malignant. A malignant tumour that keeps spreading its roots of rottenness to every part of the organism. The intelligent physician recognizes immediately that there is only one remedy: a major operation. The stupid, or dishonest, physician recommends bromides, unguents—perchance even prayers and tears; there are many quacks among physicians: many charlatans greedy for profit and power."

Southerby smiled. "But the intelligent, the honest, physician—he is often deemed a brute, a despicable fellow—knows that only the knife will suffice. Cut it out. Cut the tumour out—and without delay."

North squealed mirthfully. He glanced at Mr. Jarrow. "Watch how I'm going to trip him up. Just watch me! I say, Southy old slug, have you ever heard of a malignant tumour that could be cut out neat and whole? Aren't you forgetting that little matter of metastatic deposits? Or in plain language so that a layman like Jarrow can understand—what about the roots that may be left behind in new sites? Mightn't these, at some later date, cause a recurrence of the trouble?"

"So they might, North. A malignant tumour is always a messy business. Roots are bound to be left behind, and the trouble, as you say, will recur. But isn't that inevitable? Isn't that to be expected? But there is a remedy for this condition."

"See! That's Southy. A remedy for every illness. Yes, Southy old tin, let's hear the remedy."

"Alertness, North. There's your remedy. Now, let's change the analogy. Let's view the thing in another way. We have just taken over a slum house. It is in a horrible condition, so we proceed to clean it through and through, from top to bottom. And now, at last, it is quite free of vermin; it is clean and painted and redecorated. We are ready to occupy it. But—ah! Now, pay heed. Is our task of cleaning done? Do we expect to live in our house and never again trouble about vermin? Never lift a broom to sweep or never use a drop of Jeyes fluid? Never use our Flit gun in dark corners or dust our mattresses with Keating's? No, North. As any good house-wife knows, the task of keeping a house free of vermin is never ended. Alertness. There must always be alertness. A checking over after the major job of cleaning—the initial agony, turmoil, of putting our house right. The lice and bedbugs and the fleas and cockroaches have been eliminated, but the invisible nits and maggots lurk forever in crevices awaiting favourable conditions to hatch and pullulate. Therefore we must keep a sharp eye out, and from time to time pounce here, spray there, dust here, inspect, ferret out. Alertness. Always alertness.

"The requisites, North, of a successful human civilization are four: Strength, discipline, alertness—and the fourth? Elasticity. Provided your world community is strong, healthy, down to earth; provided its habits are well-schooled and regulated to avoid unwholesome excesses; provided it is efficiently—*not hatefully*—vigilant for inimical, destructive forces; provided—here comes the elasticity—it doesn't shackle itself to rigid formulae of thought and behaviour but can accept, absorb and reject, discard with equal ease; provided these things, such a world community—such a civilization—would be as near perfection as we unstable, unpredictable human creatures could ever hope to have it. Such a civilization could be achieved, but only by means of a drastic operation.

"When I say that," smiled Southerby unconcernedly, quite unemotionally, eyes gleaming merrily, "I'm bearing in mind, of course, that a drastic operation at this stage of mankind's scientific development could produce one of two results: complete and satisfying success—or utter failure involving a virtual dark age. Such an experiment, I should add, would be a success if carried out in a spirit of true benevolence and sincere compassion for the lot of humankind; it would be a failure if carried out in a spirit of hatred or because of a selfish lust for power on the part of one individual or a small group of individuals."

Mr. Jarrow had begun to laugh. He continued to laugh. Tapped his stick on the floor and laughed. And from outside came the muffled coughing crash of a lump of snow as it fell from roof to ground. The old gentleman kept on laughing until North, also laughing—shaking in his seat with stuttered sniggerings—leant forward and said: "I say, old fellow, I hear—hoo, hoo, hoof!—I hear you used to go wandering about on the common at night in the fog. Is that—hoo, hoo!—true or untrue?"

"Eh? Oh, that's true. Ho, ho! Too true!"

North, suddenly tense and unlaughing, asked: "Ever come upon anyone interesting? Anyone who might have needed a drastic operation?"

"Eh? Oh, yes, yes," said the old gentleman, also tense. "Every night I used to meet such characters. Including the Major himself."

"The Major? Old Rudstow, retired British Army?"

"Aged sixty-two. Served in First Great War."

"Yes?"

"Yes. Met him one night when I was in a particularly alert and vigilant mood. Bashed the old vermin hard on the bokum. Anaesthetized him on the spot. Then I operated on him drastically but in a spirit of true benevolence and sincere compassion."

"You did? Then . . . ?"

"Then I lugged him home here, and shackled him away safely and rigidly under my bed upstairs. Oh, yes. No elasticity there. No elasticity, I can assure you."

"None at all? All cold, rigid?"

"All cold, rigid, frigid. I say, did you notice my old black overcoat hanging on a peg in the hall?"

"Might have done. Must have done." Tensely still. In a bated voice. "Southy and me—we note everything, everything. What about your old black overcoat? Tell me. Tell me quick!"

"Nothing, nothing. Just a mad, vain remark. Guilty but insane. Ssh! I washed it thoroughly a week or two ago—that's my old black overcoat. Soaked it overnight in a bucket of paraffin—then next day gave it a going over with soap flakes and water. Swish-swash. Then another soaking in paraffin. Then another going over with soap-flakes and water. Took me fully four days to do it. Cleaned off all the vermin—and the nits and maggots. Not even the Government pathologist's microscope could find any clues on it now. Tut, tut! I've been too alert. Sssh!"

"Sssh! Hear that, Southy old trout! Clever fellow, Jarrow. He washed out all the clues. Tut, tut! Clues to what, I wonder? What do you think, Southy?"

Southerby flicked some ash toward the fire. It fell on the rug. "Take," he said throatily, "the question of environment. Our psychologists want to make out that bad housing conditions, poor medical attention, lack of recreational centres and similar factors contribute to the production of criminals; some of them even go the whole hog and say that such factors not merely contribute to the production of criminals but are entirely responsible for the fact that there exists a type of person who can't be decent and 'normal' in his behaviour. And virtually all psychologists tell us that should we wipe out the factors already mentioned all would be well with people; there would be no more criminals, prostitutes and wrongdoers, and we should then live, presumably, as a sweet and happy family with no need for policemen or door-locks. Or V.D. prophylactics.

"Now, if this is so—if it is these poor conditions of living that go to make criminals—why is it that *all* the people who live under such conditions don't steal and rape and murder? Why do some—only a small percentage, at that, too—succumb, and others—a very large percentage of others—succeed in overcoming the stress of their environment and find it possible to live decent, honest, peaceable lives? And why is it that many brutes and sadists—and criminals of every type, too—spring not from the slums but from the well-off and pampered classes of society? Seddon, Crippen, Heath, Haigh—did they come from the slums? No. Then why didn't their superior environment prevent them from indulging in the horrors they indulged in? Take again the Negroes of southern America—haven't they been for decades, centuries, oppressed, humiliated, frustrated? Haven't they been living under unspeakably depressing conditions ever since they were 'emancipated'? Why haven't they all, en masse, degenerated into thieves and murderers and sex criminals and prostitutes? Doesn't it begin to look as though our psychologists have been making too much of this environment business? Doesn't it begin to seem as though heredity is what decides whether a man turns out to be a criminal or a mad killer or a raper of young girls? In other words, doesn't it seem apparent that vermin is born vermin and can't help being vermin?"

"Methought I heard a voice cry," hissed the old gentleman, leaning forward.

"Sssh! Don't speak," hissed North, leaning forward. "Sleep no more! Macbeth does murder sleep!"

"The innocent sleep?" asked his host—in a whisper.

"The guilty sleep," answered North.

"When shall we three meet again? In thunder, lightning or in snow? Or will it be in the shadow of my old black overcoat?"

"Is this a dagger I see? Or a gun?"

"A cosh it is. Oh, my old black overcoat! Was there a rent in its ravelled sleeve of care?"

"Was there?" asked North, leaning further forward.

"Oh, dream! Oh, reality! Are we dreaming, or are we really here?"

"Was there?" persisted North.

"Oh, sanity! Oh, insanity! Where does sanity begin? Where does insanity end? Are we three mad or sane? Who is to judge?"

"Was there?"

"There was. But I mended it. Oh, I mended it carefully after cleaning the overcoat. Oh, that overcoat! I didn't even hide it in the coalhouse as I did the Major's corpse. Or was it under my bed I put the Major when I lugged him here? Peace dulls my memory. I'm so peaceful, my Paula. Like the snow piled up outside. Cold, detached and at peace. Were you saying something, Mr. North?"

"Whispering something—but never mind! All is peace. The peace of snow. Sssh! We must be going, Southy and me. Stealthily we came, stealthily we go. Lots to do. Always busy as bees. Come, Southy old drip. Away we go. Two happy lunatics leaving a third. Thanks, Mr. Jarrow. Thanks a co-trillion. You've been very helpful. You've supplied us with information of great value. So great value that soon we may be calling upon you again. Soon. Oh, soon out of the passive snow we two shall once more emerge. Soon. Soon. How soon!"

4

All night it had snowed, but less heavily than the night before. Toward dawn it had turned to sleet, and now at nine o'clock there was weak sunshine. Everywhere, in large and frequent clumps, from weighted branches, off eaves, the snow slithered and dropped. Outside the newsagent's, in the High Street, the Stephens' Ink thermometer registered 37, and was rising slowly. The wind had veered to south-west.

"It's thawing," said Mr. Holme. And Hyacinth said: "Yes, it's thawing. And look at my shoes. Nothing but slush, slush everywhere you walk. Slippery as anything."

"You should wear wellingtons like me. At least, they'll keep your feet dry."

"When I'm your missus you'll get me a pair, won't you?"

"Sounds very much as if you're proposing to me." He tried to sound bantering, but flushed. He put on his mackintosh—his mackintosh served as winter coat, too—and from a chair took up his canvas shopping-bag.

She did not respond as he had expected. Instead of giggling, she turned away, looking glum and discomfited, and he paused as he was about to move toward the door.

She was drawing a bucket of water at the sink. The water kept gushing furiously out of the tap. And suddenly mixed with the gushing was a dull thud and powdery hiss as a clump of snow fell from the roof just outside the window. They both glanced toward the window. He took a pace sideways and standing immediately behind her, held her arm and squeezed it. The bucket was overflowing into the sink, and she reached out quickly and turned off the tap. A stillness pervaded her body. The sleeves of her bodice were rolled up above the elbows.

"What about Dick?"

"What about him?"

"When are you going to marry him?"

"How many times are you going to ask me the same thing?" She spoke without turning her head, and kept looking at the water in the bucket, icy-cold and gently waved, reflecting in shifty flashes the light that filtered in through the pale purple window panes. "Haven't I told you I don't want to marry him? And I mean I don't." She uttered an impatient sound and began to lift the bucket out of the sink. He put out his hand and took it from her, lowered it to the floor. She exclaimed, asking him what he was doing, and found that he was holding her against him, easily, not at all awkwardly, as though he might have been doing it for the films. He looked into her eyes, his own amused but soft, and she had to lower hers shyly. She began to pull away from him, but he held her—gently but very strongly—purposeful and male, so that a surprised ache moved alive in her. A small crab's claw it was at first behind her ribs, then a multitude of urgent straws that prickled delightfully within the soft worlds of her breasts, turning her breathless and uneasy with fears yet holding her entranced. She knew she was going to squeal, and waited for the squeal to come. She smelt the tobacco in his moustache as he bent and kissed her, and the squeal hovered, an arrested ghost behind her lips. Or had it been drawn up like grey lightning into his breath? She heard herself moaning in the depth of the blue whorl that danced in the gloom of her shut eyes. It was as though she were enveloped in a swooning vacancy and could not be certain what was happening. In her fancies, in her day-dreaming, she had been self-possessed and clear-headed when he held her and kissed her. But now . . . She managed, at length, to pull away enough to say: "I don't—why did you do that?", the words coming out of her in a mumbled stammer.

He was still holding her arm, though he had pushed her away gently from him. He frowned past her and said: "I'm going out now." But he still held her arm, making no move to go. They listened to the water dripping slowly from the cold tap; she had not turned it off properly. Clink, it went. Clink. He kept looking down into the sink, frowning. "See you when I come back," he said, quietly, tenderness in his voice. But he stood where he was, making no move. They could hear a muffled, mysterious trickle of water outside. Clink, went the cold tap. Thud, went a snow-clump somewhere not too far off.

"Must run out to do my shopping," he said. He released her arm and went out. He had to walk with great care, for the ground was slippery with the flesh of melting snow that covered it. Flesh must not be hurt, he thought, and wondered at his aberration. Then he remembered. Trouble stirred in him. I ought to fall and hurt myself, he thought. Flesh ... He could feel the cold through his mackintosh. At any other time he would not have felt it. Because I've done what I oughtn't to have done, he thought. This is guilt. I'm ashamed. Shame and guilt make a man feel in danger of falling as he walks. Shame and guilt make a man feel cold when he shouldn't. Yet, he thought, have I done something wrong? I wanted to hold her and kiss her, and she wanted it. I had to do it. I couldn't stop myself. A cloud closed over me. All my youth and heat swarmed back upon me. I don't even remember it happening like this with Millicent in our first days. I was never a hot-blooded fellow. Now in my old age I'm getting hot. I don't understand it. I don't ...

He opened the gate, stepped out into the lane—and Grace Jarrow nearly walked into him. So unexpected was the encounter that he uttered a grunting exclamation, and Grace gasped, stumbled and slipped. He reached out, caught her arm and held tight or she would have sat down abruptly in the slippery lane. He himself slipped, and for an instant it was a struggle to keep his own balance, but they both succeeded. She was very pink in the face, and apologized stammeringly. "I—I wasn't expecting you to—to come out—oh, it's really too stupid of me."

"Not at all, Miss Jarrow. As much my fault as yours. I should have given a look around before charging out into the lane. And the slush—it's a wonder anyone can walk out of doors at all this morning." It suddenly occurred to him that he was still holding her by the elbow. He released her—but not with a gasp of confusion. He did not flush. And he knew that the incident in the kitchen had given him a new confidence in himself as a man; in the background of his awareness he felt flattered and elated at his courage in kissing Hyacinth; he had the feeling that he had just acquired a *savoir faire* with women. A warmth of superstition glowed within him. This incident must have been fated, he thought. It was predestined that he should step out of his gateway at the precise instant that Miss Jarrow went past. It was a test for him. Siegfried . . .

"Going into the village, Miss Jarrow? Your usual shopping?"

"Yes—as usual. And—and I have to take two jerseys to Mrs. Randolph—that's why I came out a little earlier than I generally do."

"I'm on my way to the High Street, too. Shall we go along?"

She glanced down at his canvas bag as they moved on. "No paraffin to-day? Where are the tins?"

He laughed. "No. I got about four days' supply yesterday. Made two trips."

"Oh!" She slipped and he gripped her elbow.

"This is terrible."

"No use," he said. "We've got to be prepared to slip and slide our way along. Ah—could I offer you my arm, Miss Jarrow?"

"Your—oh. I—oh, thank you, Mr. Holme. I—yes, of course."

He could feel her hand quiver as it slipped past within the crook of his arm. Her lips, too, he noticed, quivered. To put her at ease he said: "It will help us both to get along better if you take my arm like this. I'll save you from falling when you slip, and you'll save me when I slip." He laughed. Laughed with assurance. There was a bubbling within him. A cool tinkling as of icicles cracking and thawing in a furnace of unbearable feeling. The last fragments of the guilt he had felt on emerging from the kitchen melted out of him.

He had not enjoyed a walk so much since he was a schoolboy. They had to step with elaborate care, trying to avoid spots where the snow was undermined with little rills or pouches of water. Feeling their way, slipping every few seconds, supporting each other, laughing, they went. Once he thought: This couldn't be true. It isn't happening. Another moment: This is true. Real. This is the way people should live always. Just walking and laughing on a cold morning in melting snow. It's real. All else is dream. Bad dream. All else? No. No, let him pause. Kissing Hyacinth in the kitchen had been real, too. Yes, very real. Guilt tried to ooze up out of the snow, but he pushed it away. Guilt was what religious people felt. He was not religious. What could be sinful in kissing one woman in a kitchen and the next minute walking arm in arm with another in the lane! Why couldn't he be fond of two women at the same time! People robbed themselves of so much of the beauty and warmth of living by limiting themselves to a stupid, rigid morality. If they would only remember that the minutes were going. With every tick of the clock one got less young. Less vital. Nearer the arctic circle of disenchantment.

In Great Oak Road it was worse, for cars had ploughed great canyons in the snow, and the narrow pavements were pocked with numerous foot-shaped troughs of half-melted snow that were difficult to avoid. It was slip and squelch, slip and squelch, all the way. Once they bounced into the holly hedge, and a feathery-cold cascade of snow came whispering down around them. She gave a soft shriek, and he saw that there was snow specked in her hair. He told her, and she said: "In yours, too," with a quick glance at him. His self-possession had infected her; she had lost much of her initial shyness. Her cheeks glowed pink and her eyes sparkled.

And then they came out on to the London Road, with the High Street just beyond where the three roads converged. Their arms fell apart—by silently mutual agreement. The fun was over. Here were people moving on the pavements. The shops were open in the High Street. How could they walk arm in arm in the High Street? People would stare. People would think it odd—and irreg-ular. There would be giggles. If only there weren't people with nasty, envious, stilted minds! He felt anger moving in him. One had to be cheated of so much that was beautiful in life because of the dull, cramped, baleful minds of other people. If only he could have had the courage to ignore other people. Tell them to go to the devil. Tell them to shove their shoddy conventions and stultifying morality up their behinds and mind their own petty business.

I have no courage, he told himself. It's not only people. It's me, too. Let me admit it. I'm not the fighting, dashing kind. I'm not a born rebel. That's why I admire Hyacinth for her fire and guts. That's why I sometimes imagine myself Siegfried striding over the common at night. Because I'm not a hero I would like to be a hero. It's always what we are not that we want to be. Why must this be so, I wonder?

He could not wonder any longer, however. He had reached the limit of his probings. He had always had it in him to ferret out the truth, but the depths to which he could go were never great. Early in the excavations he heard the clank of metal against stone. His pick-axe had struck a slab—a granite door—beyond which he could dig no further. He must cease trying and turn away resignedly to plod on in the daylight he knew. What lay beneath the slab—beneath the unknown rock strata—must remain forever a mystery to him. I have my limits, he thought. It would be foolish to try to exceed them. Yet . . .

Yet he could sense within him a whirring discontent, a resentment against some creature or force, a refusal to surrender tamely.

The traffic rushed past with a wet swish and hiss. Two high ridges of mauled and dirty-grey snow bordered the road, one on either side. Where he stood with her, however, there was a gap, like a miniature mountain pass, where pedestrians had trampled a way through. Patiently, side by side, they stood, awaiting their chance to cross over. Two other people had joined them, and waited, too. An elderly man well muffled up and wearing a tweed cap, and a stoutish woman in a shabby black overcoat, shopping-bag in hand, purple veins like rivers in a map on her stolid cheeks, her blue-green eyes as chilly with reserve as the snow. Just a village house-wife. The man looked like a retired hall-porter, aloof yet somehow unctuous and subservient. They all four stood waiting.

"I think we can do it now," Grace suddenly murmured as a lull followed the last car. She moved forward through the gap. The stout woman and the elderly man moved after her.

Instead of following them Mr. Holme turned slightly and plunged into the ridge of snow. He heard her gasp of surprise. Sensed the turned head of the stout woman and the elderly man. But he did not heed them. He ploughed with loud squelches through the heaped-up mass of snow. Staggered, slipped, righted himself, squelched on until he was on the brown, slush-coated roadway. Without stopping he plunged on into the ridge on the other side, again ignoring the gap, and stumbled his way on to the footmarked pavement, itself soft with melting snow flattened down to a messy paste.

He laughed uneasily, but triumphantly, as he fell into step with her once more.

"But why did you—?"

"Just felt like walking through the snow," he interrupted her. "Was determined not to go through that gap."

"Oh. Yes, of course," she said. But he could see the baffled look in her eyes. Could discern the vague rebuke in her manner because he had not trodden with her—and the others—the beaten track.

5

By the following morning the pavements had been shovelled clear, though on the roads, at odd intervals, stood great heaps of snow and mud. On hedges, too, in fields, and on the common, white clumps and elongated drifts persisted like the foam of a stilled and defeated surf. The cold spell had not yet broken—the thermometer never went above 39—and the forecast was that more snow was on the way. "A cold, north-westerly stream of air," declared the B.B.C., "covers the British Isles."

"This," said Mr. Jarrow, at breakfast, "is revelation weather."

"What did you say, Dad?" asked Grace, alert at once. Suspicious.

Her father repeated the remark, adding: "Snow, for a while, covereth all, then it thaweth and revealeth all."

"What do you mean?" she said, but now there was relief in her voice. For an instant she had thought that, in some way, he had come to hear of her beautiful experience yesterday morning and was poking fun at her. Until the last hour of her life she would remember that walk in the snow along the lane and in Great Oak Road; until the final dazed second when the dust of death was settling upon and covering her mind she would regard that walk as a sacred event: an image-memory to be pedestalled and immured within a special temple of her privacy. She would feel desperate—desperate unto suicide—should her father make trivial or smutty allusions to it. She might even attack and kill him.

"Ha," said the old gentleman, "you ask what I mean, eh, my child? Wouldn't you like to know! Well, I'll tell you since you're so curious. I had a dream last night."

"A dream?"

"A vivid dream."

"Oh," murmured Grace, not at all interested.

"Grace."

"Yes, Dad?"

"Aren't you going to ask me what the dream was about? Suppose someone happened to be eavesdropping outside the window there don't you think they'd be disappointed that you didn't press me to tell you about it?"

Grace sighed a routine sigh. "Very well. What was it about?"

"I dreamt I was taking a walk on the common. It was foggy and I was in a very alert and vigilant mood. Wait a moment." The old gentleman rose and took two paces to the window, opened it and looked out, then closed the window again and resumed his chair. "No, no one is eavesdropping. As I was saying, child. It was foggy in my dream, and I was vigilantly following an elderly gentleman, my gloved hands deep in my overcoat pockets. I was taking the old gentleman to a hut in the Berkshire woods—or to put it better, I was accompanying him to this hut. As we were getting near to the hut—we had both been there before so we knew our way—as we were about ten yards from the hut, to be precise, I suddenly withdrew my hands from my overcoat pockets, and— ah, you're interested, I see. And as I withdrew my hands from my overcoat pockets I heard a voice thunder forth at me from the surrounding woods. And it did say unto me: 'Old man, lo and behold! This is the weather of revelation! In the hour that ye think not there cometh revelation and resurrection!' That's what it spake unto me. Then I woke up. Can you interpret dreams, Grace?"

"No. No, I'm afraid I can't."

Her mother smiled, entertained and happy. She wagged her

head tenderly, and seemed only by an effort of great will to restrain herself from stretching out and stroking her husband's head.

"You've lost interest again, child. A pity. I wish I knew of some-one who could interpret dreams."

Grace, ignoring him, lapsed once more into her sentimental reverie. In her fancy she could feel the stiff smoothness of the mackintosh rubbing against her gloved hand and her wrist. She could feel the hard hip as it briefly collided with her soft hip. How many times within the past twenty-two hours had she not repro-duced in her imagination the ecstasy of yesterday's event! Since its occurrence she had been living in a mist—a white, cool, wist-ful mist. A mist, indeed, of thought. Of turgid musings. Alive in the now of now, she yet dwelt in the now of then. One moment safe and protected, another whiningly ravished under an alien tester. "Oh, what do I want? Where shall I lie?" she had cried often and silently in the silent spaces, in the half-lit uncertainty, of her tremulous virginhood. "If only I could be sure what I want! With him alone in his room, in his bed? Oh, I should shriek, shriek! I couldn't stand his delving into my flesh. Oh, never, never! Yet . . . oh, yet I want him. How I want him! Let him take me and do with me as he wishes. I'm his serf. His humble concubine. I could shout it down the lane. His concubine! His concubine! Oooh! Oooh-hoo-hoo-hoo!"

Now—in the now of breakfast—she thought: "I must be con-trolled. I must be calm. Whatever is to happen will happen. If the future holds fire for my loins then fire will come. If it holds safety and soft cosiness then it will be that I shall have. It's like the weather, I suppose. Wind, fog or snow, we can do nothing. We can only wait and take what comes."

"I can understand," said Mr. Jarrow, "the revelation part of it. But it's the resurrection that baffles me. Why resurrection? A resurrection means a rising from the dead. Can a human corpse rise from the dead in 1950? I wish I knew of someone who could interpret dreams."

Grace continued to ignore him, concentrating on her bacon—and her reflections. After a silence, the old gentleman wiped his mouth and grunted. Turning slightly in his chair, he tapped with his stick on the floor, frowned at the boiler and said: "This evening it is meet and right that we should hold a séance."

"A séance?" said Grace, with a start. "Oh. Yes, very well."

Mrs. Jarrow clasped her hands, moisture in her eyes.

"Yes, a séance. I want to ask my wife's spirit to interpret my dream. If heaven is all it's puffed up to be, they ought to have given Agnes some tuition in dream interpretation."

His wife unclasped her hands, then clasped them again, almost visibly writhing, almost audibly purring, with happiness.

"Grace?"

"Yes, Dad?"

"I'm taking a walk after breakfast."

"A walk?"

"Yes, my child. The snow has thawed sufficiently. I now feel I can move about without fear of leaving footprints. I don't like leaving footprints when I walk. The police have a sly habit of measuring footprints. Even taking plaster casts of them."

"The police? But why should you be afraid of the police?"

"Did I say I was? You will misconstrue my meaning. A perverse child. I'm not afraid of them, but I still don't like leaving footprints when I walk. Nor finger-prints. I'll wear my gloves. It's a cold day, so I have good excuse for wearing them. I used to wear them every night when I walked in the fog. And when I did my occasional shopping in the High Street I wore them, too. Oh, yes, that last night, especially, I took great care to wear them. Are you listening to me, Grace? I wore them even in the house here, up in my room when I was preparing my operational paraphernalia. Oh, your old father is not as stupid as he looks."

"What are you going out for this morning, Dad?"

"One or two little jobs to do. Peeping into other people's garbage bins. Picking up an odd carcase here, an odd bone there—perhaps even an old envelope here and an odd scrap of paper there. We have to be economical, child. The country is in a bad way. There's the dollar-gap to be bridged. We must salvage, salvage. Let us salvage all we can, all day and every day."

Within the past minute some of Mrs. Jarrow's happiness had faded. A slight glaze of anxiety now dwelt in the lady's pale grey eyes. She watched her husband with serious concentration rather than concentrated sentiment. She heeded his every word. Grace, too, watched—and heeded.

"I do hope," said Grace, at length, "you won't go and do anything—anything indiscreet. The police are still on the watch in the district. And now there are those two private detectives—Mr. North and Mr. South."

"Wrong. Mr. North and Mr. Easterby. You must learn to be accurate, Grace. Names are important. I have nothing to fear from the two gentlemen. In fact, I want to co-operate with them in every way I can. I like cooperating with private detectives. And these two are no ordinary ones. One glance at them should tell you that. Clever fellows, Mr. North and Mr. Westerby. Only a shade less clever than your poor old father. Ha!" added Mr. Jarrow, tapping with his stick against the table leg.

"How long will you be gone, Dad? Will you be back in time for lunch?"

"Of course, I'll be back for lunch. Do I ever miss my lunch? You're a cruel, carping child to ask me a question like that. After my roamings, besides, my stomach will be screaming for food. Ha! And it may be colder this evening than it was last evening. I'll want a good supper, too. Solid calories. To fortify my old system against the cold—and the near future."

"The near future? What do you mean?"

"I mean the near future. Ho," said her father, tilting his head and regarding the array of cracks in the ceiling plaster. "Exciting events are billed to take place in and about this cottage—in the very near future."

"Exciting events?"

"Or diverting," said her father, nodding solemnly. Mrs. Jarrow's hand clutched tremulously at her bosom.

"Oh," murmured Grace.

"Some," enlarged the old gentleman, "will consider them exciting, some merely diverting—some grisly. Don't you know the old Middenshot proverb, Grace? Every mind maketh its own mirror."

"If you could only stop being so obscure and say what you mean!"

"Don't you like mystery? It's mystery that makes us all merry.

Think what a drab world it would be, child, without our mysteries!"

"I'm sure we can do without this kind of mystery. If you would only give me the key for the coal-house and stop prowling about the neighbourhood we—we could all be so much happier in here."

"But, Grace! It's my Mind! Are you forgetting the Accident!"

"That accident didn't do anything to your mind. You were as sane as ever after it—even Mother knows that. And all your pretence at limping about the place and being affected by humming sounds. Don't you think we aren't tired of your foolish, pointless pranks!"

"Grace dear, please!"

"I don't care, Mother. It's time he got a good talking to."

"Ha," said the old gentleman, wagging his head. "No sympathy for a poor invalid. And mind you, that accident is part of my environmental case history. Don't you believe, Grace, in the influence of Environment?

"How do you know," asked the old gentleman, "that when I was a youngster my father didn't frustrate me horribly by forbidding me to play marbles in the coal-house? Eh? How do you know it isn't that heinous action of my father that subconsciously has urged me now in my sixty-third year to lock you out of the coalhouse? And hasn't it occurred to you that my mother might have thrashed me soundly for straying out of the house and taking late-night walks—me a mere stripling of five! Mightn't it be the irreparable damage she did to my id that night that urges my old ego now to disobey my super-ego and go roaming over the neighbourhood in search of corpses and old envelopes? I can see your education has been shamefully neglected, Grace. Your mother ought to have sent you to America to be educated. That lady, Miss Pettridge, didn't teach you any psychology. It's becoming only too painfully evident."

The old gentleman rose, shaking his head and tapping his stick deprecatingly on the floor. "Time for me to go out," he said. "Time for me to go and do as my environmental past dictates. I won't remain in here a moment longer to be insulted by a child so dismally deficient in her knowledge of psychiatry!"

"Yes," he added, glaring at her. "Psychiatry!"

6

All that morning the old gentleman tramped about the village, peering unobtrusively over gates and fences, pausing to watch the traffic in the London Road, muttering to himself, a peaceful smile on his hook-nosed, hawk-like face. People, when they saw him, smiled at and with him, chuckled indulgently, affectionately, for they were accustomed to him; they were fond of him. He was an institution. "Old Jarrow on the rampage again," they said. "There's old J. Haven't seen him for a week or two." Carr, the butcher, cycling past, called out: "Any dead dogs to sell me, Mr. Jarrow?" and Mr. Jarrow looked at him, and his peaceful smile widened more peacefully. He waved a friendly wave.

In the High Street—it was shortly after eleven—he paused to watch Dick Barke who was leisurely trundling his barrow toward the square. Dick glanced in his direction and winked, and the old gentleman winked back and remarked: "Cold day. Cold day. Any carcases in your barrow, boy?"

Dick showed his teeth briefly. "Summer's the best time for them, sir. You ought to know that by now."

Limpingly, casually, the old gentleman crossed the street, and Dick halted. Dick was always willing to halt when working. "Haven't seen you about for a week or two, sir. How's the dead rat business?"

"Not too good. Seriously thinking of nationalizing it. How's that girl with the rump?"

"Who you mean? Hyacinth?" Dick scowled. "Hmphh!" he said, taking a flattened-looking cigarette end from behind his ear and lighting it.

"Aha," commented Mr. Jarrow, giving the barrow a tap with his stick.

"Aha about what?"

"Things not going too good, eh? The old bull pawing around her."

"Pawing around her?"

"And pawing her up, in all likelihood."

"What are you talking about? Which old bull is this?" Suddenly Dick smiled. Went further and uttered a raw coughing laugh. "Is that what you call the Holme bloke?" he said, scratching his neck. "Good one, that. Must tell Cinthy that one."

"She won't like it. I believe she has her eye on the old bull."

"How do you know that?"

"I know. Intuition."

"You ever see anything funny?"

"I see everything funny." Mr. Jarrow scowled at the tobacconist's shop across the street. "Got to buy some tobacco, but I'm not going into that shop. A girl in there whose face I can't stand." He fumbled in his overcoat pocket and brought out two half-crowns. "Do me a good turn, Dick?"

"What's that?"

Mr. Jarrow held out the two half-crowns. "Go across there and buy me an ounce of pipe tobacco. And keep a sixpence for yourself. Can't stand the sight of that girl behind the counter. I believe she's sickening for goitre—either that or she's pregnant in the larynx."

Dick took the coins. "What brand you smoke?"

"Any brand. I'm not fussy about tobacco. So long as it's Virginia."

Dick left his barrow and crossed over to the tobacconist's. He had hardly turned off when Mr. Jarrow leant over and began to fish around in the barrow. He swiftly selected two soiled envelopes, tucked them deftly into an empty Quaker Oats carton. He lifted the carton out of the barrow with a casually critical air, and examined it, holding it lightly, but close, against his chest. In turning it over, he let the envelopes fall out—fall out and lodge within the gaping front of his overcoat the upper part of which he had unbuttoned a minute or two before addressing Dick.

When Dick emerged and approached with the tobacco Mr. Jarrow was still examining the Quaker Oats carton; he had buttoned up his overcoat. "Thank you, my boy. Just couldn't stand the sight of that girl's face."

"Her face or her throat?"

"Don't quibble, boy. A face and throat go together—same as a rump and hips. I'm relieving you of this carton. Think I can find some use for it. Any objections?"

"Take it. Ought to hand it over to the salvage people, but what's a carton less here or there!"

"What, indeed! And I can put it to so many different uses. I must be going home. Cold morning. It will be snowing by mid-afternoon, you see if I'm not right. And keep your eye on that old bull. He's after your cow." With a sigh, Mr. Jarrow moved on, leaving Dick chuckling indulgently.

Later that day, however, when Dick told Hyacinth, Hyacinth's only response was to stare sombrely down into her tumbler of light ale. She and Dick were sitting at a glass-topped table in the public bar of the Ram and Cross. Dick had come in and found her there, and had exclaimed: "Blow me if it isn't a ghost! You in here at this time of day! Well, who would have thought such a thing!"

Hyacinth had just given him a sour look and turned her attention back to her ale. So Dick had ordered a glass for himself and joined her. Then he had said: "What's happened to you to-day you're not having tea with the old rove?"

She had ignored him.

Dick, not at all upset, had chuckled. Then he had told her about his encounter with Mr. Jarrow. "The old bull, that's what he called him. Pawing round you. That's what he told me. Pawing you up. He says: 'You have an eye on that old bull. He's got his eye on your cow, the old bull has.' And he says you've got your eye on him. How do you like that?"

Hyacinth stared sombrely down into her tumbler of ale.

"Well, I like that! What's been happening this morning? He put you across his knee and give you a spanking? I believe he must have done."

Hyacinth took a sip, staring across the room past Dick's head.

Outside, a few tiny flakes of snow were coming down sparsely, intermingled with sleet. It was very cold. The Stephen's Ink thermometer at the news-agent's registered 34. But it was warm in the Ram and Cross.

"What's he been doing to you? Tell me about it. Come on."

"Stop making yourself a bloody nuisance, Dick."

"That's more like yourself. Sit there looking like you been

bashed one in the head by a blooming railway engine. Why haven't you gone to make his tea this afternoon? You had a row with him?"

She shook her head and sipped, staring past him.

"Then what's it? You coming with me to pictures to-night?"

Again she shook her head. She looked at him and said: "You want to know the truth, Dick? I've got it bad for him."

"You've what! Look, what's all this you're saying?"

"I've told you now."

"You don't mean as you're getting serious about an old—an old codger like him!" The banter vanished from his manner. He sat erect, looking at her.

"Everything's over between us, Dick. You may as well know from to-day."

"But ... look, Cinthy, what's gone and got into your head! Haven't we been walking out these how many years! He's put the question to you?"

"No."

"Then what you mooning over him for? What's happened?"

"I shouldn't talk about it," she said—remotely she saw herself a character in a heavy film drama; without knowing it she slouched in her chair with what unconsciously she imagined was an air of sophisticated dejection. "I really shouldn't talk about it to a soul, but the two of us have been friendly for a long time, and it's only right I should give you an explanation. He kissed me. He held me in his arms and kissed me."

"He! That old—that old ... the blooming cheek! So old Jarrow's right. The old rove *has* had his eye on you. I laughed at him, but I can see now he was right."

"Old Jarrow is a mad fool. He has a dirty mind, that's what he has. Mr. Holme never had his eye on me. It's me."

"You? What you mean it's you?"

"It's me who had my eye on him. It's me who tried to hook him."

"You?"

"Yes, me. And now he's—he's getting soft on me. He kissed me."

"He's getting soft on you? A minute ago you said it was you who had it for him. Did he tell you he was soft on you?"

She moved her head slowly from side to side, gazing down into her glass. "Not in words, he hasn't. But people haven't got to use words to say everything. Actions can speak louder than words. You never heard that?"

"You're just imagining it up, that's what you're doing. He'll never ask you to marry him. He's got it for that Jarrow thing up the lane. I heard he was walking out with her yesterday arm in arm in Great Oak Road."

"That's not true. It's dirty gossip."

"It's true. Bill was pushing the grey cart up Great Oak Road, and he saw them. He told me himself. Walking arm in arm and laughing and talking, they was. It's her he'll be asking to marry before long. She's his class. You're not his class."

She said nothing, but she blinked, and the corners of her eyes began to get moist. She raised her glass and took a long sip.

While they had been talking someone had entered the bar and ordered a stout. Abruptly that someone was standing at their table. They looked up and saw him. He was smiling a bright, friendly smile.

"North," said North. "Albert. May I share your table?" He glanced at Hyacinth's glass; it was nearly empty. "Another ale, Miss Withers? On me."

Dick and Hyacinth gave him blank looks. He smiled: "Action. That's my motto. Brief word—then action." He turned off, went to the counter and ordered a light ale, and hardly a minute later was back. He put down the glass before Hyacinth and said: "Yours." And at that instant another figure entered the bar. A shortish, merry-eyed gentleman with a large, round head, in a buff overcoat and scarlet woollen scarf. He ordered a stout, and North, now seated at the table with Dick and Hyacinth, winked and said: "See that chap? Met him in the High Street this morning. Struck up a friendship with him—just like that! Phew-ff!" He snapped his fingers and winked again. "Ten to one he joins us here. Watch and see."

"Are you the private detective chap I've heard about?" Hyacinth asked.

"Sssh! That's it. Private detective. But it's strictly between you and me and this fellow here—Mr. Barke. Hush-hush. Not a word to a mortal. Just the three of us sharing the awful secret—with the village. Ah! What did I tell you?"

Southerby stood by their table, glass of stout in hand, merry smile on round face. "May I share your table?" he asked huskily, very confidentially.

"You don't mind, do you?" asked North, glancing swiftly from Hyacinth to Dick. "Good chap, Southerby. John. Little chip on the shoulder, but never mind. Family man. Wife and four children. And a spaniel. Always note the spaniel. Sit down, Southy old chump. Miss Withers and Mr. Barke don't mind if we join them. Snowing outside, isn't it? Eh, Southy?"

Southerby nodded and sat down. "Take," he said, "the *crime passionelle*. Here is an instance where we can extend our sympathy and careful consideration. An act of violence is committed in the heat of emotion. Anger, jealousy or severe provocation of some kind was behind the deed. It was not planned in cold blood—no question of malice aforethought—hence we must pause and investigate the matter, for the mind behind such an act may not necessarily be a deficient or diseased mind. Such a mind, however, is in need of discipline, and this is the remedy we must apply on discovering that the past record of our offender bears no evidence of inherent disease. Here is an instance where we must try to remove the environmental conditions that were directly responsible for the deed. If it is a jealous lover then we must do what we can to convince him or her that while we recognize that love is a strong emotion and while we are sympathetic, we feel that a serious breach of mental discipline has occurred; we feel that, as a civilized human being, our offender has allowed his basic instincts and emotions to triumph over the rulings of his superior human brain; we must point out that while our offender is in such a state he cannot be considered fit to mix with the rest of his fellow men. He must be put through a hospital course of discipline; he must spend a few months in confinement so that specially trained doctors may work upon his mind and impress upon it the value of emotional restraint. And at the end of his term of treatment he must be released—not given a term of penal servitude nor in any way victimized. For such an individual is not verminous; it was merely temporary circumstances that turned him into a killer.

"Naturally," smiled Southerby, unemotionally, quite impartially, without the slightest desire to sway, "we must be wary in such cases. For it is not impossible that our offender *could* be a specimen of vermin. There may have been other incidents of violence in his past. It is our business to find out. Should we find that this is so we must take a grave view of the matter. Anything that is *habitual* is serious; it is an indication of heredity. Bad heredity. Our offender, in such a case, must be considered a menace to the community. Yes. Sad but true. Vermin. Only one expedient in such a case. The Prick. A hypodermic needle with morphia or cyanide would do it without making a mess. All over without pain or bother to offender or executioner. A clean, hygienic, clinical extermination."

"There you are!" cried North. "See him! That's Southy. Hard nut to crack. But harmless as a dove. I say, Mr. Barke, I thought I saw you having a word with Mr. Jarrow this morning. Interesting old man, eh?"

Dick grinned self-consciously and nodded. "He done something?"

"Something? No. Nothing. Nothing at all. Charming old man. We're just wondering what you talked to him about—or, rather, what he talked to you about. Point of general interest. Students of human nature, Southy and me. Interested in everything human. By the way, our card!" Dick took it and read what was printed on it, and Hyacinth peered over his shoulder. Hyacinth had a dismayed, half-amused air as she glanced from North to Southerby. Much of her gloom had departed.

"See? Busy as bees, Southy and me. Interested in everything. From garbage to eccentric old men; from pins and needles to Quaker Oats cartons. Mr. Jarrow went off with a Quaker Oats carton, didn't he?"

"Yes. Yes, that's right. He asked me for it."

North leant forward eagerly. "Did he mention what he wanted it for?"

"No." Dick grinned and tapped his forehead. "He's not all right up here. Haven't you heard?"

"Oh, we've heard, Mr. Barke. We've heard. We hear everything, Southy and me. Acutely sharp ears. We never miss a sound. Not even the wailing of a siren. Not even the crash of thunder overhead. Everything, everything we hear."

Dick and Hyacinth looked one at the other. Dick gave a sputtering sound. A man in a heavy brown overcoat came in. His greying hair and his shoulders were flecked with snow. Hyacinth giggled.

"You were telling me, Mr. Barke. He took away the Quaker Oats carton but he said nothing to you about what he intended to do with it. Insist on correcting me if I have made a misstatement."

"No, he didn't say what he wanted it for. Suppose to put some dead rat in."

"A dead rat?"

"Don't you know his hobby? He picks up dead things and puts them in boxes or buries them in his garden."

"Interesting, interesting, but we'd heard that already. But tell me, what did you talk about with him this morning? Anything special? Was it about cabbages or cobblestones? About polar bears or ball-room bores?"

Dick spluttered, exchanging a look with Hyacinth. "Nothing," he said. "We just said hullo, and he asked me to buy him some tobacco."

"Ah. You bought him some tobacco. I see. He sent you into the tobacconist's across the street, and as soon as you'd turned off he rummaged in your barrow and brought out this Quaker Oats carton. We've got that clear. But just one thing more. Is he in the habit of stopping you for a chat and a rummage in your barrow—or your grey cart? Has he done so before on several previous occasions that you can recall?"

"Umpteen times," said Dick.

"Ah. Umpteen times. And what does he generally take away? Boxes? Dead rats? Quaker Oats cartons?"

"Yes. Mostly old boxes. I can only remember him once asking me to hand over a carcase. A dead mouse it was."

"I see. So should you be asked at any time, you would say that what happened in the High Street this morning was nothing out of the ordinary. You weren't surprised at all that he stopped you and then went off with a Quaker Oats carton?"

"No. It's happened lots of times before. He done something?"

"No. Nothing. Nothing at all. I'm just making conversation. We're fond of conversation, Southy and me. Men of few words.

But telling words. Conversational artists. What do you say, Southy old twirp? Am I right or wrong?"

Southerby nodded. "Take religion," he wheezed, resting his glass. "Religious sentimentality, we may say, is behind most of the weak attitudes we assume toward criminals and persons of verminous mentality. The Christ-like policies of turning the cheek when struck and of not hating our enemies and of being humble and surrendering—these policies have been allowed to undermine our reason, the result being that we look upon every rational attitude as suspect: the emanation of a cold, scientific brain. Now, it is excellent—indeed essential—not to hate one's enemies; hate is destructive. Humility is not only a commendable quality but it is the hallmark of a truly civilized man. To turn the cheek, to surrender—well, no, that is masochism and must be eschewed. Let us say, then, that we are fully in favour of not hating our enemies and of being decorously humble. Good. But—heed carefully—are our enemies also interested in these noble ideals? No. Sad but there it is. Our enemies are ruthless, without pity, without humanitarian scruples. Hence, since we are up against such enemies, we have only one recourse. We must be detachedly ruthless in opposing and wiping them out. To be Christ-like would be sheer folly. Such an attitude could result only in our downfall and their triumph. In our annihilation."

Southerby took a sip. "What we need," he smiled, amiably, unexcitedly, quite unexcitably, "is an education free of religious bias and based on the elements of courtesy. A wide subject, courtesy. Covers the whole field of humane and genuinely civilized conduct. No community thoroughly schooled in the graces of courtesy would want to seek war as a solution to our problems. Instead of instilling into our children a fear of God and a love of this same intangible God, instead of filling their imaginations with superstitious myths, suppose we taught them to be courteous for the sake of being humane, to be courteous for the sake of being dignified animals, to be courteous for the sake of the spiritual well-being of the human species, to be courteous for the sake of being loving one to another instead of hating, envying and killing each other; suppose we taught them these courteous refinements and omitted all mention of confusing dogma relating to a Trinity-God and a crucified Saviour, don't you think we should produce a far more wholesome race of beings? Don't you think that such tuition would do far more good in ridding our world of its false values of greed and power than a tuition which features an ethical code based on religious dogma about which no two schools of thought can agree entirely? Courtesy is a quality possible of attainment by all humans everywhere, but can we ever hope to unite the world of men in religious thought and myth? A doctrine of simple good conduct can be taught to every man and woman of every race and nation and be comprehended. But can we say that it would be as easy to convince men of every race and nation of the correctness of this or that particular religious attitude? Then why do we persist in perpetuating from generation to generation the mushy, impracticable religious doctrines that the churches uphold? Why must we attempt to be decent creatures for the sake of God instead of for the sake of our own practical good? God is an idea about which there is much dispute and uncertainty; how many of us find it easy to believe in God? Humans, on the other hand, are concrete, irrefutable entities; we don't require much effort to convince ourselves of the fact that we exist. It is true that our metaphysical philosophers can prove that all we see about us, including ourselves, is, in reality, a mere figment of our thought processes. But our thought processes happen to be capable of disturbingly tangible feats; so much so that should I knock in your teeth with my fist you would in no wise be inclined to consider it a mere figment of your thought processes. Let us, therefore, I say, try to be sensible about the sum of phenomena which we call life. Let us make this sum of phenomena as pleasant as possible while it continues to be a vital and inescapable figment of our mental perceptions."

"If you watch carefully," whispered North into Hyacinth's ear, "you'll see a halo around Southy's head. Sssh! Old Southy is a prophet. Modern saint-prophet. No one heeds him, and that makes him an even better prophet and much less a saint. Great lad with the ladies, Southy old twig." North winked at Dick. "But prophets can be tripped up. You watch how I'm going to send him sprawling! I say, Southy old scone, tell us this. You advocate the eradication of religion, but haven't you heard it said often and often again that the human species must have some sort of religion, that without a God to worship and put their confidence in men would find life unbearably empty? Now, if this is so, tell us—and I have an idea the question has been posed before—what are we to substitute for religion?"

Southerby held out his open cigarette case. North refused. Dick and Hyacinth put out their hands, but Southerby withdrew the case quickly. "Mind! They're mentholated. Good for my throat, but might be bitter for yours." He selected one and snapped the case shut. Dick spluttered. Hyacinth giggled. Southerby lit his cigarette and said with a smile: "The human species believes it needs religion, and this belief came into being, originally, out of fear. Fear of the unknown forces of life. Because primitive men didn't understand what caused thunder and lightning they held this phenomenon in awe and dread. An awe and dread far above what mere physical exigency called for. It was a mystery. It was a threat in the sky. It was intangible. It could strike at any moment. *It was a god!* It was a fearsome Being somewhere in space. It struck at men with a spite that was purposeful with intelligence. Human intelligence. No! *Super-human* intelligence. Mankind was up against Something. What was the solution? Well, the god must be propitiated. Offer sacrifices to it. Build an altar to it. A temple. Flatter it with ritual incantations, and perhaps it might help us and frown upon our enemies.

"See what I mean?" asked Southerby. "A religion has been born. The god may be thunder and lightning. Rain. The sun. The moon. A tree. The human mind can imbue any object with divine qualities. Especially when that mind is stimulated by the threat of danger. Danger tangible or intangible. Had primitive men felt no fear, the human imagination would have invented no gods. In the beginning God was a bogey. To-day that bogey is a Hydra of a thousand heads, each head presiding over its particular sect of worshippers. And each worshipper is a worshipper *because he fears*.

"Educate," said Southerby, "a community of children along purely rational lines, emphasizing always the idea of courtesy one to another; teach these children how to appreciate the beauty and richness of pictures, poems, symphonies; mention nothing about religion, except as an incidental commentary on certain

historical and sociological aspects of *primitive* man—do this,"
smiled Southerby, "and see if your children, when they become
adults, will hunger after religion; see if they will find life empty
because they have no God to believe in. Oh, no, North. Mankind
only needs religion because religion seems the safest and cosiest
burrow into which, rabbit-wise, to scurry when reality seems to
offer uncomfortable dangers. The emptiness we feel is the emptiness we create by our own failure to put to good use the stuff
of life that lies around us. Would a man who is enjoying a happy
sex life, who is in an interesting job, who can enjoy books, music
and pictures—would such a man tell you he discerns an emptiness in life? Would such a man feel that he has nothing to believe
in and nothing to inspire him to further efforts? Would such a
man feel that unless he became interested in an x quantity—or
quality—called God; unless he could persuade himself into being
passionately in earnest about the existence of this Quantity—or
Quality—his whole life would collapse around him?"

North shrugged. "There! See! Defeat. Always the same. Take
my tip, Miss Withers. Mr. Barke! Be warned. Never become
involved in a debate with old Southy. He'll floor you. Just like
that! Whuff!" North looked at Dick. "Have another ale, Mr.
Barke. On me."

Dick refused, and North said: "Don't let Southy put you off.
Can't help himself. Chip." He put out a hand and touched Dick's
shoulder. "Right there. Chip on the shoulder, old Southy. Always
with a grouse. Always inviting battle. Shall I—?"

North broke off, glancing up. Mine host stood by their table,
missive in hand. "For you, sir," he said to North.

"For me?"

"Just cleared the letter-box, sir. Found it there. Seems as if it
must have come by hand."

"Thank you. Good. I like receiving letters delivered by hand.
And this one strikes me as being an interesting specimen. Sssh!
Excuse me," he said to Dick and Hyacinth. "Must read it without
delay."

He did not slit it open at once, however. He examined it. It was
a soiled envelope bearing a stamp. But the postmark—a Woking
postmark—was four days old. And the address—Mrs. H. Breen,

4, Miller's Lane, Middenshot, Surrey—had been lightly scored out with pencil. In green ink, in block letters, at the left bottom corner, was written: *A. North, Esq., Ram and Cross, Middenshot.*

North whistled. He took from his overcoat pocket a lead pencil and with its point slit open the envelope.

Dick and Hyacinth watched—Southerby, sipping, regarded the cream-painted ceiling, a detached but pleasant smile on his round face—while North took from the envelope what looked like the torn-off corner of a newspaper.

North read the words—in green ink—written in block letters on the unprinted-on margin. They were very few, but they caused him to sit erect with a shrill chirping sound.

"Abracadabra," he said. "Cadabra-abra. Southy, we're at the end of the trail. Action! Up, Southy old bin! Wellingtons and away!"

Silently, unexcitedly, quite unexcitably, Southerby, smile on face still, stretched out and took the slip of paper from North. He read: *Tip: Hut in woods. Old well—now cellar. Entrance outside hut—not inside.* And rose. "We must go," he said hoarsely.

"We must go," agreed North.

They went.

<h1 style="text-align:center">7</h1>

Indefinite little paws, midget ears, frayed coins—florins, pennies, shillings—and many tiny toes, incredibly puny snails and an infinity of broken finger-nails: like the ghosts—ghosts are invariably white—of all these, tangled in an After-world of chaos, the flakes came down from the padded grey wintry sky, settling in silence on the ground but tip-plipping, plip-tipping on window-sills and against window-panes. Oh, the lovely, desolate whiteness of it all, thought Grace, watching it from the backroom window. White like my not yet sullied virginity. Oh, who will sully my virginity for me? Who would dare sully it?

In slanting flurries, noiselessly frenzied, now from the north-west, suddenly from the north, swirling amidst the tree-tops, down through the leaves—invisible leaves, on bare limbs, visible only as ghosts: cascades of winter ghosts fluttering down from heaven through the wintry air; bleached replicas of summer's living greens, fragments loose and wandering in the churning cold winds from the north. Leaves, twigs, buds that never burst-crippled, killed in last spring's frosts—bits of bark and tree-top sprigs pixie-snipped at mid-summer's midnight: like the ghosts of all these tangled in an aimless pother, the flakes came down from the woolly grey wintry sky, settling in silence in the back-garden but tip-plipping, plip-tipping on the window-sill and against the window-pane. Oh, the wild, white loneliness of it all, thought Grace, watching it with wide eyes from the back-room window. White—oh, white like my unfondled breasts. White . . .

. . . white like the sheet hanging on the line.

How careless of her! She should have brought it in before the snow began. She must go now and bring it in. It had been hanging on the line since the thaw had set in yesterday morning. Her mother had tried to take advantage of the weak sunshine. Yes, she must certainly go at once and fetch it in. Look how it was snowing! Never mind, she must go.

Putting on her coat, she went out by the kitchen door, hurried past the coal-house door, and, while the flakes hissed nervously about her, whispering unintelligible secrets, she unpegged the sheet—flakes fell in powdery flocks off its washed whiteness—and bunching it together, began to make her way back toward the cottage. Going past the coal-house door, she slipped on the slippery ground, but managed to retain her balance. Pausing for that brief instant, she noted something. Oh, she thought. The flakes whispered fiercely about her. Her eyes stared wide in horror. Oh, she thought, as the flakes tried to tell her of terrible deeds committed under drooping testers, of virgin-knots split in the darkness of many a snowy midnight past. Split asunder, said the flakes. With pain and signalled parturition. Oh, dread signal! Oh, she thought, her breath coming in a swift gasp.

Instead of moving on, she stood quite still and turned her head slowly. She looked at the coal-house door, two or three feet on her left. And once again there drifted to her nostrils the sickly-sweet smell.

A smell of putrefaction.

She moved a pace nearer to the coal-house door. Yes, she had no doubt. Despite the cold, the smell persisted. A smell of a body rotting. She bent and put her nose right up against the small oblong hole that was the keyhole. She recoiled with a puffing grunt of repugnance.

A certainty. The coal-house. It was from in there the smell was coming! She shuddered in all the follicled oases of her skin.

"Oh," she said, the flakes falling in a tremulous frenzy around her.

But surely . . . Could it be . . . Would it be . . . a dead rat? A dead cat? A dead dog that her father had perversely put in there? Yes, perhaps . . . Oh, but she had never known him to put dead things in the coal-house. Then . . . then could it be . . . ? No, no. She could not believe it could be . . . Not *that!* A rat. A cat. A dead dog. But not *that!* Oh, she was foolish to be alarmed. She must really not let her fancy form fearful pictures. Let her hurry inside. How cold it was, and how the snow came down! So thickly furious, so densely, dispassionately, persistent. Passively antagonistic.

She moved on toward the kitchen.

As she was entering, she laughed and murmured: "How very silly of me! A cat, of course. A dead rat." Didn't he, she thought, go wandering about the neighbourhood this morning? He must have picked up a carcase somewhere. A dead dog. And brought it home and put it in the coal-house. A silly dead rat. Poor fellow. It was his Mind. He couldn't help it.

Her mother came in from the hallway as Grace was locking the outer door. "Oh, thank you, Grace dear. I'd forgotten all about that sheet."

"Yes, I thought I'd better bring it in. I really ought to have remembered it. Mother, I—Mother, there's—oh, never mind. It doesn't matter."

"What's it, my child?"

"I—oh, nothing, but I was passing the coal-house . . ."

"The coal-house?"

"Yes, Mother. I—somehow, I just thought . . . Oh, it was silly of me, but I thought I noticed a peculiar smell. I think there must be a dead dog in there. Oh, if only Dad would give us the key!"

"A dead dog?"

"Yes, a dreadful smell. I'm sure it's a dead cat."

Her mother stared at her, white. Like the snow outside. Tip-plip! it went against the window-panes. So insistent.

"He—he must have found it this morning and put it in there, Mother."

Plip-tip!

"He's—he's so absurd. I don't know what to say." Tip-plip-plip! From her mother came a whispering. Just audible.

A mimicking of the snow on the sills, against the panes. Plip-tip!

Similar in timbre to the noise of Hyacinth's breath as she blew snow from her sleeve. The sleeve of her overcoat.

"I thought you weren't coming," said Mr. Holme, opening the door.

She blew more flakes from her overcoat sleeve, making no reply as she came in.

"Weather turned nasty again," he said, and helped her to take off her coat. "Thought the thaw might have continued, but no hope of that now."

"Have you had your tea yet?" She asked the question without glancing at him. She kept looking at the floor.

"No. I was just thinking of putting on the kettle. I missed you. Said to myself you've run out on me to-day."

She accompanied him into the kitchen. Still without comment.

"Where've you been to, Hyacinth?"

"I was in the Ram and Cross," she murmured. Half-shyly, yet with some defiance.

"Met Dick there?"

She said nothing. She took up the kettle, rinsed it out, filled it.

He seated himself at the small table and watched her. He took up the evening paper which he had been reading when her knock came on the door.

She began to giggle in smothered bursts.

"What's biting you now?"

"You never told me," she said.

"Never told you what?"

"How funny they were."

"Who are you talking about?"

"Mr. North and Mr. Southy—the two detectives."

"Oh, you've run into them?"

"They were in the Ram and Cross. They came in and joined Dick and me at a table." She put down the kettle and went off into another fit of giggles.

"They're mad. Should be in a mental home, those two fellows."

"They were so funny! I nearly died laughing. I was in a bad mood, but they put me in a good mood."

He watched her shaking with laughter. Her hips. Her stomach. Her breasts. A symphonic pattern of shaking. Plip-tip-tip! A furry flurry of flakes blew against the window. His gaze darted toward the window, then back to her. His hand holding the paper sagged. The fingers began to curl slowly inward. The paper touched the table with a lisp, sister-sound to the harmless noise of the flakes. Tip-tip-plip! So diligently sibilant . . . He rose and sprang at her.

Swish-plip-tip! On. Always onward. No faltering. Busy as bees. What was a flock of little icy, white fragments sailing down in the dark! Only snow. Soft, innocuous.

"Sure we're on the right track, Harry lad?"

"Don't you be afraid, sir," said Harry. "I know this common and these woods like the palm of my hand, I do. We'll be at the hut in half-an-hour."

"Good. Good. As long as you're sure of your bearings, Harry old bin. How're things with you, Southy old bum? Standing up to the weather?"

"I'm all for the open air," said Southerby. "What we need," he added hoarsely, "is more open air life and less indoor coddling. Less shutting of windows in railway compartments and more exposure to the fresh winds and snows of Nature. When we coddle our bodies we tend to coddle our minds."

Swish-tip-plip! The flakes flicked lightly against their hats, and their wellingtons ploughed earnestly through the piling carpet as they advanced over the common toward the Berkshire woods. It was very dark, but Harry Coombe, their guide, a gardener who worked at Rogan Hall, moved with sureness; there could be no doubt that he knew his way about the common.

"This hut," said North. "You've actually been there before?"

"Many's the time, sir. Since I was a boy I've known it."

"Did you know there was a cellar under it?"

"Cellar? Never heard of one, sir."

"Old well. Converted into a cellar."

"Never heard of it."

"Excellent! That means it really was a secret known only to a sinister few."

"Is it something to do with the Executioner, sir?"

"Perhaps—and perhaps not, Harry. We never know. Oh, life is a dithery business. But we've had a tip, and we mean to drain it dry of its possibilities. Tap every tip. That's our motto, Harry. On! Onward, lisping soldiers! Excelsior!" He glanced at Southerby. "What do you say, Southy old tack?"

"Take environment and heredity," said Southerby wheezingly. "They're related to each other as conductor to composer. A bad conductor may dull the brilliance of a fine composition—but it still remains a fine composition. No matter, however, how good the conductor, he can't convert a bad composition into a satisfying performance. Bad music is bad music and will always be recognized as bad music."

"Are you listening to that music, Grace?"

Grace and her mother turned as their father entered the kitchen. Mrs. Jarrow was still very pale. She still made whispering noises.

"Not particularly, Dad. You can switch it off if you like until it's time for the weather forecast."

"Grace."

"Yes, Dad."

"I've come to a decision."

"What's that, Dad?"

"We must hold the séance immediately after tea."

"Oh."

"Yes, child. We can't wait until after supper. That smell . . ."

"Yes, Dad? What did you say?"

"Did I say something?"

"You began to say something about a smell."

"Did I? Well, don't encourage me to talk about smells. I'm surprised at you. I thought your mother and I had trained you better than that."

"I . . ." Grace gulped and said: "Why do you want to hold the séance after tea and not after supper?"

"Don't you see how hard it's snowing outside? Do you think it would be considerate of me to expect your mother's soul to come down out of her warm heaven into the hellishly cold night that is obviously before us? It's your mother I'm thinking of, Grace. The sooner we hold the séance the sooner she'll be able to set out on her return trip—that is, of course, if all heaven-bound planes aren't grounded for the night. In that event we'd have to put her up until morning. Couldn't very well turn her out into the snow."

"Dad!" Grace stamped.

"Grace dear, please . . ."

"Mother, don't you think it's time he stopped all this—this stupid foolishness! I'm tired! I'm tired of it, I tell you!"

"Aha. Breaking point is near," said her father. "Come, child. Hurry up with tea and let's get started on that séance. Who knows if it might not be our last!"

"Our last?"

"Our last. Ho!" exclaimed the old gentleman, and tapping his stick sharply on the floor, turned and left the kitchen.

Sharply to the left. Now this way. "Turn this way, sir!"

"This hut, Harry, if you don't mind me reverting to Theme One—how did it come to be in the woods? Who built it?"

"The Rudstows, sir. Major Rudstow's father. Where it stands now used to be part of the old Rudstow estate. Now it's government land."

"Ah! Now, now! There's something! The old Rudstow estate, eh? In other words, it would be quite understandable if this hut were very well-known to Major Rudstow?"

"Oh, yes, sir. He must have known it as a boy and a young man. Only about fifteen or twenty years since the estate passed into government hands."

"Excellent! Exceedingly superb! You're an asset, Harry. The situation momently brightens, lightens. What do you say, Southy old flake?"

Southerby brushed a few flakes of snow from his chin. "Let's look at it this way," he said huskily. "Assuming—and it is an extremely feasible assumption—that medical science succeeds in reaching the heights of achievement at which it aims and doctors are able to prolong human life far beyond the limits possible to-day, what would we do about our old people? Think of it. Here are our old people living on and on to ninety, a hundred, a hundred and ten, just as a matter of course, and in the meantime children continue to be born, the world grows more and more cluttered up with people; death is on the wane: death becomes rarer and rarer. Now, wouldn't this mean that some drastic step would have to be taken to control the situation? Even Mr. Malthus didn't take into account people living to a hundred and a hundred and ten, as a matter of course. How would we provide food to feed an ever-growing, hardly-ever-dying population? Either the old people would have to agree to commit a pleasant and graceful suicide after they have outlived their usefulness or babies would have to be killed off at birth—or not allowed to be born for long periods, thus lowering the ranks of our youthful, virile reserves. What would our religious sentimentalists do when faced with such a quandary? Wouldn't they eventually have to reconcile themselves to a sane, practical system of elimination?"

"Wisdom! Hear it, Harry! Wisdom on Brameley Common with the cold snow flakes swirling all about us. Frightening but true. Too true!"

The kitchen seemed to swirl around her. "You frightened me," she said. "Springing at me like that."

"I couldn't help it," he said. He was still holding her, still stroking her hair and her cheek and her throat. For him, too, the kitchen seemed to swirl. He could feel the shape of her stomach against him, a navel-pitted patch that palpitated with a pain of unendurable pleasure.

Tip-plip-plip! Monotonously, mysteriously. Projected into his senses, the little flakes melted, for his senses had built around the surface of his body a belt of aching torridity, insulation against the most persistent, insistent chilly flurry.

"I couldn't help myself," he said.

"I don't mind. I like you to hold me."

"Just couldn't help myself."

"I wish you could hold me like this the whole night."

"You make me feel as if I'm mad. I don't want any tea."

"I don't want any tea. Just hold me like you're holding me."

Tip-plip-tip! Assiduously.

He glanced at the window, then back at her—at her face under his. "I feel as if I've gone mad, Hyacinth. Mad. I want to undress you."

"I feel mad myself. You can do anything you like with me. Undress me."

Plip-tip-tip. Unheedingly.

"Hear how it's snowing!"

She moved against him. He could feel the separate detailed dents and all the smooth, small cushioned softnesses of her body. The whole palpable female mass of her had, for him, become an ache. Shapeless. Placeless. A stirring warmth about to put forth wisps to bind and softly, deliciously, submerge him—the lean pillar of him swaying in the magic of an over-powering rhythm.

"I don't know what I'm saying," he said, looking about him. "Hear how it's snowing!"

"But it isn't cold in here. Undress me."

"I've gone out of my head, Hyacinth."

"Me, too. If you only know how bad I've got it for you."

She tried to pull away from him slightly, whispering: "Let me undress." But he held her to him tighter, afraid that if he let her go he would grow madder—or less mad. He wanted to remain at this exact level of madness. All the years behind him dead . . . If he had only known madness could be so delicious!

He felt her wriggling and trying to fumble about with her clothes, her hands clawing at her back, her hips shifting against him as she turned and twisted. And his madness, passing through an unseen distillery, assumed the quality of a turgid dream—a dream in which he toppled off the cliff but did not fall. He drifted. What aerial delight to drift! Not down but across and over. Not down but slightly up, up. Level. Over. Up again. Dizzily he could tell what she was doing. Unhooking. Detaching. Deftly undressing despite his holding her. It could be real, this—but it was not. Such things never were real. One inevitably awoke. To feel the over-warm mattress beneath, the over-warm blanket-sheet mixture itchy at the neck. Oh, how the dark mocked one's bliss-that-might-have-been! No. Oh, no. Never real! Yet this ... Wait ... Tip-plip! Plip-tip! Little paws, peas, little fleas, perhaps, mere shades—shroud-white phantoms in the freezing Outer Dusk. Making mock beyond the panes. Beyond the Pale.

A lisp and swish and a turmoil of cloth slipped. Continued to slip. He tried to grasp, to encircle, the warm flesh that might elude him if he were not careful, but it was the slipping that gave the dream its inner tremors. Tremors that reached his knees. His loins.

Plip-plip! Swish-swish! Drapery on the move. Down—not up. Not over, not across. Always down. She wriggled. She gasped and giggled. Her giggle had such vibrancy, husky and creamy and female. Overburdened with the power of the flesh. Insanity inciting. And continuously, persistently, the clothes about her, once an actuality, a marshalled, stable actuality, dissolved into a tantalizing instability. Always slipping. Unremittingly. Monotonously. Tip-plip! Slip-slip! Folding eccentrically like waves receding and merging with advancing waves.

Tip-tip-tip! Minute, invisible beyond the purple panes. Why should he care? Especially as now she gave the final, the most deft and animated, wriggle of all. And his breath turned to gasps. For his hands grasped smooth, cool back. Real. Female-real. Skin. Firm, smooth shoulders. Cool—yet warm with blood. And two breasts were pressed against him. Tangible globes of human flesh. No illusion. With red-brown nipples and tiny dotted bumps, infinitesimal, inimitable, sand-dunes, on the spreading areolae. He had beaten the dream. This was the palpable reality.

He managed to speak her name. Very softly.

Plip-tip-tip!

That sounded so unimpassioned. But not his voice speaking her name.

"Hyacinth."

She put up her hands and pressed her palms against his cheeks. Rubbed them down slowly. She moaned.

Tip-plip! Maddeningly monotonous. With unceasing detachment. Frenziedly but unheatedly.

"Hyacinth."

"I love you. I love you like hell."

"The living-room. There's a fire in there. Let's go in there."

So they went in there. Pulled the sofa up before the fire. The sofa with the mended leg. But it bore their weight without collapsing. And the fire drowned the sound of the soft tip-tip outside. The crackle of the flames and the agitation of their breaths blotted out all sounds of the cold snow in the dusk outside. The saturation of cold in the world beyond the curtained windows. On this sofa there was a saturation of warm softness. On this sofa two full white breasts—and a rump shapely and firm. Of village renown.

8

"A snowy night," murmured the old gentleman, his gaze on the stone.

"A snowy night," echoed Grace solemnly, in a trance of anger.

"A snowy night. All is hidden in the snow. English snow. When shall we three meet again—Grace, Agnes and poor Herbert? When shall we three meet again in snow, snow, snow?"

"In snow, snow," murmured Grace, gnashing her teeth.

Sharp glance from her father.

"Oh, where am I? Oh, what am I saying? Agnes! Oh, Agnes, come and rescue me, my love! Come, my plain-faced love! Come and make me a cup of tea!"

Mrs. Jarrow pushed the door softly in and entered the room.

Her husband was silent, staring at the stone.

Plip-tip! Tip-plip! At the windows. Not an instant desisting.

"Oh, listen to the snow! Tick-flick! Flick-tick! When shall we three . . ." The old gentleman broke off. His stick, balanced in his lap, rolled forward and fell to the floor with a clatter.

Grace gave him a startled glance. It was an unprecedented accident.

"Oh, revelation! Grace."

"Yes, Dad?"

"Oh, resurrection! Grace."

"Yes, Dad, what is it?" asked Grace—impatiently. Scowling.

Her father ignored her impatience—and her scowl. He sat tense, his gaze on the stone. He said: "Grace, your dear mother is here."

Grace was silent, her face set. Her head trembled slightly—with suppressed anger.

"Oh, resurrection! My dream, Grace. Remember that dream? 'Revelation and resurrection,' quoth the voice in the Berkshire woods. This is the revelation, Grace. And behind me is the resurrection."

"Behind you?"

"Behind me. Your mother is here, child. That's what I mean. In the flesh. She is risen from the dead. Grace."

"Yes, Dad?" She looked at him with sudden curiosity, some of the anger fading from her face.

"Grace, aren't you going to stand and sing 'Halleluiah'? Your mother is risen from the dead. After seventeen years she has come back—in the flesh. Praise the Lord, Grace."

Grace stared at him.

"She stands behind my chair. Agnes Jarrow, sound and solid. This is her Easter Day. Halleluiah!"

Mrs. Jarrow, too, was regarding him with astonishment. This was not in the ritual of the séance. This was a departure. A distinct innovation.

Slowly, Mr. Jarrow rose and turned. He smiled at his wife. "Agnes! Oh, Agnes beloved, you're back! Back from heaven, my love!" He put out his hand and touched her on the shoulder. Lightly. "You're real. No illusion. My old Agnes—as plain as ever. In the flesh and bone." He stretched out again and pinched her cheek. "Real. There's blood in your cheek. Oh, a miracle, a miracle!" The old gentleman moved forward a pace and took his wife in his arms. Mrs. Jarrow shuddered—then sobbed and returned his embrace. She sobbed and sobbed.

"Oh, Herbert! Herbert, what does this mean?"

"It means that you're risen from the dead, Agnes. It's a resurrection of modern times, my love. Biblical history has repeated itself in Middenshot. Oh, holy village!"

"Oh, Herbert! You've never touched me in all the past seventeen years!"

"Because you were spirit, Agnes, during that time. Now you're flesh."

"Oh, Herbert, Herbert!"

"Oh, Agnes, Agnes! We're mimicking the snow-flakes, my dear."

"The snow-flakes?"

"Their repetitiousness."

"Oh, Herbert, I'm—I'm overwhelmed. Is this—will this last? You won't look upon me as dead again?"

"Never, Agnes. We two—pardon, we three, meaning Grace as well—shall live happily ever after. Isn't that how all popular stories end? Don't you want our story to end in the popular tradition, Agnes?"

"I just can't believe this is happening," sobbed Mrs. Jarrow.

"It isn't, Agnes—and it is. All is illusion and delusion, my dear."

Grace regarded her parents with pleasure and alarm. She was delighted and happy—for her mother's sake. But she was disturbed—for this was not in accordance with the accepted trend of their household routine. Her father's pretended madness she had always frowned upon, but now she realized that it was something she had come to look upon as part of her life: something for which she had almost cultivated an affection. Her mother as a ghostly presence only recognized by her father on the occasion of a séance had also become a part of her life: a circumstance irritating but one which familiarity had imbued with an aura of fondness. Now, at a single wave of his hand, so to speak, her father had shattered the seventeen-year-old conventions. He was introducing a drastic change in their household arrangements. It was most upsetting. Changes alarmed her. Suddenly—it came almost as a magnesium flash of intuition in her awareness—she realized that she could never become the wife of Mr. Holme. No matter if he besought her with tears she would have to refuse.

Change! Oh, how terrible was change of any kind! The adjusting of oneself to the new conditions! All the old cosy details of one's private imaginings to be flung to the winds and new, unfamiliar ones collated and marshalled into the freshly adopted routine. Oh!

"Oh!" she exclaimed aloud.

"What is the matter, Grace my child? Aren't you glad to see your mother and me united once again? And Christmas is only a week or two off, besides. Isn't it wonderful to be resurrected and united at Christmas?"

"Oh!" Grace exclaimed again. "How upsetting! I—oh, I really don't know what to say."

"Even my madness seems to be fading fast, child. Haven't you noticed that this past week or two I haven't cringed and moaned at the sound of passing planes? Oh, I'm well on the way to being cured of my neuroses and psychoses. I can even venture to say that after this evening no one would dare accuse me of being manic depressive in manner. I have a feeling I won't walk with a limp, either. Oh, it's a miracle, Grace!" The old gentleman gave his wife an affectionate hug. His wife's sobbing grew louder.

Mr. Jarrow gently lowered her into a chair. "There's much we two have to discuss, Agnes. Much. I vote we go into conference this minute—with Grace as our secretary. Grace, seat yourself, my child. We're going into family conference. There's no time to be lost."

Both Grace and her mother gave him quick glances, for it was obvious that he was in earnest about their going into conference. He said: "Agnes, do you believe in me?" His hands, they noted, were trembling.

"Believe in you, Herbert? What do you mean, dear? Of course, I do."

"Good. I wanted to make sure."

Grace and Mrs. Jarrow stared at him. His face kept twitching and his eyes seemed to shift in his head as though electrically agitated. In this instant Grace knew for certain. He was really insane. He had always been insane. He had not been pretending all these years. Grace felt herself gulping down a lump of air.

"I'm glad you believe in me, Agnes. Grace, what of you?"

"Yes," said Grace, gulping again. "Yes, of course, Dad."

"Why do you ask that, Herbert?"

"Because, in the eyes of the law, I've committed double murder."

"Oh!"

"Herbert!"

"In the eyes of the law, I say. But, as I see it, Agnes, it was not murder but a sane, practical good deed—a deed for which the community should want to thank me, not hang me."

"Herbert, you didn't . . . You've killed the Executioner—and the Major?"

"Captain John Leigh-Houghton and Major Alfred Rudstow. I killed them both, Agnes. By injecting them with a carefully prepared solution of hydrocyanic acid."

"My God!"

"Oh, heavens!"

"I've rid the community of two menaces to its safety. Captain Leigh-Houghton was sent to Broadmoor for murdering his wife and child and raping and strangling the child of their housekeeper. And he murdered five people in this village within one week. When caught—or I should say, if caught—he would have been sent back to Broadmoor, and, who knows, would have escaped again at some later date and committed a few more murders. And Major Rudstow, himself an old criminal, aided and abetted Leigh-Houghton's escape. He accommodated him for several hours at his farm house at Ashbole on the morning of his escape, and after that allowed him to use an old hut in the woods that once belonged to the Rudstow family before the land passed into government hands eighteen years ago."

"But, Herbert, you aided and abetted him, too, by letting him use our coal-house."

"I did—but with the ultimate purpose of getting rid of him. The means justified the end, Agnes. Besides which, I was glad he committed five murders in this village, for it all goes to show up the arrant stupidity of the law that permits such characters to be kept alive."

Grace and her mother shifted in their seats. Mr. Jarrow shifted, too.

"I'm telling you, Agnes. Grace. On the night I killed Major Rudstow, the Major came here to this cottage with a parcel which I was supposed to deliver to Captain Leigh-Houghton. In that parcel was a complete housebreaking outfit. Are you heeding me, Grace? Are you heeding me, Agnes?"

The two women could say nothing. They merely looked at him.

"So there you have it, Agnes. If you believe in me—if you believe I did right—you simply have to support me in what I tell the police when they call here, as inevitably they are going to call, and all will be well. If you feel I did wrong, if you feel I ought to have let the law take its senseless, sentimental course and keep two such specimens of vermin alive, then you can give the police the answers they want and have me charged and convicted. Have me hanged by the neck. Crick! Like that!" The old gentleman snapped his fingers.

The two women still said nothing.

In the silence they heard the snow. Tip-plip! Plip-tip! Monotonously, repetitiously persistent. Unflagging. A remote whisper beyond the misted panes.

"You haven't long to make up your minds. The police may call this very evening. At the latest, tomorrow morning."

"Why do you think they will, Herbert?"

"Because the bodies of the two men will be found this evening. Perhaps they have been found already. I gave a tip to our two friends who called here the day before yesterday—Mr. North and Mr. Southerby. They are not men to be idle for long. Active men, Messrs North and Southerby. Hee, hee!"

"You gave them a tip?"

"Yes, Grace. I told them in an unsigned note dropped in the letter-box at the Ram and Cross where to go to find the bodies."

"Why did you tell them?"

"Because I think it wiser that they should find the bodies. They are not ordinary detectives, Agnes. I believe we shall get a call from them before the evening is much older. I feel convinced of it." The old gentleman rose and sat down. Gave a quavering giggle.

The two women stared at him.

"Well, Agnes? Grace? What do you say? I am in your hands now."

"But-but, Herbert . . ."

"Yes, Agnes?"

"Murder. It's a terrible thing. To take upon yourself . . ."

"I know what you want to say. To take upon myself to dispose of the lives of two of my fellowmen. Why not, Agnes, if these two fellowmen have proven themselves unfit to live among decent men! Why should I be considered wrong in having put an end to their lives! What about the airmen, my dear, who were sent with an atom-bomb to drop on Hiroshima! At one flash they wiped out eighty thousand human beings—virtually all of them ordinary simple townsfolk going about their usual day's routine. They weren't menacing anyone. They weren't active soldiers armed with tanks and guns—just towns-people. Mothers and small children, schoolboys and schoolgirls, bank clerks, shop assistants, old ladies and old gentlemen sitting quietly in parlours—or the Japanese equivalent of parlours. At one flash— eighty thousand people done to death. Were the airmen who performed that splendid deed sentenced to death? No. They were probably decorated. They were killing eighty thousand people for the good of the rest of mankind. Oh, Noble Allies we! How justified we were in sending them on to Nagasaki to do the same thing. All, mind you, for the good of the rest of the world. For freedom! Well, if that is so, why ought I Herbert Jarrow to be sentenced to death for killing off *two* humans—two humans with twisted brains who have raped, strangled and killed! Tell me, Agnes. Go on. Don't stare at me. Tell me!"

Mrs. Jarrow said nothing. Nor did Grace.

"Well, Agnes? Grace?"

"What's it you want me to tell the police, Herbert?"

Her husband smiled: "You've decided, then? You're on my side?"

"Murder, Herbert . . . I—yes, I'm on your side, my dear. You know I am. How could I be against you? But—oh, I don't know what to say. You've sprung this on me so suddenly. I wish I had time to think it over."

"No. It's something you must not ponder on, Agnes. Conditioned as you have been, brought up with the set of values our civilization has accustomed you to, you would only experience greater confusion of mind if you attempted to think it over. You must decide on the spot. Now. Will you give the police the answers *I* want you to give them?"

"Yes, of course, dear. Certainly. But what are these answers? When I said 'think it over' I didn't mean I hadn't made up my mind about backing you up. I . . . Oh, I don't know what I meant at all."

"Grace? What of you? Are you with me?" He shifted about. "Bound up with your grisly old sire in love and harmony? Tell me."

"Yes, Dad. I'll tell them anything you say." The thought of her father being arrested struck terror into Grace. How could she have survived such a *change!* It was bad enough that he now once more recognized her mother's presence, thus breaking the seventeen-year tradition. But to have him taken away and charged with murder—why, she would never again experience a cosy moment in bed. Such a change in the status of their home would ruin her security for good.

"Very well. Then listen to me carefully, both of you." He leant forward. "If asked, say you have never known me to have in my possession any drugs or surgical instruments. Your father's drugs and instruments, Agnes, never came into this house; they were disposed of shortly after his death. No one but you and Grace know that I took them over and kept them here—"

"But aren't they here any longer, Herbert?"

"No. They are where no one will ever find them. I buried them somewhere in the woods. Buried them three feet deep, under a heavy stone, and spread soil and leaves over the spot. I literally doubt whether I myself could find the spot. And even if they were, by some odd chance, unearthed no one could connect them with me. I handled everything with gloved fingers, and made sure the phials and instruments were polished clean of all traces of human finger-prints of any kind. As for the two hypodermic needles I actually used to put Rudstow and Leigh-Houghton out of the way, those are lost in the sewerage system of Middenshot. I slipped them through a grating in Great Oak

Road and heard them fall with a splash into the running water below. They are now in Satan's hands. Safely tucked away on some secret shelf in Hell."

"But, Herbert, I just can't see—how ever could you have succeeded single-handed in killing—in injecting these two desperate characters with hydrocyanic acid?"

"We can do anything we want to if we have the will to do it, Agnes. If we have the fierce, purposeful determination of years behind us we can perform what may appear miracles. And that's what I had behind me. The savage, powerful determination of years. I'll tell you, my dear, what happened on the Tuesday night Major Rudstow vanished. The Major came to this cottage with, as I've told you already, a parcel of housebreaking tools. At the time I didn't know what was in the parcel, and I didn't care. I simply knew that he was coming, and it was the opportunity I'd been awaiting during the whole period of the fog. I could have got rid of Leigh-Houghton quite easily long before that Tuesday night, but I knew he had an accomplice and I was determined to get his accomplice as well.

"The Major arrived at about eight o'clock, and I met him near the coal-house. He handed to me the parcel he had brought and which I was expected to give to Leigh-Houghton hiding in the hut. I took it, but told him I wanted him to accompany me to the hut because Leigh-Houghton was ill and was calling for him. He hesitated at first, because he was fearful of the police discovering his part in the affair and didn't want to risk being found near the hut if it could be helped. But eventually I persuaded him—I had to use a few threats—and he came with me.

"When we were about fifty yards from the hut I suddenly tripped him up, pounced on him and knocked him half-conscious with a single blow to the chin. I had been tensed for the attack, and everything in me went behind it. When he was gasping on the ground I emptied a needle of hydrocyanide into his neck, and in a few minutes he was subsiding after the paralytic fit cyanide instantaneously produces. I'd given him enough to kill four men. I've spent years studying your father's books, Agnes, and I knew what was the right dose to kill, and I knew how to allow for deterioration. Remember, I had had those drugs for many years.

Hydrocyanide, unless properly stored, deteriorates in strength. Oh, I'm clever, my dear!

"Next, I caught him by an ankle and hauled him the rest of the way to the hut. I left him about ten yards from the hut, approached the hut and called softly for Leigh-Houghton. I heard a movement in the hut, and a weak voice answered me. I went in, flashed the little electric torch I had into the gloom inside the hut, and saw Leigh-Houghton lying on the floor. He seemed weak and ill. He was shivering. He hadn't had any food for over forty-eight hours. I was to have taken him a food parcel the night before, but I purposely didn't. I asked him what was wrong, and he began to swear at me. Then I saw that he had a pile of his belongings in the corner nearby, and among them was a revolver—a revolver the Major had supplied him with; he told me so himself. As he was talking he reached out toward the revolver, but I rushed forward and kicked him hard on the side of his face. Everything in me went behind it, because I knew I was dealing with vermin, and I knew what to expect from vermin. I kicked him into insensibility and emptied a needle of cyanide into his veins. I had taken with me four five-c.c. needles—just to be on the safe side.

"When he had grown still, I slipped off my overcoat from his body. He had been using it since the first night I met him on the common in the fog. To gain his confidence I had had to let him have it and take his in exchange. At the moment I was wearing the one he had given me—that fawn coloured overcoat of rather expensive cut the B.B.C. told us about. It was a big risk but I had to take it. A man like me can take risks. A man who lives with fire never fears heat, my dear.

"Well, all that was left for me to do was to haul his body outside and drop it down into the disused well that had been converted into a sort of cellar under the hut. That was where he used to hide. That was why the police couldn't find him. The Major had given him a paraffin heater to keep him warm down there, but he must have run out of paraffin and it would have been much colder and damper down there without heating, that's why he probably came up during the last two or three days and remained in the hut itself where I found him. I threw his body down into the well-cellar, then hauled the Major up and flung him down there, too. I threw in all their belongings with them, including the parcel with the housebreaking tools and the revolver. Then I put back the garden seat that disguised the trap-door entrance to the well-cellar, and made off. I put on my coat and took over my arm the fawn coat. I arrived back home here about half an hour later, went upstairs and cut up the fawn coat into eight pieces, then came downstairs, and while you and Grace were asleep burnt it in the living-room here, piece by piece. Burnt it to ashes. Next day the ashes were swept out. The police won't find any left to take to the government pathologist for analysis. And then, as you observed yourself, I soaked my old black overcoat in paraffin, washed it in soap flakes, soaked it again in paraffin and washed it again. I've always been very thorough, Agnes. I've left no foolish clues lying around as criminals in detective thrillers do. I defy any policeman to come here and discover the One Clue I Had Overlooked."

"But what about the note you sent to the two detectives, Herbert?"

"That? An old envelope bearing a stamp postmarked Woking and addressed to Mrs. H. Breen, 4, Miller's Lane, Middenshot. And the green ink I used to write in North's name and the message came from a pot I bought about two years ago. I emptied it into the brook on the common. That's where the pot itself lies now. As for the paper bearing the message enclosed, that was a piece of *Daily Express* torn off at the corner. Over four million copies of the *Express* are issued every day. Why should it be from *my* copy that this piece was torn?" The old gentleman smiled and winked. Rose and sat down. "And, in any event, Agnes, there's more about those two eccentric detectives than you see. Mr. North and Mr. Southerby—they'll be calling on us before the evening is very much older. Interesting fellows. Too interesting. Hee, hee!"

They sat still, and gradually the tiny sounds of the flakes returned into their hearing. Tip-plip! Plip-tip!

"But, Herbert . . ."

"Yes, Agnes?"

"Why did you . . . what made you want to do it? What happened in your younger days to bring alive in you such a detestation of criminals?"

"Ha," said her husband. "That is another story. That is something I have no inclination to talk about. It happened before I met you. Let's leave it where it is—in the long past. To think about it gives me pain. To think about it . . ." Mr. Jarrow broke off. He was weeping.

"And all these years," said Mrs. Jarrow. "Seventeen years. You might have been in a foreign land—far away from me, Herbert."

Mr. Jarrow was murmuring to himself—and weeping.

Grace looked all around the room, as though seeking a ghostly presence that might have entered slyly—perhaps through an unsuspected crevice in the ceiling, or in the door, or in the floor. A weeping demon. A demon shedding frozen tears, that melted in her perfervid fancies. She trowelled up a lump of coal and threw it on the fire. The fire crackled with acid response.

Mr. Jarrow started, leaned forward and trowelled up a lump of coal, too, and threw it on the fire. He put down the trowel and stared at his daughter, and then at his wife. Weeping and muttering to himself.

"Herbert," said Mrs. Jarrow, "speak. Say something. Please. Do you understand what I'm saying? Are you hearing me?"

"I'm weeping," said her husband. He spoke in a murmur, but the murmur was audible—and instantly intelligible. There was no need for them to ask him what he had said.

"Weeping for the stupidity and the futility of my deeds," said the old gentleman. He smiled at the fire, wagged his head, the tears still, one by one, oozing in a slow trickle down the drought-dried, wrinkled cheeks.

"Sentimentality and weakness," he murmured. "How can Herbert Jarrow cure the world of its ills and foibles at one stroke! How! Tell me how!" The old gentleman leaned forward and threw another lump of coal on the fire. He lifted the lump with two fingers, ignoring the trowel this time. He murmured something to the fire, evidently meaning only the coals to hear it.

"Herbert, speak to me. You're with us again—you're with me, dear. You've come back, haven't you? You won't leave me again?"

"Never again, Agnes. You and Grace and me—and the fire. The snow. We're one. Inseparable. Listen! Be very silent and hearken! Snow is gentle. To hear it we must be very silent. Listen!"

They sat still, listening.

Gradually the thin voice of the falling flakes returned into their hearing.

Tip-plip! Plip-tip!

"So gentle," smiled the old gentleman. He had stopped weeping.

Tip-plip! Tap-tap!

"Oh!"

"The window."

"Someone is tapping on the window."

"Aha!"

Dimly they could see two faces through the misty panes. Then the faces vanished.

Tap-tap!

"The front door," Grace murmured.

"The front door," agreed her father. And rose.

9

"Did you see us? We saw you."

"Saw me?"

"With our little eyes we saw you."

"Your little eyes?"

"Standing outside your window in the cold, white snow."

"Ah. Now I see what you saw. Come in, come in! Welcome!"

The old gentleman led them into the living-room.

"We must thank you for your tip."

"Tip?"

"Sssh! Hush-hush. The soiled envelope. The slip of news-paper. Sssh!"

"Ah! I see what you mean. Who sent it to you?"

"Sssh! A poor limping old man sent it."

"Oh. And did the horse win?"

"You bet it won. We bet on it and it won. Didn't it, Southy old corpse?"

Southerby nodded. "Force," he said, "is always the deciding

factor. We think it uncivilized to hold such a view. Barbarous. But it is the truth. We can't avoid the elemental laws that govern the universe. Force. Force will to the end of time decide every issue. Not kindness. Sad but true. He who is strong is saved. He who is weak is lost. Yet take democracy. Excellent ideals. Ideals worth aiming at. But look what we've done with our democracy! Look how we've tarnished our ideals. And all through weakness. All through a rotting, pampering process. A lack of discipline. How Disraeli must groan in his grave! How Abraham Lincoln must writhe! . . ."

"To my grave I'll remember this. Oh, I will."

"I feel I've done you a wrong, Hyacinth."

"But I wanted you to do it to me. For me it isn't any wrong. I love you. I love you like hell."

"I love you, too, Hyacinth. I believe I loved you since that day when you flared up in here. Remember? When you said criminals should be wiped out?"

"I remember. Kiss me. Kiss me again."

"Did you tell Dick you were coming here?"

"Yes, I told him before we parted at the Ram and Cross. He was mad at me. Don't let's talk about him. It's you I want to talk about."

"I'm sorry for Dick. I feel I've done him a wrong."

"Him, too? Oh, forget it, darling. Kiss me. Kiss me."

"Before we forget, tell me. Did you find your way to the race-track alone?"

"Alone? Oh, no. We had a guide. Harry Coombe was our guide. We've just returned. We sent Harry on to the police station to break the news."

"Ah. So you yourselves haven't seen the police yet?"

"No. Oh, no. Sssh! We're private detectives. Very private. We're never too eager to take tales to the police. Hush-hush! That's why people hire us."

"How did he take it?"

"Who? Dick? Haven't I just told you? He was mad at me. Said I was making a regular fool of myself. Said he had a good mind to come here and tell you off."

"Poor fellow. It isn't fair to him."

"But suppose I don't love him. We were friends from school-days. I feel about him as I'd feel about my brother. Except . . ."

"Yes?"

"He's good at rough-handling me. I like a little rough-handling."

"Rough-handling?"

"Oh, never mind! One day I'll teach you. Kiss me, darling."

"We mind our own business, and let the police mind theirs. For instance, have a look at what I'm going to do."

He took a pace toward the fireplace, and from his overcoat pocket produced the envelope containing the slip of newspaper with the message in green ink. He took the slip of paper out of the envelope, and with the flick of a hand deposited both envelope and message into the fire.

"See! Watch it burn! The police will never see that. And if they ask us how we got the tip we'll say a man in a pink fez dropped in to see us at the Ram and Cross. He was cross-eyed, wore green spats and spoke with a Finnish accent. And if they get at the landlord or Dick or Hyacinth and they hear that a note was delivered to me and they ask us any questions, I'll tell them it was a message from an old aunt telling me of the death of Oodles-doodles, her Siamese cat. I destroyed it immediately after sending a wire of condolence." North winked. "See what I mean! Southy and me, we're no orthodox detectives. We hold our own views about crime and criminals. Views the police don't hold. Haven't you heard old Southy spouting his philosophy? His philosophy is mine. Mine and yours and Hyacinth's. Really remarkable how we all happen to agree, eh? Indeed, astounding! Almost like a fairy-tale! Who knows if the dead men themselves didn't hold our views! But sssh! Hush-hush! The sentimental are many, the sentient and sensible few. Too few. Eh, Southy old tome?"

"If," stage-whispered Southerby, "we are going to let ideals based on primitive myths and mawkish sentiments influence and govern our way of life then we must resign ourselves to a state of unending disharmony, unending wars, unending corruption. Our civilization of to-day, like the civilizations of the past, is only a gilded barbarism—and how easily the gilt flakes off! No community can call itself truly civilized until it has completely discarded the shackles of sentimentality and superstition and has established itself as a strong, disciplined, humane body, able by its very strength, humaneness and integrity to forbid other communities from attacking it and from attacking each other. Such a community would put an end to exhausting wars, and eventually teach its neighbour communities how to be truly civilized. In strength, in discipline, in humaneness lies the solid gold of civilization."

"You're solid, Hyacinth. I used to think you light and silly, but now I know you as you really are."

. . . no, he was not for me, thought Grace, staring at the fire. Remember how he plunged off into the heaped-up snow instead of walking with me on the beaten track? Perhaps he meant to show me that he and I were not intended to tread the same path in life. He spoilt our beautiful walk. Now I can see it all clearly. He spoilt it at the very end. No, he was not meant for me, nor I for him. Here is my place—safe and cosy in this cottage with my secret dreams and fancies that no one can spoil . . .

"I'm not solid. I am light and silly. But you're nice and I love you. You can do anything you like with me and I won't mind. I'd love you even more if you can beat me sometimes. You'd make me happy . . ."

. . . so happy. Oh, if you could only know how happy you've made me this night, Herbert. I'd forgive you anything, thought Mrs. Jarrow, ignoring the conversation of the men and staring at the misted windows. Yes, even murder. My love for you is as deep as that. And you're not brutal at heart. I know you're not. What you've done you've done because you honestly felt it was right . . .

. . . safe and cosy with my knitting and my household chores.

How happy I shall be knitting and knitting by the fire, and whistling and dancing in the kitchen with only the pots and pans for company, with no one to smile or sneer at me. Or scold me when I hug myself. Remember that evening when the wind kept howling down the chimney and seeming as if it would lift the roof off? How snug and secure I felt sitting by this fire! There will be many more winds like that, and how I'll snuggle deeper into my seat and hug myself with cosy delight . . .

"Hug me again. Hug me. I wish you could hug me the whole night."

Crash!

"Oh, God! What's that?"

Crash!

"Someone is stoning my greenhouses!" He sprang up. "The dirty dog! It's Dick. I'm sure it's Dick."

"I'm going out. Wait here."

"I'll come with you."

"Naked like this? Don't be foolish."

"I'm tough. I'll throw on my coat and come with you."

They went out. He kept muttering frantically: "My greenhouses. My greenhouses." The night greeted them as a wedded couple, generous with its confetti. Confetti specked her disarranged hair. Confetti found its way down the chasm of his trousers that he kept hauling up agitatedly as he walked. It kept falling down. He tried to flash the beam of the electric torch around with one hand and haul up his trousers with the other. "Oh, my greenhouses. My greenhouses," he muttered.

"Oh, we're not green, Southy and me. We're not green, Mr. Jarrow. We're men with a Mission. We're intellectual detectives. Eugenist detectives. Down with Vermin! Up with the wholesome! Oh, have no fear about us. We're grateful to the limping old man who gave us the tip, and we congratulate him on what he's done. Now we shall collect our fee from the late major's wife and call it another case. We shall go home and chalk up the score. Two more ticks! How we disapprove of ticks! Lice and ticks! But I say, Mr. Jarrow, can you clear up a little point for us?"

"What's that?"

"This old man who limped across the common at night in the fog, how do you think he succeeded in stamping out two desperate specimens of vermin all on his own?"

The old gentleman adduced his theories on the matter.

"Ah! Ah! Light breaks over the hills. But wait! That hydrocyanic acid that belonged to his father-in-law, wouldn't it have deteriorated after so great a number of years?"

"It would have—if it hadn't been properly stored. Oh, the limping old man might well have done some extensive reading up on the subject of poisons. And suppose he tested out the strength of the hydrocyanide from time to time on odd dogs and cats and rats in the neighbourhood just to keep a check on how the hydrocyanide was faring—to keep a check as to the degree to which his stock had deteriorated in potency."

"Ah! Ah! Light. Light keeps flooding over the hills. Now we know how some of the cats and rats and dogs in the neighbourhood died. Now we know why this limping old man took such an interest in carcases."

"Oh," said Grace.

"Yes, Grace?"

"The Laytons' cat! Dad, did you . . . ?"

"No, child. The Laytons' cat died from sheer old age. I'm sure the limping old man had nothing to do with that. I feel sure he would only have experimented on mangy stray cats and obviously starved and miserable dogs. As for rats—well, rats are always rats. Vermin. I'm pretty certain he had no mercy on those."

"But . . . oh!" exclaimed Grace.

"Yes? What's it now, child?"

"That smell. I've just remembered."

"In the coal-house? It's the Laytons' cat. I recovered it from the old bull's door-step that first night of the fog and put it in the coal-house for the police, in due course, to find. I had a feeling the police might want to search the place before long, and it's only fair they should find something. This morning I even left a little message beside the carcase—a message I scribbled on the inside of a Quaker Oats carton. I'm a man," added the old gentleman, "with a great consideration for his fellow creatures, Grace."

"Great heavens! Look! Look, Hyacinth!"

"Oh, what a shame! He's smashed the roof in two places. He's a dog. Wait till I see him again."

"But look! Look, Hyacinth! My orchid! My precious orchid!"

"What's wrong with your orchid?"

"The shoots with the buds that took so many months to grow out—they're smashed. Snapped off."

"Oh, what a dreadful shame! He deserves a horsewhipping, Dick does!"

"All my dreams ruined. It may never put out more shoots in years."

"Oh, poor man! I'm so sorry. Never mind! Let me comfort you. You have me, haven't you?"

"My orchid! Oh, my dream orchid! I'd had such hopes for it!"

Was that a horn-call he could hear out in the smothering snow? Oh, Siegfried!

"Let me comfort you. Poor dear. I love you so much."

"You're so good, Hyacinth. Hyacinth, will you marry me?"

"Of course I will. Oh, I'd like nothing better. I'll take good care of you, you watch and see if I don't!"

Was that the death *motif* sounding on the bassoons? Oh, Brünnhilde!

"You don't think me too old for you, Hyacinth?"

"Too old? But you're young. Young and strong. After what you did to me on the sofa how can you think you're old!" She giggled. "You're young and strapping. You're—ooh! Careful! Your trousers are dropping again!" She helped him pull them up, giggling. "Oh, I love you. I love you so much. Hug me. Hug me!"

"Hyacinth, you'll take cold. Let's hurry inside."

"Yes, it is cold out here. Oooh! I'm shivering. I know what! Let's go in and have a hot bath."

"A hot bath? The two of us together?"

"Yes. The two of us together. And then we'll go to bed. What do you say? Shall I go and run the bath?"

"Yes. Yes, please. Oh, Hyacinth, you're so good. So good and solid. I don't mind now about my orchid."

"Oh, you're sweet! Hug me. Spank me. We'll be happy ever after!"

. . . oh, ever after I'll be safe and protected in this cottage . . .

. . . oh, Herbert, my eternal beloved . . .

"Time for us to be going," wheezed Southerby.

"Listen!" hissed North. "The snow!"

Tip-plip!

"Once it was the fog," murmured the old gentleman. "Cold and enclosing."

Before that the wind, thought Grace, trying to lift off the roof.

Plip-tip!

"I say, Mr. Jarrow!"

"Yes?"

Tip-plip!

"That message for the police . . ."

"Scribbled on the inside of the Quaker Oats carton?"

"Sssh! Hush-hush! What's the message?"

"Quiet. Hark! The snow! Two or three weeks ago it was the fog."

And a week or two before that, thought Grace, the wind.

Plip-tip! . . . Insistently.

"The message?" persisted North.

An ectoplasmic leucorrhoea . . .

A quarking pterodactyl thing of dread . . .

"Quote all is illusion . . ."

Assiduously . . . Tick, plick!

". . . and disillusion . . ."

Repetitiously . . . Plick, tick!

". . . end of quote."

www.ingramcontent.com/pod-product-compliance
Lightning Source LLC
Chambersburg PA
CBHW030828020726
47499CB00006B/2111